MEAN GHOULS

A Greek Ghouls Mystery

ALEX A. KING

For Wuv, who was the best doggy nephew ever

CHAPTER ONE

WHEN THE WORLD didn't immediately end, I poured two shots of ouzo and knocked back both before relinquishing the bottle to my sister.

"Did you see that?"

"See what?" Toula said in a tone approximately as dry as one of the bigger deserts. Hooray, her sarcasm was back. Things were already looking up.

"If there is no future, then how can we possibly be doing this?" I snatched the bottle out of her hand. "Or this?" I sat the bottle on my coffee table. "Or this?" I stood up and did a jig across the room.

Normally I wasn't a jig-dancing person, so my self-awareness muttered that I wasn't entirely myself. Not surprising, given that my sister had just come out of the woo-woo closet in a huge way. Minutes ago, Toula informed me that she could see the future, and there wasn't one. Which meant either there was no future, or there was a perfectly fine future lying directly ahead but she could not, in fact, see the future at all.

"If you can see the future, what am I going to do five minutes from now?"

"Pack a bag."

"Why would I pack a bag?"

"Because you'll have to."

Not that I doubted my sister, but her claims of having the power of foresight or prophesy or whatever it was struck me as … unreal. This was Toula, for crying out loud. Her hobbies were asking to speak with the manager, rolling her eyes, and being mildly disappointed in me. She didn't engage in risky behavior, and she did her best to not believe in my own woo-woo skills—skills that had recently manifested further down the family tree in her own children.

Despite our wildly divergent personalities, no one would mistake us as anything other than sisters. Same dark hair. Same dark eyes. We both hover around 170 centimeters (five-seven if you do height in feet and inches). We're not identical, though. Toula scored the big boobs, but I think I got the better deal. I can jog down the stairs braless without losing an eye. While my sister shops for clothes at nuns-for-less, I live in jeans and leggings. Comfort is important when you ride a bicycle everywhere.

"I'm going to check my work mail and we'll see." As I spoke, I edged toward my desk and eased open my laptop's lid.

My name is Allie Callas. I'm thirty-one-years-old, and I run a business called Finders Keepers. Finders Keepers is devoted to the art (and science) of finding things. Mostly it's stuff. Sometimes it's people. If it can be found, I find it for a reasonable fee. Around ten percent of my jobs required a trip to Greece's mainland, or further. So, packing a bag wasn't out of the realm of possibility.

I flicked my gaze sideways at the screen.

Nothing. Nothing that would require a packed bag, anyway. Mostly time on eBay and crafty corners of the Internet (who knew monkey hair was something people wanted to knit with?)

"Ha," I added. "Nothing. That's good, right? It means your vision of the future is wonky and we have a future after all."

Our phones warbled at the same time.

"Check your phone," my older sister said.

My hand crawled sideways to find my phone. The screen lit up with notifications, including a frantic message from our dad. Mom had been hospitalized with stomach pains in the Caribbean. Dad begged us to come in case this was The End.

A few months ago, our parents decided they were destined to be pirates and now lived aboard a cruise ship that traveled the world. The ship was full of other retirees who had also discovered it was a sailor's life for them; so my parents were in what they considered good company. The truth was, despite being born Greek, my parents were way too Americanized to spend the rest of their lives on Merope. They wouldn't have dragged our family back here at all if my grandmother hadn't mistaken a venereal disease for cancer. By the time the antibiotics kicked in, Mom and Dad had already uprooted their teenage daughters and dumped us on this Greek island. Now Toula and I were part of Merope's landscape, while our parents dodged norovirus and other assorted plagues at the buffet.

My pulse lost its rhythm. No steady *thud-thud*. More of a lengthy pause that should have been life threatening, followed by a *swish-flub*.

"It's Mom," I said.

Toula's head was bent over her own phone. "I know. I got the same message."

"Dad wants us to come."

"I know. I got the same message." Toula sighed. "Better get packed."

"You're not freaking out. Why aren't you freaking out?"

"Because it's not fatal. Mom is going to be fine. But you need to go. I can't."

Knowing Mom's episode wasn't deadly didn't switch off any of the alarms screeching in my head.

"Why not?"

"Kids, husband, no passport."

"You didn't renew your passport?"

"I never go anywhere!"

"You might if you'd renewed your passport."

One week later ...

An empty plastic bag tumbled across the road, shoved by a finger of wind. There was no sign of its owner, no hint of its origin. There were no signs of *anybody*.

I was the only soul that had disembarked at Merope's dock. The boat had yanked up the gangplank and sailed away the moment my boots touched ground. The dock was been deserted. Even the ghosts of old fishermen and dockworkers that clung to their beloved sea post-life were absent.

A shiver started at the base of my neck and rippled outward, one tiny convulsion at a time.

Everything felt ... *off*.

Because Toula drove me to the ferry last week, I had left my bicycle at home. Traipsing back on foot was my only option. Probably the best option in the absence of a tank. The wind was savage. Riding a bicycle was asking to end up as jetsam.

I readjusted my backpack and set off for home.

I plodded along Merope's main street, looking for life signs—or death signs. This road had its own ghost, Vasili Moustakas, a geriatric flasher who had been mowed down by a vengeful teenager in a luxury car. There was no sign of Vasili or his ghost wiener. Normally I'd be relieved, but it was another indication that sometime this week, while I'd been at Mom's side, something had gone horribly wrong on Merope.

I see dead people. Usually I see living people, too. And when I can't see them because I'm cloistered inside my apartment, I can reach out and touch those living folks with my phone—frequently to order food delivery.

Alas, my phone was flatlined. No signal. No Wi-Fi. Nada since the ferry crossed into Merope's waters. That meant I couldn't call anyone to ask just what the heck was going on. The dead phone explained why I hadn't been able to reach anyone on the island since Friday.

Shops were shuttered. Houses were sealed up. The island looked like a ghost town, minus the ghosts. The weather was bonkers. Wind was lashing Merope with a ferocity I'd never experienced before.

As I struggled along the main road, a pile of garbage whipped into sloppy a funnel and spun down the street before stopping abruptly and hurling debris at the local post office.

Weird.

My eyes watered. I located my sunglasses and shoved them down on my nose to form a protective barrier between me and the airborne dust. I glanced down the narrow cobbled side streets. Shops that sold souvenirs all year round--in case of the occasional intrepid tourist--had hauled in their racks of t-shirts and spinning postcard stands. Smaller potted plants were riding out the windstorm inside. Larger flora had been abandoned to fend for their selves. Given that nobody had equipped them with weapons, they were toast. Merope's narrow streets were littered with shards of shattered pots.

Lights were on at the More Super Market. As far as I could tell, it was the only open place in town.

Hallelujah. My stomach was making rude noises. If I ignored it, they'd get louder and I'd be shunned from society.

I tried the door.

Locked.

A face appeared in the glass. One I barely recognized.

Stephanie Dolas unlocked the door and yanked me in before slamming the door behind me. She flattened her back against the glass.

That Stephanie Dolas opened the door herself shocked the bejeezus out of me. Stephanie isn't the kind of person who exerts herself or performs any actions not specifically listed under the heading of market cashier. She takes money. She makes change. And in between customers, she plucks and primps and pops any pimples that need popping. What she doesn't do is open doors or be generally helpful.

Today Stephanie wasn't herself. This was the first time I'd seen her barefaced since she was in single digits. Her eyebrows were threadbare and her lashes were invisible.

"What's going on?"

"Bad weather," she said.

"That's not bad weather. That's bad weather's demonic cousin." I eased my bag off my back and let it slide to the floor. "Tell me everything. Where is everyone?"

"At home. Nobody goes out now unless they have to."

"Why are you out?"

"Because I have to be." She scooted up onto her stool behind the counter. "On Friday afternoon it was the regular kind of windy, but then I saw Kyrios Lambros fly past on his donkey. I looked outside and everyone was either flying or trying not to fly."

"What did the weather forecast say?"

Her face blanked. "Who watches the news?"

Only every last one of Merope's denizens in the over-fifty age group. Stephanie was hovering around twenty. The news wasn't really a priority for someone who spent their free time watching makeup tutorials.

"Well, what about the newspaper?"

"The Bakas family has not printed any newspapers since Friday."

Could be that had something to do with the paper's editor taking a trip to prison. Maybe without Tomas to guide them, the rest of the family didn't know how to make the printer go *buzz-buzz*. The Bakas family tree was a stick, and along the way they had managed to breed all the brains out. Until recently, they had made no attempts to bring in new blood. But it was too late for that now; the bride-to-be was currently incarcerated, along with her cousin.

"What about the police?"

"They have been doing what they can. Telling people to stay home, mostly. Rescuing anyone that needs to be rescued. Kyria Yiota got stuck in a tree. The police were in here talking about it. They could not decide whether to leave her there or not."

Plus one to the "leave her there" column. Kyria Yiota was the worst. I felt sorry for the tree for having her stuck in its branches. Probably it would be best to wave a smoking bundle of dried sage around the poor thing to banish any bad juju.

Outside, wind was lashing the streets with Henry VIII-level glee. The gale had been joined by rain. Buckets of the stuff gushing out of the sky.

Weird, you'd think with this freakish weather, the sea would also be a churning mess. But it was still and steady, gently lapping the island the way it had been when the ferry pulled up to the dock just minutes earlier.

A tingle in my Spidey senses told me this weather wasn't natural. Not if the sea was calm and the island was chaos. I needed to talk to Betty Honeychurch, co-owner of the Cake Emporium and my go-to person for woo-woo matters and friendship. I also needed to talk to my sister about our mom, and to Detective Leo Samaras about how much I'd missed him while I was away and wanted to get naked with him ASAP.

Priority One was family. Toula was waiting for news, and I hadn't been able to get in touch with her for days.

First, though, my stomach was in tantrum mode, and I had the feeling if I didn't eat now it would be a while.

"Can I still buy deli stuff?" I asked Stephanie.

She shrugged. "If you cut it yourself. Nobody else is here to work the slicer."

Although Greece isn't a country of regular American-style sandwiches, the More Super Market does keep a constant three loaves of bread in stock. People rarely buy the sliced, bagged loaves. Nobody wants prepackaged when they can walk into any of the island's bakeries and buy golden-crusted bread, fresh from the oven. Right now my stomach didn't care. I ripped into a packet right then and there, and cobbled together a couple of sandwiches with mortadella slices and mild kaseri cheese. One for me and one for Stephanie. We stood at the door and watched a goat cartwheel past the small market. The creature landed several meters away and, after a "what the heck just happened?" shake, took off down the road.

"This is a good sandwich," Stephanie said.

"Want another one?"

"Yes, please."

I made two more sandwiches and took mine to go, determined to get to my sister. If I were lucky, the wind wouldn't pick me up and toss me out to sea.

———

Merope is a dot in the Aegean Sea, wedged between Greece and Turkey. At some point in history, Greece licked the island and decided it was theirs. Turkey, surprisingly, didn't want an island covered in Greek spit. The Ottomans (the people, not the furniture) set their sights on the rest of the country. If you ask me, Greeks should have licked that, too.

During summer, Merope is a hit with tourists. The population explodes like nuggets of corn zapped in a microwave. Whole industries thrive here in the hot months and tighten their belts in winter. Like the souvenir shops tucked under steps that lead to other tourist friendly treasures, subterranean bookstores, and countless tavernas that pump out *mezedes* days and night, April through October. In winter, the island hibernates. The locals hunker down in their homes to ride out the months until spring shows up again, bored with its annual vacation to the southern hemisphere.

I made it two blocks, although "blocks" is a nice word I used so as to not hurt the village planner's feelings. In Merope's early days, residents slapped down a market and dwellings in a loose geometrical formation, and after that things spiraled out of control. At times the island could be a rabbit warren of cobbled roads and white steps.

So. I made it two blobby blockish thingys before the rain pummeled me with its wet fists and I was forced to find shelter on a doorstep with a narrow overhang. Wind rocked me back and forth. Rain slapped me. Cold sliced through my clothing and bit at my skin. My eyes stung. Salt water shoved its way into my mouth.

Salt water.

Since when was rain salty?

When it wasn't rain.

Somehow, seawater was pelting the island without causing a commotion. The Aegean was calm, the waves were gentle, and yet here I was, drenched in its water.

As I'd decided in the More Super Market, this was definitely not a natural phenomenon. Science wasn't the answer. Which left the supernatural.

Toula would have to wait. Mom was already aboard her ship, ordering room service and living the pampered seafaring life.

I pivoted and battled the gale to the next stoop. And the next. Weather yanked on my hair. I tucked everything under a beanie and hoped the hat would hold the line until I reached the narrow alley where the Cake Emporium existed, but only for people with a touch of woo-woo. Instead of a cake shop, regular folks saw nothing but a vacant storefront.

The wind was relentless. It ripped along the alley, unfazed by buildings blocking its path. Definitely not normal. I flattened my back against the wall and inched toward the Cake Emporium, unsure if the shop would be open today. Given that Betty and her brother had alternate means of commuting from England to their business that didn't involve the outdoors, I figured they wouldn't be inconvenienced by a bit of spooky weather.

Wrong.

The door was locked. The sign said Closed. My gaze slid to the window display, which was empty. Fear bubbled up from my diaphragm and lodged in my throat. This wasn't like Betty Honeychurch. The woman *decorated*. She lived for holidays and the shifting seasons, and styled the cake shop's front window accordingly. She was Pinterest and instagram rolled into one, although I was confident she wasn't present on any social media.

I rapped on the door.

Nothing.

Nose to the glass, I stared into shop. No movement. No flicker from the fireplace. The lights were off and the cabinets were empty.

Guess who had two thumbs and wasn't getting any cake today?

This gal.

I checked my phone for a signal again. The wind did its best to knock it out of my hands. Irritation bubbling up, I managed to stuff it back in my crossbody bag.

"Cut the crap," I told the wind in two languages.

Spoiler alert: the wind did not, in fact, cut the crap. I was out of languages, so I wheeled around and staggered out of the alley.

Toula was next.

I was halfway down the main street again, when something caught my attention. Two bundles of clothing dumped in a different alley. Everything else was in motion, but the piles of fabric were unmoving.

I fell into the alley.

The wind stopped dead.

Not everywhere. Outside of this one narrow alley, the

air continued to spin and destroy. But it was still. Like the weather wanted me to inspect the clothing.

I'd experienced strange occurrences in my life, but mystical weather was new. Mildly freaked out, I hurried over to the piles before the weather changed its mind and kicked me in the pants.

A stick of wind snaked into the alley and poked at the ground. The fabric flew up, revealing a human leg, covered from foot to knee in knee-high stockings. The foot wore a navy blue slipper.

Not clothing. Well, yes, clothing. But the clothing was on people.

Without rolling them over, I recognized them instantly. When you live on an island with a population of twenty thousand, everyone knows everyone. If not their names, we recognize each other's faces. As it so happened, I knew this pair. I'd done some work for their daughter in the recent past.

Stathis and Maria Zervas.

The married senior citizens were dead.

CHAPTER TWO

In my not-even-remotely professional opinion, Maria and Stathis Zervas had both been struck in the head, probably by flying debris. It only took me a minute of searching to find a chunk of wood with a smear of blood and hair at one end. I knelt down beside the slab of dead tree but didn't touch.

What to do?

Calling the police wasn't an option. Couldn't contact their daughter Eleni. Somehow I had to make it to the police station on foot and hope that the station was manned. Hopefully the Zervases would be here when I returned with backup.

The wind kept its distance until I reentered the main road. Then it was open season on Allie. A gust tackled me, kicking me across the cobblestones, knocking the breath out of my lungs. I fell on my face. Pain zigzagged across my face. Tears rolled out of my ducts.

Mmm … dirt. Not my favorite post-sandwich dessert.

I peeled my teeth off the stones. Staggered to my feet. Something went *wah-wah*.

Siren.

Leo's police cruiser was slowly bumping over the cobbled stones in my direction.

Part of me wanted to sink to my knees in gratitude. The rest of me wanted to be cool and lean against the wall and go, "Sup?" like I hadn't just eaten dirt.

I did neither. I shoved my hands down in my pockets and jiggled as best as I could in the brutal breeze until he rolled to a stop beside me with Constable Pappas in the passenger seat. Constable Pappas rolled down his window and grinned until the wind kicked dirt at his teeth. Gus Pappas is rookie cop with a heart of gold and a penchant for women's underwear. Spaghetti physique. Buzz cut. A motorcycle that's too much metal for him to handle. His stomach is too weak for homicide, but he tries, bless him.

"Get in."

I chucked my chin up to signal a Greek "no." The Zervases were dead in the alley behind me. They needed the police to get out more than they needed me to get in.

Pappas struggled to open the door. He pushed. I pulled. Eventually we maneuvered it into position. Despite the *no*, I got in. He scooted around back, leveraging his wiry frame into the backseat where metal mesh separated the goodies from the baddies.

Leo reached over me and tugged on the door. The wind slammed it shut and continued its temper tantrum around us. Rocking the police car. Flipping debris like a short order cook.

Leo Samaras's face was grim but the tension drained out of his shoulders as he checked me out. His dark hair was scraped under a beanie bearing the local police force logo. His hazel eyes were leaning towards brown today, no doubt from the charming ambiance on Merope. He looked like he'd been awake for a week and hadn't shaved in almost as long. He stared at me like he didn't believe I was real.

"You're okay," he said, slightly dazed. "And you're back. How did it go?"

"My mother is fine. It was just appendicitis and she's on the road to recovery. There was no need to stay any longer. So here I am in time for the party. What did I miss? Anything interesting?"

He rubbed his chin like he was thinking, then he curled his hand around the back of my neck and reeled me in for a long, sweet, toe curling kiss. Below the belt things got steamy fast. Life kept intervening, and Leo and I hadn't had a chance to get naked at the same time, in the same space. Something we needed to remedy soon or I was going to pop.

There was a disturbance in the police force.

"Nice," Pappas said from the backseat. "Okay if I record it?"

"*Vre, malaka*," Leo said.

I pulled away. "I was on my way to find you. Kyrios and Kyria Zervas are … well; they're no longer worried about the weather. I was passing by on my way to Toula's place and spotted then in the alley."

His smile flickered on then off. He let out a heavy sigh that sounded like he'd been suppressing himself for a week.

"We were looking for them," he said. "Their daughter came by earlier to report them missing." He scraped his hand across his chin. This week has been crazy. We've had to search for a lot of people this week."

"Who else is missing?"

"Kyria Yiota got stuck in a tree," Pappas said. "I wanted to leave her there. Samaras did, too. Even though he won't admit it."

"No one—now," Leo said, smothering a smile. "We've

managed to locate everyone. I don't know what's going on. We've lost contact with the outside world."

"No landlines?"

"Nothing. It's a miracle the ferry got you here. No one has been able to leave. Put a boat in the water and the wind kicks it back on land."

"The waters were quiet until we reached the dock. The ferry staff pretty much pushed me off the boat and bolted." I flicked a side-eye at Pappas. "Can we talk in private?"

"It is about sex?" Pappas wanted to know. "I've heard it all before. Done it, too."

Leo put on his take-no-*kaka* cop face. "Constable, go check out the Zervases. I'll be right behind you."

Pappas didn't look happy about leaving the police cruiser's protective barrier, and I didn't blame him. But he got out, leaving me alone with Leo.

"What is it?" Leo said.

I told him what I suspected, that this maelstrom of wind and sea water affecting Merope wasn't a natural phenomenon, and that it was capable of selectively switching on and off at something's will.

A shallow ditch appeared between his brows. "Ghosts?"

"If it's ghosts, I can't see them." No point mentioning that the island's ghosts were missing. Even my own recently returned grandmother was absent. Maybe she was hunkered down in my apartment with Dead Cat, whose name was a spoiler alert.

"Then what?"

"I don't know. I need to talk to Betty at the Cake Emporium, but shop is locked up tight."

He leaned back in the seat and blew out a long, head-shaking sigh. "I'm the first guy to admit I don't understand any of what you see or know, but if this isn't natural then I'll do whatever it takes to make it stop. Let me get the Zervases taken care of, then I'll drive you over to Betty's place."

A nervous laugh squeaked out of me. "Betty isn't exactly a local."

"She commutes to Merope every day?"

"In a manner of speaking."

"Where does she live?"

My eye twitched. "Not here."

Leo pressed a finger to the spot between his brows. "Okay, let me check out the Zervases. Then … I'll do something. Don't know what, yet. Eat until I pass out, maybe."

We got out of the rocking car. The wind made a grab for my beanie. I stumbled. Leo placed a steadying arm around my waist and steered us into the alley, where the wind immediately died again. Since it was traveling in this direction, the alley should have been a wind tunnel instead of a dead zone. Pappas was standing a few meters away from the deceased couple, behind a puddle of puke. The rookie cop was handling death with his usual sour stomach.

"C'mon, it's not even a murder," I said.

"My stomach doesn't know that."

Leo knelt beside Maria and Stathis. "Their daughter was afraid of this. Both Zervases were suffering from dementia. They've been steadily declining for a long time."

"I know. They've wandered off before," I added. "One time I found them on Mykonos snorting Coke off a Maltese prostitute's peg leg. Soda everywhere when they sneezed it out."

Pappas perked up. "Was she pretty?"

"He."

That didn't dim the constable's enthusiasm. "Was he pretty?"

"He was ninety-three years old."

"Is that a yes or no?"

With my eye twitching and both eyes watering from the wind, I swung back around to Leo. "That chunk of wood over there has hair and blood. Could be theirs."

He inspected the wood and sent Pappas to bag it. "Okay. Let me call Panos." Phones were down but Leo still had a functioning walkie-talkie. When he was done calling the coroner, he looked down at me with his eyebrows high. "It wasn't murder, right?"

I felt confident enough to answer him honestly. "No."

The dead never come back before their forty days in Afterlife Orientation are up, unless they've been murdered or have serious unfinished business that prevents them from moving on. Murder victims show up almost immediately. Not that they're entirely helpful. The transition between life and death tends to scrub their day's mental browser history, so it's not like they can point the finger and tell me that it was Kyrios Patata, in the pigsty, with a souvlaki skewer. That doesn't stop them from coming back and—more and more frequently—demanding I help them.

"That's something," Leo said. "Want to huddle under an awning?"

I glanced around. "There are no awnings. The wind took them."

"How about a stoop?"

We stood on a stoop. Leo put his arms around me. For a moment I imagined things were normal.

"Great idea," Pappas said. He stood on the stoop with us. He inched closer.

"Get your own stoop," Leo told him.

I waited with Leo and Pappas until Panos Grekos, the island's coroner showed up in his van. He inspected the dead couple, came to the same probable conclusion as the rest of us about flying debris as the culprit, and then loaded the deceased Zervases into the van.

Normally the coroner was accompanied by his dead mother, a screeching banshee who stalked her son. She wasted her afterlife howling at Panos for buying nudie magazines. Maybe he was reading them for the articles, otherwise why else bother? Everyone naked was already on the internet. No trip to the *periptero*—newsstand—required.

Today nothing but silence followed him.

"I'll know more when I perform the autopsies," Grekos said. "If there is more."

His eyes twitched as he passed me. Recently I had to accompany all three men home after an incident involving a fake priest and a bottle of ouzo. Probably he was having fragmented flashbacks.

The van rolled away slowly over the cobbled street. We watched him depart, none of us eager to leave the weirdly sheltered alley.

"I need to see my sister," I told Leo. "I haven't been able to get ahold of her for almost a week. Then somehow I need to figure out what's going on here."

"I can drop you off at Toula's place, but it might be better if I don't come in."

I didn't laugh. Leo is my sister's high school sweetheart. The relationship fizzled out when school ended and Leo left the island to further his education. Majoring in goat herding or picking olives wasn't his style, so he had to leave or commit to livestock. When he returned to the island he'd changed so much that I hadn't recognized him at first. He went from tall, skinny metal-loving teenager to a buff hunk oozing sex appeal. We'd flirted, and things spiraled out of control from there. Toula was still weird about us dating. Although her marriage was mostly happy, she was experiencing a serious case of the "what ifs."

Fifteen slow minutes later, during which time the police car rattled and shook so hard I thought we'd flip over, I was knocking on Toula's door. Normal Greek protocol is to stand outside the yard and yell for whomever it is you want to speak to, but I could barely stand upright. The wind flung my words away as soon as they came out.

The door opened. I fell through. Toula's face was white with worry.

"Allie! You're back!"

In a very un-Toula-like move, she threw her arms around me. Moments later there was squealing, and I was pelted with two smallish—but expanding by the day—children: my nephew Milos and niece Patra. Milos is eight, and Patra's birth certificate says six, but really my niece is six going on thirty. Recently I discovered my niece and nephew see dead people, as often and easily as I do. Much to my sister's horror.

"Go to your rooms," Toula said, shooing them away. "I need to talk to Thea Allie."

Patra farted like a grown man and ran away giggling.

"Eww," Milos said, following her. But I could tell he was impressed and maybe a bit envious of her skills.

Toula rolled her eyes. "I don't know where they get that from."

Deeper in the house, a deep bass belch rumbled. My brother-in-law Kostas was zoning out in his favorite recliner.

"On second thought, I do." Her worried gaze found

mine. "What happened to Mom? Is she okay? I mean I know she's okay, but is she okay, if that makes sense."

"Appendicitis," I said. "They operated and she's fine. Bonus: free weight loss. She's four ounces or so lighter now."

Some, but not all of the tension drained out of her face and shoulders. "That's something." She closed her eyes. "It's started."

"What?"

"The end."

"You mean the wind that isn't wind?"

Another burp cut through the tension. "Toula?" my brother-in-law, Kostas, called out. "What are you doing? Who is it?"

Toula's lips tightened. "It's Allie," she called out. "We're discussing your birthday presents."

"Oh."

My sister's voice dipped. "He doesn't know he won't be having any more birthdays. I didn't buy him any presents, because what's the point? Better to save the money."

"If the world is ending, what exactly are you saving for?"

"Why do you always have to do that?"

"Ask questions?"

"Yes." She rubbed her temples. "I get it all day from my kids. I'm exhausted."

"Okay, okay, I'll go now."

"No, you don't have to go. Just … no questions."

"Then I should definitely go because I'm full of questions right now."

Tackling the wind again so soon wasn't my idea of fun, but I didn't want to cause my sister more anguish. If this wonky weather was the beginning of the end, as she put it, I wanted to at least satiate my desire to know what, exactly, was going on before the whole world imploded or exploded or blew away.

I yawned. Tears leaked out of my eyes. I said my good-byes to my sister, then struggled back to my apartment. Whichever way I faced, the invisible force shoved me. It was changing directions constantly. Messing with me. It was getting hard not to take this personally. What had I ever done to annoy the weather? I'd barely even complained about it until today.

Like earlier, nobody was out. Debris danced through the air before slamming into buildings. Occasionally chickens discovered they could actually fly. Everything airborne avoided me. Which was strange but not unwelcome. I didn't fancy being slapped with a spinning gate.

Across the street from my place, Merope's Best was inexplicably open. Huh. Weird. But also welcome.

The coffee shop's building looks like a Burger King, if the king of burgers was entombed in white stucco. Merope's Best is a misnomer. Nobody on the island sells worse coffee—if it's even coffee. I half suspect the employees dig dirt out of graves and splash the grains with coffee flavoring before loading up the espresso machine.

I pushed through the door. The coffee shop was empty, except for the pair of baristas, both wearing ironic t-shirts. One shirt claimed to be PANTS. The other read I DON'T CARE. They both looked like they were about to expire from boredom at any moment.

Good thing I was here to break the monotony. I didn't want their deaths on my hands.

The baristas flicked their apathetic gazes at me. They folded their arms, probably hoping I'd leave. No chance. I needed a cup of coffee-flavored grave water or I'd never get through the rest of the day.

I slapped my money on the counter. "Do your worst."

I DON'T CARE shrugged bonelessly. "We are out of coffee."

"Your other worst," I said.

"We have coffee."

"Ugh. I was afraid of that. What's today's special?"

"Affogato …"

How bad could it be? Nothing in the world ever tasted worse with ice cream.

"Take my money."

She took my money. "… But we are out of ice cream so we are pouring the coffee over a chunk of cake."

"Give me money back."

She kept the money and maintained eye contact while her coworker poured my coffee over a dense chunk of fruitcake.

"Fruitcake isn't really cake," I told I DON'T CARE. "It's a weapon."

She pointed to her t-shirt. At least it was honest.

"Why are you even open?"

"They gave us the day off, but we did not want to miss all the no-people. This is the best workday ever. Or it was." She gave me a sharp pointy look, the kind with sticks in it.

"Give me my utterly ruined affogato and I'll leave, I promise."

Her coworker shoved my coffee at me. "Go now, and never come back."

"See you tomorrow.'"

As soon as I stepped outside, the wind snatched my cup and threw it on the ground.

"Are you kidding me?" I yelled at the sky. "That's just mean!"

My fruitcake lay there, sad and soaked. But it was still technically cake, wasn't it? Therefore it deserved to be saved. Worst case, I could dry it out and give it to someone as a gift next Christmas.

I crouched down and scooped the cake back into the cup, licked my fingers. This wasn't so bad. I thought about doubling back to get a refill, but decided against it. Why ruin the employees' one good day?

Cake in cup, I shoved back against the weather and managed to ease into my apartment building's tiny lobby. Outside, the wind wailed. Inside, it was immediate relief. I peeked through the glass door. There was no sign of Kyrios Yiannis, the building's dead gardener. No sign of the live gardener either, which wasn't unusual. The ghost did most of his work.

My apartment building is three stories high and houses two apartments per floor. I live on the second floor, and Leo lives directly above me. These days I'm a homeowner, which frequently surprises me. When my best friend and neighbor, Kyria Olga, was murdered, it was revealed that she owned the building and that she was leaving me my apartment in her will. The rest of the building is now owned by her granddaughter, Lydia Marouli, who lives directly across the hall from me in her grandmother's old apartment. My heart still hurts when I see Olga's door and remember she's no longer there.

The building itself is typical for the island: A lot of white and blue. Solid construction. Real, functioning shutters on all the windows. We have an elevator that I never take because it's like being encased in a shuddering coffin. The stairs are better for me, anyway. They mitigate some of the cake damage.

Across the hall from my place, Lydia's apartment was quiet. When she was home she played a lot of music of dubious quality. I liked it anyway. A reminder that I wasn't alone. Today the silence weighed heavily. The backdrop of raging winds amped up the eerie factor.

I let myself into my apartment and dropped everything except the cup of cake onto the floor.

No Yiayia. No Dead Cat.

I was sure they would be here, riding out the windstorm.

"Anyone home?"

Silence.

I dumped the cup of cake on the kitchen counter and staggered to my bedroom, where I flopped facedown on the bed.

Betty, if you're out there, get in touch, I thought as I faded out.

CHAPTER THREE

I WOKE up an hour later to the *rat-a-tat* of someone knocking on my window.

My second-floor window.

I peered out.

Nothing. Nobody.

Weird.

Ha. Nothing had been not-weird since I stepped foot back on Merope. The last normal thing that happened was me boarding the ferry early this morning.

There was still no sign of my dead roommates, Yiayia and Dead Cat. Worry sloughed off the last vestiges of my nap. Where were they? Were they okay? Was the disappearance of the island's ghosts linked to the supernatural squall?

I splashed water on my face, grabbed my now-cold coffeecake, and jogged downstairs, determined to find a loose end to pull. This was what I did—I found things. I could find out what was going on, why Toula the future wouldn't be happening. Probably I couldn't stop it, but at least I wouldn't die ignorant. Not knowing stuff made me twitchy, especially when my fate was involved.

Given that Betty Honeychurch had shuttered the Cake Emporium, I figured there was one person on the island who might be able to help get a message to her. My old mentor and boss, Sam Washington.

As I burst out into the thick, howling daylight, water splashed over me. A bucket of the wet stuff.

Slowly, it seeped through my outer layers, heading right for my skin.

Give me a dang *break*. Enough was enough.

"Rude! As soon as I figure out what you are, I'm calling an exorcist. A real one, not the fake one that was here a couple of weeks ago, either! A serious oogie-boogie banisher! They'll send you right back to wherever hell you clawed your way out of!"

This whole thing was using up my entire daily allotment of exclamation points.

The rain that wasn't rain stopped slamming me. The wind died in a neat circle around me. The air shimmered. Pieces of a man coalesced. Big, beefy, transparent chunks. If I had to guess, I'd say he died in his parents' basement with a can of Mountain Dew in one hand and a bag of Doritos in the other. He was maybe twenty, maybe twenty-five. His peach fuzz aspired to be a real beard someday. He wore a tracksuit—blue—pushed to its synthetic limits.

"I am Vladimir," he said in a Russian accent. "You are Allie Callas, *da*?"

Fun fact: Ghosts are annoying. They're needy and desperate for validation, in their own way. They want to be seen and heard, and once they know I can see them, the pushier phantasms won't quit bugging me. So this was one of life's same-old dilemmas. To ignore Vladimir the Russian or to acknowledge his probably-Cheetos-stained fingers—or whatever the equivalent junk food was called in Mother Russia.

On the one hand I didn't want anything to do with a Russian ghost. They tended to be maudlin and enjoyed long, dreary literature and complaining about foreign vodka and turnips. On the other hand, I was burning to know why I could see this guy when all the other ghosts around the village were absent.

The cat hair in my Greek DNA activated, making the decision for me. "Who wants to know?"

He opened his mouth.

I held up my hand, not caring that it was palm-out. Given that he was Russian, I figured he didn't know about the *moutsa*.

(The *moutsa* is a charming gesture with dual meanings. In one scenario you're rubbing *kaka* in the recipient's face. In the other you're accusing them of a brain-softening amount of physical self-love.)

"I know you're Vladimir, but who *are* you?"

"I am emissary, but also partner."

"Still not much information. Let's take another run at it, shall we? What do you want?"

"You are Allie Callas?"

"Yes, yes, I'm Allie."

He spoke slowly, carefully, Russianly. "I haff come with message and request. My partners and me, Vladimir, we seek vay off this island."

"Have you tried the ferry?"

He stared at me. His face said he thought I was a ding-dong. "Do you think ve vould be here if we could get on boat? Just valky, valky vith our legs?"

"Maybe? You never know about people. We have a tendency to miss blatantly obvious solutions to our problems on a regular basis. The other day I had a sound problem with my laptop. I tried everything. You know what fixed it?"

"*Nyet.*"

"Turning it off and back on again. Can you believe it? Should have been obvious, but nope. I missed it."

"Ve cannot get on boat."

"Okay, you can't get on boats. Who are your ... uh ... cohorts?"

"You heelp us? *Da* or *nyet*?"

"Why should I help you?"

"Because you are good person, da? And also I hear you are person who finds things. Ve vant you to find us vay off island."

I groaned. "Yes, I find things. For paying clients. That means money or whatever it is you have to barter with."

His face fell and hit chins. "That is beeg problem. Ve have no pockets, no bank accounts. Vhere to keep money? Beink ghost is not easy like people think."

He'd just made the decision easy. "Okay." I stepped around him. "Got to go."

There was an annoyed *pop* and the Russian spook vanished. The tempest picked up again, leaving me to fight back the wind.

Great.

Five minutes later, I had exchanged my sopping clothes for dry leggings, several top layers, and a heavy coat. I grabbed my sad coffee-soaked cake, plucked the sandwich out of the fridge, and stuffed it into my bag.

Time to take another stab at reaching Sam's house.

Once more unto the windy breach.

Late afternoon. Night would be here soon. I didn't want to battle the wacky weather after dark, so I hurried as hard as I could toward Sam's place. No point pulling my bicycle out of the lobby. The wind would toss it out to sea.

Eventually I arrived on his doorstep and thumped with my gloved hand.

"That better be a pizza," Sam called out from inside.

"I'm so much more awesome than a pizza."

"Nothing tops pizza."

"I can go home and make a pizza with all the no ingredients I have, or you can let me in and I'll give you a sandwich."

"What about dessert."

I thought about the coffee-soaked fruitcake. "Do you like fruitcake?"

"Nobody likes fruitcake."

"That's a problem, because all I have is fruitcake."

The door opened, revealing my former boss and always friend, Sam Washington. Years ago, Sam took a chance on a nosy, know-nothing teenager. He gave me a job as his intern and sidekick, and sent me off on my own with a smile when I was good enough to fly solo. Sam is tall, Black, thin, and unrequitedly in love with Luther Vandross, who is long dead and has never returned as a ghost, as far as I know.

He squinted at me. "Get in here and show me that fruitcake—and the sandwich. Anything good on it?" He rolled backward in his wheelchair, giving me room to get out of the wind. As I shut the door, the wind around me died.

"Mortadella and kaseri."

"Mustard?"

"Nope."

"That's okay, I've got brown mustard in the refrigerator. Straight from home."

Like me, Sam was an American. The difference between us was that moving here wasn't my choice, although Merope was home now. Sam fell in love with the island while he was on a missing persons case. So he decided to stay.

I offered him the second sandwich I'd made at the More Super Market and my coffee fruitcake. He peered into the cup.

"Nasty, and not in a good, fun, eighteen-plus kind of way. That cake shop of yours closed?"

"Like almost everything else."

He blew out a long sigh. "I've seen some things in my life, but never anything like this."

"I don't suppose you still have a connection to the outside world? Everything else is dead. No phone. No internet. We're lucky we've still got power."

Sam grinned. "What if I do?"

"I need to call someone. But first I want to know if this crazy weather is limited to Merope or if it's part of a freak weather pattern."

"Let me get a spoon," he said.

"To make a call?"

"To eat this fruitcake."

"I thought you didn't like fruitcake."

"Just because you don't like something, that's no reason not to eat it, especially when you're out of cake and pie."

He located a spoon and stuck it in the cake. A soggy chunk vanished into his mouth. He slapped the cup on the counter. "Not that bad. Not that good, either. Keep your weird coffee fruitcake. Let's head to the bat-cave and see if we can reach out and touch whoever it is you want to touch."

Sam rolled into his office and I followed. The wheels were a relatively new, post-Merope accessory. A few years ago, Sam was the victim of a hit and run. The driver was a boy in single digits who was driving his great-grandmother to the store. She'd asked the wrong child and the kid didn't see any reason to correct her.

My old boss didn't waste time wallowing—not for long, anyway. He quit the PI business and turned to the tech industry. If information was out there, Sam was the guy who could find it. That he had a link to the outside world didn't shock me. I was counting on it.

His hands danced over the keyboard. He did a bunch of mouse clicking. "How was your trip?"

"Stressful. Mom had appendicitis and Dad panicked. He needed one of us there, but Toula doesn't have a current passport. So I went."

That got an eyebrow rise out of him. "Toula the control freak doesn't have a passport?"

"That's what she said."

He swiveled and tapped on a different keyboard. "Sure she does."

"Wait, what?"

"Yeah, your sister got her passport renewed last year. Hasn't been anywhere, but she's good to go if the need arises."

"Maybe she just didn't want to go. I mean, what would she do with my niece and nephew?"

"Leave them with their dad?"

"When it comes to parenting, Kostas is in over his head. Or at least that's how he plays it. Milos and Patra would be scoffing candy for every meal, while he's tied up in the closet as a human sacrifice to Walt Disney."

He raised both brows at me. "A beloved aunt?"

I laughed. "Toula would rather cut off her arm and hit

herself with the soggy end than leave her kids with me for more than a few hours."

"You too much fun or something?"

"Like everyone else, I'm too much not Toula."

He grinned. "Okay, so what are we doing?"

"First thing, is this kooky weather happening anywhere else?"

"All right. We're looking for freak weather like ours. Crazy winds, occasional buckets of rain—"

"Not rain."

Up went his brows. "Have you looked outside? The streets are wet."

"It might be falling from the sky, but that's seawater."

He shook his head. "This gets weirder and weirder." He worked his Sam Washington magic. "Looks like we're it. Merope is the epicenter of a weather pattern no one can explain because the world doesn't know about it. Nobody out there is even talking about this thing. Never been anything like it, as far as I can tell. Not since mankind created meteorologists to dissect and report on bizarre weather phenomena."

"And before that?"

"Do I look like I have a time machine?"

"No, but you look like a guy who could find someone with a time machine, if one exists."

"That's why I like you, Callas. You've got faith in ol' Sam." He tapped his fingers on the desk. "What's next?"

"I need to make a phone call. Can you make it happen?"

He reached over and picked up an old fashioned handset. "Got a number for me?"

I gave him Betty's number and waited while her phone rang. When she answered, the line was clear. Could have been we were standing in the same room. Sam left to give us privacy.

"Allie! My goodness, love, I've made a mess of things."

"I knew it," I said. "I knew this wasn't natural."

"I wish it was. Weather passes on its own. This isn't going anywhere, I'm afraid."

"Can you come to the shop?"

She hesitated. "That's impossible right now. We had to lockdown our business, didn't we, love?"

"It's locked down? Why? What's going on?" Despite spending most of his day in his wheelchair, Sam owned a regular office chair. A high dollar swivel that made me feel productive merely slouching in its capable arms. "Tell me everything."

"It's a disaster, that's what it is. And they plotted it right under our noses." There were tea sounds. "You know the Cake Emporium exists in every civilized time and populated place, yes? Anyone with the slightest woo-woo powers can find it if they know where to look. Three of our customers crossed time and space to meet up in our shop to plot something, didn't they? And now they've done it and taken over your island. We're closed for the foreseeable future so they can't double back and go somewhen or somewhere else."

I felt around in my bag for pen and paper. "Who are they? What else do you know?"

"Oh, love. Part of me was hoping you'd take this on, but another part of me is terrified for you. These aren't your ordinary cake-eating people. They all met up when they were alive, but they put their plan into motion once they were dead."

"So … *ghosts* are making wind and holding the island hostage?"

"Something like that. I don't understand it fully myself.

I never listened in on all their planning—with my ears or my mind."

Betty can read minds, or at least active thoughts. She tries not to listen in on mine, but sometimes they pop right out of my head. I guess I'm a hard thinker.

"Do you know who they are?"

"All I know is that they're from different times and places, and at least two of them are people of some significance. Or at least they put on a show of being important. It's hard to tell with people. They were telegraphing a serious amount of self-importance and confidence in their plan. But that's a lot of people in this world. The third one is a strange fellow. Russian, I believe."

"Vladimir," I said.

"You've met him?"

"He's the only ghost I've seen since I got back to the island." That reminded me … "Where are the other ghosts? Even Yiayia and my cat are missing."

"Hiding, if they're smart. These three … they're different. Not your usual spooks. I'm not sure what's driving them but it's something fierce. Promise me you'll be careful."

I crossed my heart and hoped not to die, and avoided the whole sticking a needle in my eye part. One should always be careful with their eyeballs.

Three cunning and calculating ghosts were responsible for all this. Something had to be done, and the only person on the island who could do that something—probably—was me. Not just because I could see the dead, but also because finding things, including solutions to problems, was kind of my thing.

I needed a plan.

Step One: Talk to the ghosts. Establish a rapport.

Step Two:

Step Three:

Step Four: Success!

The middle part of my plan was missing, but I had absolutely no confidence that it would eventually show up. Which meant I'd have to wing it. Merope's people couldn't take much more of this, and they shouldn't have to. This was their home. Three interloping ghosts weren't going to keep everyone locked away, no matter how fancy or self-important their credentials.

I'd encountered Vladimir after yelling into the wind outside my apartment. To speak to all three ghosts, I decided to take it out of the village. Merope is one of those stereotypically Greek places where everyone knows everyone, and there's no business like everyone else's business. The last thing I needed was people making up stories about crazy Allie Callas, who can find anything except a husband—and no wonder, because she's a whole lamb short of a party.

I schlepped toward the center of the island, one tedious step at a time, where there wasn't much except a cemetery, olive trees, and a whole lot of scrub and dirt. Branches lashed out at each other. Layers of Merope's dusty soil twirled in dense clouds. It hadn't been fake raining out here. The air tasted like a litter box.

"Vladimir?" The dust vacuumed the words right out of my mouth. "We need to talk!"

The wind died. Not gradually. It dropped completely dead in a three-meter circle around me the way it had earlier. Vladimir, he of the mighty girth and cheese puffs, materialized.

"Allie! We meet again. You are ready to help, da?"

"Here's the thing. You want off this island, and I want you gone. So let's dance."

He looked down at his feet. Or down where his feet would be visible if his favorite food wasn't food.

"You don't actually have to dance," I told him. "It means let's do this deal, let's talk."

"I already tell you vhat we require."

I rotated my hand in a circle to hurry him up. "Yes, yes, but if we're going to do this, I need to talk with your pals, too. If I understand what happened, I have a better chance of helping you."

A wrinkle appeared between his ghost brows. He figured I was trying to con him but wasn't sure how. "Vhy talk to them? They are nothink. I am emissary."

"Yes you are, and you're doing a great job." I gave him what I hoped was an "atta boy" smile. If I was going to get them off this island, I had to meet with his buddies. I wanted to see for myself who had managed to bamboozle Betty and throw Merope into turmoil. "But this is about information. The more I know, the easier and faster this will be."

He lost some of his bluster. He held up one finger. "Vait."

Pop. Vladimir vanished.

Wind swirled around my protective circle, churning up dirt and dust.

A protective circle.

Doh!

Now there was an idea. If ghosts had one inconvenient enemy, it was salt. Pour an unbroken salt circle around a spirit and they weren't going anywhere. If this whole wind thing was ghost-driven, maybe I could put the main street in a salt circle. Or draw one around the Cake Emporium so Betty and I could figure this out if my parlay failed to produce results.

Where could I acquire that much salt?

The More Super Market sold salt in small kitchen-friendly boxes. Maybe Stephanie had enough on the shelves for me to work with. Or the Cake Emporium itself. Bakers use salt, seeing as how it's a natural flavor enhancer. Surely Jack Honeychurch's kitchen contained a bag of salt. Maybe even a big one. If that didn't pan out, I could call in favors, raid some of the local taverns. Not a literal raid. I'd pay for the salt.

The ground shuddered. Outside my circle, gale force winds heaved on the trees. There was an almighty crack as a widow maker branch tore off and cartwheeled across the dirt.

Vladimir winked back into existence. He bowed as low as he could, which was basically a head nod, then drifted sideways. Two forms slowly materialized. The calm circle widened, and two dead men stepped into the peaceful clearing.

Virgin Mary, what the heck?

The dead man on the left was some kind of old timey washerwoman. He had a pile of laundry on his head. Reminiscent of a Sheik's turban, but *more* turban-y. From the fuzzy beard down, he was covered in a plush velvet robe that I suspected wasn't supposed to be nightwear but looked like it anyway. The other guy was also in a robe, but his was gauzy. Someone had been shopping at Fredericks of Hollywood and slammed into Gloria Swanson, resulting in a fabulous mash-up. His narrow face ended in a long, black beard, dangling from the tip of his chin. This mass of hair was braided. Easy to mistake him for the back end of a show horse.

The way they moved, I could tell they thought they

were somebodies. Whether they were or weren't, the verdict was still out.

Vladimir's head popped up like a squirrel with its cheeks packed full of nuts. Copying moves he'd borrowed from a stage magician, he presented his buddies.

"Mehmed II—"

"Mehmed the Conqueror," Mehmed, probably, said.

"A thousand apologies," Vladimir said. His face said no —no apologies. "And Xerxes."

"Do you have a number after your name as well?" I asked Chin Braid.

"The Great," Xerxes said.

"I can't count that high," I said. "Does that come before or after a zillion?"

He stared at me in Persian dictator. Good thing he had no power over me or I'd be sniveling and scraping on the ground.

I swung around to Vladimir. "And you are?"

"Only Vladimir. I am nobody. But vun day people vill hear about me. Maybe they vill say good things about Vladimir, eh?"

Yeah, that seemed unlikely, given that he was already dead.

"Okay, we've got Vladimir the nobody, Mehmed the Conqueror, and Xerxes the Great. A Russian, a Turk, and a Persian. That sounds like the beginning of a joke. A Russian, a Turk, and Persian walk into a cake shop ... how does the rest of it go?"

"You know of the cake shop?" Mehmed demanded.

"I can see you, can't I? Only people with certain skills can see the shop. A little birdie told me you can see the shop, too, otherwise you wouldn't have been able to go inside. So what's your woo-woo superpower?"

Mehmed stared down his razor thin nose at me. "Woo-woo? What is this woo-woo?"

"She means paranormal abilities," Vladimir said in his slow, careful accent.

Xerxes held his arms out. Possibly on the verge of prancing down a runway. "I have no need of these woo-woo abilities. I am divine."

"Nice eyeliner," I pointed out. "How do you get a clean cat eye? Never mind, I don't care. But you should meet the woman at the More Super Market. The best she can manage is a feral cat eye."

"You are insolent." Xerxes sounded surprised. Obviously we hadn't met before.

"I've been called worse. And better. You have to have woo-woo powers or you wouldn't have been able to see the shop. So what is it?"

Xerxes stared at a tree. The tree ignored him. Vladimir fidgeted. Mehmed scratched his bushy beard.

"In life, I had the sight," Mehmed told me. "I could see the past, present, future. Very useful for my poetry."

"I, too, can see the past and present. That's how my family knows not to put me in a nursing home yet."

"Mehmed the Conqueror writes poetry," Vladimir said. His face told me he'd heard a lot of the Ottoman's poetry in recent days. His face also indicated that the quality of Mehmed's poetry was on par with the sound of cats hocking up hairballs.

"Would you like to hear some of my poetry?" Mehmed asked in a hopeful voice.

Yikes. "Uh, maybe after we talk business?"

He pouted. His laundry pile wobbled. "All I want to do is write poetry and enjoy the mouth of an attractive young man on my *cuk*, but instead I am here, negotiating with a woman."

"Well, excuse me," I said. "I didn't invite you to my island."

Xerxes brightened up. "This is your island? I will take it from you! Or you could give it to me."

"I don't own it, if that's what you mean. I just live here."

"Oh." His disappointment was palpable. "Do you have any Spartans?"

"Not that I know of."

"Wells?"

"We have wells."

"I would like to avoid those. Nothing good happens to Persians when there are wells around. Or Spartans."

I did the backward hand circle again. "Okay, let's go back to the power bit."

"I am a god," Xerxes said, as though his divinity was obvious.

"Yeah, in a book. In real life you were just a garden-variety conqueror. History is full of guys like you. Vladimir?"

"I can move things."

"Like furniture?" I asked.

He frowned. "Sometimes furniture, yes."

Now that I was semi-acclimated to hanging out with historical figures, I hit them with a hardball question. "Why are you on this island, causing all this … weather?"

Mehmed shrugged. "We are conquerors. We are conquering."

"Yes, we are conquering," Xerxes said. "That is what we do. Nations have bent down and kissed my feet."

His feet were gnarly. Probably he should spring for closed shoes instead of those man-sandals.

"No, you're making wind," I pointed out. "You've conquered nothing."

With a smirk, Mehmed's hands landed on his sizable hips. "Where are your people?"

"In their houses, where it's safe."

"Hiding. Afraid. Because I—"

"We," Xerxes said.

"—Have forced them into their homes. In time they will come to love me, even though people all over Europe cheered when they heard of my passing. They hated me." His face fell. "Everybody hates me."

"Vladimir does not hate you," Vladimir said.

"He is lying," Mehmed said. "His nose is brown. See? Brown."

Vladimir's nose looked white and see-through to me. "So your big plan is to conquer … Merope? Why? We're one tiny island."

Mehmed belly-laughed. "No, first we want the shining star of Europe, the cradle of civilization that is not Turkish—"

"Or Persian," Xerxes added.

"Greece," Mehmed said. "And we will have it as soon as we get off this island, with your help."

I raised both brows. "And you're going to conquer Greece with a stiff breeze?"

"And rain," Mehmed said.

"We are working on earthquakes, too," Xerxes said.

"Wery clever," Vladimir said.

Ooh boy. Talk about delusional and behind the times. Well, someone had to break it to them, and it looked like that someone was me.

"When were you last alive?" I asked Mehmed.

"I died very boringly on May 3, 1481."

"And you?" I asked Xerxes.

"2500 years ago. But my death was not boring. I was

killed by one of my men and a eunuch. Do you still have eunuchs?"

"Only in politics," I said. "What about you?" I asked Vladimir.

"My life and death matter not at all. I had ewerythink and then died with nothink ven I lost it."

Someone needed a consultation with a mental health professional and a prescription for antidepressants.

I addressed the two dead conquerors. "Things have changed in the world since you two last walked around in your meat sacks with your skeletons keeping you upright." My eye twitched. "I can't believe I'm going to say this," I muttered to myself. "I hope nobody still alive hears me." I raised my voice. "The thing is, Greece is lovely, yes. Gorgeous country. Wonderful people. Great food. But it's lost some of its …"

Eyebrows raised, the conquerors stared at me expectantly.

I gagged slightly. "… Political cachet. It's not what it used to be. This isn't Spartans and Athenians and Alexander the Great anymore. It's Greece digging itself out of a financial ditch with the rest of Europe's help. We're not the center of the civilized world anymore."

"Ditch?" Vladimir said. "Vot is this financial ditch?"

"Finance. Money. Greece ran out of money," I explained.

"That is too bad," Xerxes said. "I like money."

"I have money," Mehmed said.

"You're dead, you don't have anything," I said. "Not even the clothes you died in. Haven't you heard the expression 'you can't take it with you'? That's where you're at. Whatever you had while you were alive, it's not yours anymore."

"I had Europe," Mehmed said.

"Not anymore."

"That is a problem."

"No, it's progress and change." I shoved my gloved hands in my coat's pockets. Even in this quiet circle it was winter on Merope, and the cold continued its relentless attack on my wardrobe. "Now, pack it up and head up to the Afterlife. I hear it's quite nice up there. They might even let you conquer something. A table, a parking space, that sort of thing."

"Let me confer with my, uh, this person," Mehmed said, waving at Xerxes.

"Xerxes the Great," Xerxes reminded him.

Trouble in their partnership? Or a case of too many conquerors in the kitchen?

In their robes, they huddled together, murmuring like a pair of mean girls.

"They are wery secretive," Vladimir told me.

"I can see that."

"They do this all the time. Vhisper, Vhisper. Is, how you say, rude, yes?"

"So rude."

The conquerors broke their huddle and returned.

Mehmed cleared his throat. "One question. Which country is the new Greece?"

"In Europe? Germany, probably. Although there was a time it was the Romans. Global superpowers tend to rise and fall. Outside of Europe there's the USA, China—"

"Take us there."

"Which one?"

"The best one."

"No."

Mehmed threw his hands in the air. "What can you do?"

"I can help you get to the Afterlife. You're dead. That's

where you belong. Did you three even do your orientation?"

They stared at me. Yeah, that was a definite no.

"The only way you get to delay orientation and stick around is if you were murdered or have another serious unfinished business. Xerxes was murdered, yes, but since we know who did it, it's no longer unfinished business."

Xerxes glanced around. "Where is my angel then? I cannot go without my angel. Every soul in my religion gets an angel escort."

"That's not how it really works. You die, and then you go to Afterlife orientation. That's what limbo is. Orientation, where you learn the ropes, benefits, and rules of being dead."

"You know nothing, woman," Xerxes said.

These freakin' ghosts. "I know more than you."

"I heff unfinished business," Vladimir said.

"What?"

The dead Ottoman's turban was wobbling on his head. "Take us to your China! Or USA! Or Germany!

I folded my arms. "No. Afterlife or nothing."

Mehmed shrugged. "Okay, then we will keep doing wind until you change your mind."

Inflicting them on the rest of the world didn't seem smart. I mean, what was their endgame? Roam around the planet, blowing on things? What was the point? They couldn't conquer anything without bodies. They were dead. They needed to move on like other ghosts.

"I won't," I said.

Summoning his inner drama queen, Mehmed II swished his hand through the air and vanished. Xerxes performed a fancy arm wave that made his robe sleeves flutter. *Bam*. He was gone, too. Now it was just me and Vladimir, who didn't seem particularly theatrical.

"You need new friends," I told him.

"Men such as those do not have friends, only allies. Today ve are allies. Tomorrow, who knows?"

"Bleak."

He shrugged. "It is vhat it is. Ve vill speak again soon, da?"

"I won't change my mind. I'm not unleashing you or your pals on the mainland. It's time to move on."

"I haff business." He tried swishing his hand. Nothing happened. "Vait. I vill try again."

He tried again. More nothing happened.

"Close your eyes?" he asked me.

"No."

"Okay." He held his breath—not that he had breath to hold—and disappeared.

The wall of calm collapsed. A wild burst of wind kicked me in the pants and knocked me down. It wasn't all bad, though: the ground caught my face.

CHAPTER FOUR

BY THE TIME I reached my apartment building, I was a limping, panting mess. My face hurt. My body ached. Tears rolled out of my eyes non-stop, desperately trying to hose out specks of dirt. A monster coalesced in the lobby's glass door.

I jumped back. "Argh!"

The monster leaped with me.

Wait. No. Just me and my battered face.

With my cranium throbbing, I dragged my pathetic carcass up the stairs, hoping I wouldn't run in to anyone. Especially Leo. I wanted him to think I was pretty, not hamburger meat.

My luck ran out at the top of the stairs. Lydia was sitting in the hallway, butted up to Jimmy Kontos. Legs stuck straight out; heads together. Probably conspiring to produce porn.

Jimmy is Leo's cousin. For reasons I don't understand, he lives with Leo, and I like to imagine he sleeps in a drawer or a dog bed. Jimmy is the island's only dwarf. He compensates by keeping his facial hair big and blond and wild. Lydia is a platinum blonde, although today her darker roots were playing peek-a-boo. Didn't detract one bit from the fact that she's utterly gorgeous in a porny pin-up kind of way.

Eyes on the floor, I tromped up to my door. Maybe they wouldn't notice my purpling cheek.

Nope. Not that lucky either.

"Nice bruises," Jimmy said. "You catch the ground with your face?"

"Actually, yes."

"I was joking."

"I wasn't. Why are you two in the hallway? Don't you have homes to go to?"

"Keeping our relationship in the open," Jimmy said. "We don't want people to think we're sleeping together."

My eye twitched. Jimmy is the star of a series of skin flicks called *Tiny Men, Big Tools*. They're popular among a certain subset of the porn-watching world that doesn't include me. As for Lydia, she'd dated a lot, and she had maybe one standard that may or may not be animals.

I stuck the key in the lock. "Okay."

"Because we're not," Jimmy went on.

"Okay."

"We're taking it slow," he said.

"She doesn't care," Lydia said.

"I really don't," I said.

I fell into my apartment and slammed the door before Jimmy could throw more words at me. Exhausted and bruised, I poured an inch of ouzo. Flopped down on the couch. Closed my eyes for a moment while my face went *womp-womp*. At least I could sit here and watch a movie.

I turned on the TV.

No signal.

Great. Just great. The dead conquerors were plotting to

inconvenience us with wind and boredom until I caved and inflicted them on another, more pivotal nation.

Wasn't going to happen. I could live without television.

I grabbed a book. I went to bed.

I got up again because I needed to pee.

Thanks to little-known 90s flick called *Deep Rising*, I never sat on a toilet without looking first. Good thing I did.

Tonight there was a waterspout forming in my toilet.

Vladimir's voice burbled up through the pipe. "Take us vhere ve vant to go."

I dropped the lid and flushed.

"*Ty che, blyad!*"

It was 8:00 AM and I'd slept hard all night, despite the absent comforting heft of Dead Cat. Now I was uncomfortably awake.

An inconvenient fist was pounding on my front door.

I staggered to the living room still fully dressed from the night before. My toilet hadn't quit swirling; so I'd been forced to make other plans that I would never, ever speak of in polite company. What else could I do? I couldn't sit on a toilet that made voices and weather.

The peephole revealed a stiff, buttoned-up man who could have been a butler in a grand British mansion. Instead, Alfred had left jolly old England to be a butler in a sterile Greek villa, owned by my client and almost-a-friend, Angela Zouboulaki. Alfred looks like he toppled off a long production line of butlers—slender, balding at the front, thin but neat mustache. Choosing a different career would have been contrary to his genetic programming.

I opened the door. "Good morning, Alfred."

"Pardon me for saying so, but what is good about it, Miss Allie?"

"We still have electricity."

The lights flickered.

"We still have electricity—for now," I said, correcting myself.

Mentally I was calculating the effect losing electricity would have on Merope. Most homes on the island were heated via overhead pipes that vented hot air from wood-burning ovens. Others had pellet stoves. Some had regular fireplaces or radiators. Houses were built solid and thick with spectacular insulation against the heat. That meant they also excelled at keeping out the cold. Most of us would make it. *Most* wasn't good enough.

I had to find a way to get the ghosts to the Afterlife without inflicting them on another nation, before anyone was hurt. Besides the Zervases. It was already too late for them.

But first, Alfred. Who was staring at me with his usual deadpan expression.

I sighed. "What did Angela do this time?"

"Mrs. Angela would like to employ your services again. She wants this wind to stop and she would like you to find a way."

His face said her idea was preposterous, but he was willing to deliver her message because he was madly—as mad as a man who wore starched underpants could be—in love with his employer.

Since his expression said what his mouth wouldn't, I said it aloud for him.

"That's preposterous."

"I am only the messenger. Mrs. Angela wanted to come herself but I convinced her to stay home where she is safe."

"It's weather." It wasn't weather. "What, exactly, does she think I can do about it?"

The poor man looked constipated. "The way Mrs. Angela explained it, she is certain you can call somebody to find out when this weather pattern will pass. Perhaps you have an *in* with a noteworthy meteorologist."

And there it was: the real reason for Alfred's visit.

"Does she have a particular noteworthy meteorologist in mind? What am I saying? Of course she does."

For a man with a poker face, he sure used it to tell a lot of tales.

"The man in question is George Diplas."

George Diplas. Greece's favorite weatherman. Notorious for charging face-first into storms and delivering his reports while clinging to a tree or the nearest sturdy object. George was attractive in a weather-beaten tough-guy way that sent loins all over Greece a-quiverin'. If the gossip columns were accurate, when he wasn't out chasing storms he was at home with a legendary collection of books. The complete opposite of Angela's type. She had a penchant for rakes and other assorted tools.

"So she wants me to bring George Diplas to Merope on the grounds that we have freakish weather, and then she can make her move?"

Alfred stared at my nose for the longest time. I touched it and winced.

"Wind knocked me over," I explained.

"Perhaps you need a physician."

"What doesn't kill me only makes me stronger."

He blinked. "Yes, Mrs. Angela has plans for this Diplas character."

"And she knows phones aren't working, right?"

"Mrs. Angela said, and I quote, 'There is no one more resourceful than Aliki Callas.'"

Things were serious if she was using my full first name.

I blew out a long, frustrated sigh. A manhunt wasn't on my agenda right now. Not with this weather and weirdness.

"I can't call anyone. I can't go anywhere. I'm terrible at miracles and pulling rabbits out of hats. The only thing I've ever pulled out of a hat is a louse—and it wasn't my louse. Although I suppose it was afterwards."

"Mrs. Angela has complete confidence in you." He nodded once. "And so do I."

Angela regularly got the hots for flimflam men, so her opinion was suspect, at best. But Alfred was different. That he believed in me held some weight.

"I'll do what I can, when I can."

He touched my nose. My pain receptors freaked out. I might have yelped.

"See a doctor," Alfred told me.

The electricity held.

I made coffees—two—and carried them upstairs to Leo's apartment. I knew he was home because his cop car was snugged up to curb in its usual spot, leaving enough room for two donkeys or a compact car to squeeze past. I also knew he was up because I'd heard his heavy footfalls on the ceiling above. Our apartments were mostly sound-proof, but occasionally noise leaked through when Leo was working out. In the early days I'd mistaken him for a guy with a revolving bedroom door instead of a weight rack.

Jimmy threw the door open. He was in footie pajamas. Hair done up in a man bun. Beard running wild.

"Nice. The giant brought coffee." He grabbed both coffees and kicked the door shut.

That sawn-off little weasel. Nobody steals my coffee. *Nobody*.

"I spat in mine," I said through the door.

The door opened. He slapped both coffees back into my hands and held the door open.

"Yeah, you better not mess with my coffee," I said. "The reason you're not still hiding in garbage cans, stalking Lydia, is because of me."

His face flushed. "Can't even take her on a proper date because of this wind."

"Where's Leo?"

"Shower."

The thought of Leo sluicing water and soap over his naked body was doing things to me.

"Why don't you take Lydia over to Merope's Best for a coffee-like substance? They're open."

He was this close to jumping at the idea, but not completely sold. His eyes narrowed. "Are you trying to get rid of me?"

"Yes."

He considered that for a moment. "All right."

"Order the affogato. It's amazing."

He shot me a dubious look and raced off to get changed. He returned in a jeans and an itty-bitty puffy jacket.

"Affogato?"

"Affogato."

"I love ice cream," he said and took off.

Leo emerged from the bathroom, hair wet, skin clean. Everything about him made me want to pounce. But I had this coffee and he looked like he needed it. The sacrifices I made, I swear. I was practically a humanitarian.

He stopped short when he saw my face. "Honey …"

"It's just makeup."

"Really?"

"Sure, why not? I'm auditioning for Community Theater."

"What really happened?"

"I tussled with gravity. If you think this looks bad, you should see the ground. It took a serious beating."

"Stop doing that." He kissed me softly on the lips. "I worry about you." He eyed the door. "Merope's Best, eh?"

"It *is* open," I said.

"Is there any ice cream in that affogato?"

"In a manner of speaking, yes. Also, in a manner of speaking, no."

He laughed. "What did they substitute? A rock? Dirt?"

"Fruitcake."

"I'd rather have the dirt." He eyed the coffee in my hands. "Is one of those for me?"

I handed him a cup.

"Does it have fruitcake?"

"I have too much respect for coffee to inflict fruitcake on it."

He buckled his holster to his belt before taking another long drag. He made sounds like the coffee hit all the rights spots on the way down.

"Work?" I asked like it wasn't obvious.

He nodded once. "What's on your schedule today?"

"I need a sounding board. Normally I run this kind of thing past Betty, but Betty can't get to the shop right now."

"Because of her commuting issues," he said.

"Because of her commuting issues. Exactly. Which means I don't have anyone to bounce ideas off. Unless you're willing."

"For you I've always got time. Plus you brought me this coffee."

Boy, was he probably about to be sorry.

Deep breath. "This wind, none of it is natural."

"Okay …"

I forged ahead. "It's ghosts."

No question mark: "Ghosts."

Oh boy. I was losing him. "I know I said it wasn't ghosts because I couldn't see them, but it *is* ghosts. Somehow these guys are able to create weather—or at least a bunch of wind. I don't know how. They're old. They had time to plot this and hone all kinds of skills."

"Guys?"

This was where things were about to get weird. Leo would either take it all in stride or call for the men with the strappy jacket and the needle full of chill-out juice.

"Mehmed the Conqueror, Xerxes the Great, and Vladimir."

His face gave nothing away. The guys with the strappy jacket were still on the menu.

"Just Vladimir?"

I waved my hand. "He's a flunky. Looks like he was born and raised in a basement. Also, he's Russian."

"Russian."

"You can use more words."

"I don't have more words."

"Okay, so these three ghosts are threatening to keep this wind storm going until I give them what they want."

"Which is what? A country? A continent? A potting wheel and Demi Moore?"

"Pretty much. They wound up on Merope by accident, I think, not realizing it was an island, and now they're trapped here. They want me to find a way to get them off the island and to a country of their choosing. They wanted Greece but changed their minds when they realized …" My words fell off a cliff.

"Realized what?"

"Nothing."

"Something. Have you noticed that I'm a policeman?" His voice turned to honey. "I have handcuffs. I have ways of making you talk."

Oh boy. "Maybe I don't want to tell you now."

He located the cuffs, dangled them in the air. "I'll get your confession, one way or another. The torture is going to be rough. You'll break."

"I don't break."

"You will when Jimmy sings the Oompa-Loompa song."

I shuddered. "Anything but that. Fine. I told them that Greece is no longer the epicenter of civilization."

He tipped his head back and laughed. "That's it, that's the thing I'm going to hold over you when I want to get my way."

"What makes you think I wouldn't just let you get your way?"

His eyes scraped me from top to bottom before flicking to my lips then back up to meet my gaze. I felt like he'd undressed me—in a good way. "You say that now, but wait until I want you to do that thing I like."

"What thing?"

He leaned in close. His breath was warm on my ear and burned all the way down to my hoo-ha. My pulse went nuts.

"Make coffee in the morning."

I went to play slap him, but he was too quick for me. His fingers clamped around my wrist and pulled until my hand was settled on the back of his neck. His mouth pressed down on mine. Hot. Firm. Delicious. He tasted like coffee and Leo. He pulled me onto him.

"My ghosts …"

"Can wait."

I pointed out the obvious. "No, but your phone can't."

He said a lot of words that were mostly benign on their own in a dictionary or a spelling bee, but strung together they suggested appalling sexual shenanigans with a variety of household objects and long-extinct animals. He snatched up his phone. "Come."

Given that the common Greek phone greeting wasn't an order for me, I hopped off his lap, sipped my coffee, and tried to compose myself while he listened to whoever was on the other end.

His face grew grimmer by the second. By the time he hung up with a terse "I'll be right there," he was in full cop mode. The guy I'd been kissing was locked away for later.

"Murder, death, intrigue?" I asked.

"The Zervases. The cranial injuries were post mortem."

That got my attention. "How did they die?"

"Poisoned."

CHAPTER FIVE

Leo and I took our coffees to go. He dropped me off at
Sam's place before battling the elements to meet up with
Panos Grekos, the coroner.

Sam raised his eyebrows at me. "Back so soon?"

"I need to send an email. You're the only person who
can get correspondence on or off the island."

"Mi computer, su computer."

"Thanks. I'll bring double the pie and cake next time."

"I'm gonna hold you to that, Callas. I couldn't handle
that fruitcake again."

Through a series of back channels, I managed to
scrounge up a personal email address for George Diplas
and let him know about Merope's loony weather, hoping
that would be enough to trigger the cat hair in his DNA.
Then I called Betty again and told her I'd identified the
goons who'd cooked up their plot in her shop.

"Those cheeky buggers! If I'd known who they were, I
wouldn't have let them through the door. But they came in
wearing disguises, didn't they? The question now is will
you help them off the island?"

"And inflict them on an even bigger population? That's not going to happen. They're getting a one-way ticket to the Afterlife. First I need to contain them before they do more damage."

"Salt," we both said at the same time. Me because it was my idea and Betty because I was thinking the word so hard it flew right up in her face.

"Does the Cake Emporium keep mass quantities of salt, by any chance?"

"Jack tells me there's a twenty-five kilo bag in the storeroom you can have."

"You want me to break into your shop?"

Her laugh tinkled. "No, love. Jack says he'll let you in. But we can't risk those dead fools trying to make a run for the shop, otherwise who knows where they'll end up this time? There's already a salt barrier baked into the foundation. The circle breaks when the door opens. You'll need to close that gap and Jack will let you and only you in."

The mysterious Jack Honeychurch. I'd never met the Cake Emporium's master cake craftsman. He rarely left his kitchen, and only then to commute between his workspace and home.

My brain was already working on a solution. "I'll make a smaller salt circle around the entrance."

"That's the ticket."

"What time?"

"He said when you're ready, knock on the door and he'll be there."

———

For woo-woo emergencies, I keep a small saltshaker in my bag. A gift from a man I called the Man in Black. *Man*, because he appeared to be male. *Black*, because his entire wardrobe was devoid of color. Probably he had a real name, seeing as how most people do unless they've been raised in the woods by wolves or primates. But thus far he hadn't ponied up his name, so I had to improvise.

The Man in Black was tall. Dark of hair and eyes. Brooding in the style of a Darcy or a Heathcliff, without the alcohol and opium addictions. He made regular appearances in my life, usually to dispense obscure advice. A couple of times he'd saved my bacon. Which was nice. Bacon should be saved. But the last time I flirted with death, he didn't show up. He'd been absent since he'd shown me a glimpse of the past and explained that time was a fistful of beads on a smooshed string.

Because I needed salt to acquire more salt, I kicked and punch the wind all the way to the More Super Market. Exhausted, I tapped on the door and jiggled to stay warm.

This time Stephanie wasn't playing butler. A man shoved the door open and pulled me in.

"Are you crazy?" he said. "Nobody should be out in that."

He had some nerve, given that he'd clearly risked being "out in that" to get to the More Super Market himself. Who was this clown? He wasn't one of ours.

I replayed his voice in my head.

Ungh. Now I recognized him. When I spoke to Adonis Diplas on the phone before things blew up with the Bakas family, he was making noises about coming to Merope to claim his bride and his prize: the More Super Market. Ownership of the market had been part of Effie's dowry. Effie Bakas was locked up now and wouldn't be marrying anyone ever, but Adonis Diplas already had the deed to the shop. And now here he was, opening doors for his customers.

Not exactly the tall, dark, smooth charmer I'd pictured when we spoke on the phone.

Adonis Diplas looked like he could throw a punch and catch one with his face without flinching. Fair-hair slicked back and mostly hidden under a ball cap. Brown eyes. Stocky build. A guy whose confidence never wavered. Sexy if you liked them dirty.

"You must be Kyrios Diplas."

He smiled. It was a crooked thing that had probably ripped off a lot of flimsy panties. Good thing I was wearing heavy-duty underwear.

"I know you." He sounded like a cup of hot chocolate with a shot of whiskey. "We talked on the phone. Allie something, right? I looked you up after our phone call."

"Yes, that's it. Allie Something. What are you doing here? Your fiancée is in jail."

His sweatshirt tensed and flexed across big shoulders as he shrugged. "I wanted a change of scenery. As luck would have it, I own this shop. So here I am."

Stephanie flipped through her magazine without looking up. "I do not like him."

He leaned on the counter. "What do you make? I'll give you a raise. A good one."

She flipped a page. "I love this man. He talks raises to me."

I rolled my eyes. "Is that how you work, you just buy people?"

"Why not?" Adonis said. "People like money. Now I have some to share."

"I *do* like money," Stephanie said, eyes still on her magazine.

Stifling a second eye roll, I focused on my task.

Salt … salt … salt …

Salt. I grabbed four small boxes from the shelf, leaving

two in case someone else was suffering from an electrolyte shortage. Given how much salt Greeks threw into and onto their food, that was a weak possibility.

Adonis Diplas glanced at my purchase. "That's a lot of salt."

"I'm making ice cream."

"In winter?"

"Ice cream is for every season, not just summer."

"Are you really making ice cream?"

"I guess you'll never know."

"What, you're not going to invite me over for dessert?"

I grabbed a *tsokofreta* wafer bar off the shelf and dumped it on the counter in front of him. "There's your dessert."

Toting four boxes of salt, I wended my way toward the Cake Emporium.

I was halfway there when there was a telltale *pop* and Vladimir appeared.

"Vhat are you doink?"

"What does it look like I'm doing?"

"Valking." He dragged the word out in that laconic, languid Russian way until my "valk" became a crawl.

"Give the man a Snoopy."

"Vhat is Snoopy?"

"What do you want, Vladimir?"

"To see if you have changed mind about heelping."

"You mean if I've changed my mind about helping your two power hungry buddies."

"And me."

"No—not you. Whatever scheme they've cooked up,

you have to know that you're only the messenger. You're their servant."

He spat on the ground. Tricky feat for a guy without spit. "Not true."

"So they see you an as equal, as a fellow conqueror?"

Silence.

"What, exactly, have you conquered? Countries in the first Civilization game through however many they're up to in the series now don't count."

"I only play first game, then I die."

So he'd died in the 1990s. I filed that away in my mental filing cabinet. "Tell your overlords that if they drop the gale force winds, I'll find a nice way to send their ghosts to the Afterlife. Otherwise we do it the hard way."

He opened his mouth.

I stuck my index finger under his transparent nose. "That's my best deal."

"They vill not be heppy."

"Do I look like I care about their happiness?"

"*Nyet.*"

I gave him a look that said, Well, what are you waiting for?

Pop.

Vladimir evaporated.

I fought the wind, and the wind nearly won. By the time I arrived at the narrow alley that housed the Cake Emporium, I was oozing sweat and wishing I'd chosen the blanket fort life. I could be at home right now under a cozy canopy, reading books. Instead I was battling woo-woo weather. I had chosen poorly.

Betty had told me the foundation of the Cake Emporium contained a perimeter of salt, making it easy to seal off the shop from intrepid ghosts and oogie-boogies with a sprinkle to the front door step. I kept that in mind as I poured a thick line of salt in a semi circle in front of the Cake Emporium's front door. Instead of the wind whipping it away, it stopped dead in its tracks, creating a calm pocket.

Huh. Nice.

I stepped over the line.

Gravity regained control. My hair dropped back into place. I put away my sunglasses and rubbed my eyes. Before long, they began to feel like eyeballs again, instead of burning marbles. I yanked the hair tie out of my hair and did my best to scrape it into a tidy, presentable tail that wouldn't have Jack Honeychurch thinking I was a deranged derelict, begging for cake. I tried to look professional, like the fate of the island's weather was in competent hands.

I knocked.

Waited.

Wondered about the mysterious Jack Honeychurch. What was he like? A Betty clone? A delightfully British cherub? Same ancient look in his eyes?

There were footsteps inside. The door opened. My jaw slackened. My raw eyes bugged.

"You had better come in," the Man in Black said.

CHAPTER SIX

I WAS TOO STUNNED to follow his instructions. "You're Jack Honeychurch?"

"Am I?"

"But … you're a *baker*?"

"Interesting."

"You don't look like a baker!"

He peered down the length of his aristocratic nose. "What, precisely, does a baker look like?"

I waved at his long, black coat. At his black pants, high riding boots, shirt. They were not the clothes of a man who spent his time with his hands in flour.

"They don't wear black!"

"Will it help if I assure you that I do not wear black while I am baking scones?"

"I don't know." My brain was buzzing with confusion, and part of me wanted to shake Jack for being an evasive jackass. Why keep his identity hidden from me all this time? "I don't know anything right now."

He took stock of the alley. "Then come inside until you reach a conclusion. It's dangerous out there."

I shrugged it off and stepped over the threshold. "It's just three ghosts throwing a temper tantrum until they get their way."

He inspected my face. "You are injured."

"People keep saying that. It's just my new look. I'm a trendsetter."

His face said he wasn't buying it. "How many spirits have you met in your life?"

"Are you looking for an exact number?"

"Approximate will suffice."

Phew. For a moment I thought this was going to be some sort of pop quiz. I was woefully unprepared for one of those.

"Hundreds, maybe."

"Hundreds. And among those spirits, have you seen any that can cause … *weather*?"

"What are you saying?"

"Either these are not mere ghosts, or they have a powerful ally."

On a regular day, the Cake Emporium's cabinets were filled with sweet treats. Today, the lights were off and the cabinets sat empty. The store's fireplace, always glowing or blazing, depending on the temperature outside, was cold and dark. The lack of Betty downgraded the atmosphere to funereal.

"Come with me," the Man in Black, aka: Jack Honeychurch said.

"To your misty moors, or wherever it is you go?"

His pillowy bottom lip quirked. "To the kitchen. You require salt, do you not?"

Still reeling from the whole Black-is-Jack revelation, I trotted along behind him to the Cake Emporium's kitchen. The space was larger than the building would allow, so I knew there was some kind of spooky space warping going on.

Not my first trip to the kitchen. I'd been here before, when an Englishman dropped dead in the Honey-churches' cake shop. That day it was deserted. Today was more of the same. Surfaces gleamed. Tiles shone. No snacks for enterprising rats in sight. A germaphobe could eat directly off the counters and floor without flinching.

Jack opened the massive pantry and hauled out a sack of salt.

"What do you mean to do with the salt?"

"Make ice cream?"

He almost smiled. Almost.

I rubbed my hands together. "Okay, so my big plan is to trap the ghosts until I figure out how to send them to the Afterlife. At least if they're contained, Merope's people can have their lives back."

"Contain them how? Where? Do you have a plan?"

"That was my plan. Did you not hear the part where I mentioned my big plan?"

He stared at me. "That is not a plan. What you have is a first step, and a small one at that."

"Everyone's a critic." I squinted at him. "You're not usually this chatty. Most of the time you're vague and wishy-washy."

"Most of the time I am a busy man."

"Baking."

"I have a job to do, Allie Callas. The same as you."

Was he mocking me? Hard to say. While Betty was made of sunshine, Jack was snippets and snails and shad-ows. But there was no denying both siblings were vastly more than what was on the surface. Sometimes when I looked at Betty, I got the distinct feeling she'd been around since the beginning. At the very least she'd been playing on the Maker's floor while He, She, or They were sketching plans for the universe.

I let out a long stream of air and shoved my hands down in my pockets. "There's no real plan. Yet. It used to be the dead mostly left me alone because they didn't realize I could see them. Lately, they've been coming to me to help them resolve unfinished business. But these guys? They're something else. They don't want a ticket to the Afterlife. They want to finish what they started: conquering the world."

"A difficult task from beyond the grave."

"Unless, like you said, they have help. Who would help them? And if they're not regular ghosts, what are they?"

"Who can say what powers and allies they might have collected during the centuries since their passing?"

"I could use some more of your vague warnings right about now."

"I have no vague warnings to give. This is a most serious situation. Take care, for I cannot easily come to your rescue. Not without compromising my business."

"You can't just walk outside, lock the door behind you, and step over the salt line?"

His dark eyes bored through me.

"I'll take that as a no," I said. "But wait, I have more questions that I suspect you won't answer in plain, honest English. Why do you occasionally come to my rescue?"

"Everyone needs a hobby, Allie Callas. You are mine."

"Not the answer I was expecting."

"Nonetheless, it is the answer I have to give you."

I glanced around the kitchen, looking for answers that weren't here. "I don't suppose you have a plan, or some idea about how I can send these spirits to the Afterlife once I've caught them."

In the past, I'd watched a black swirling hole suck up

bad players once their business was resolved. Could the swirly hole suck up Mehmed, Xerxes, and their Russian sidekick before their plans came to fruition? Or did I have to see this through? I needed answers. Something told me I would have to do what I usually did: work the case until I found a solution.

I didn't want to work the case. I wanted the wind to go away. I also wanted to have sex with Leo, find things, and snuggle at night with my ghost cat.

As I expected, the Man in Black—Jack—shook his head. "They need to move on, that is all I know. How they get there when they are this resistant, I am not sure."

"When we spoke last time, you showed me your time bead thingys, remember?"

He nodded once to indicate that his memory was just fine, even though his mouth didn't function like a mouth should.

"The anomaly. What was it? Is this the anomaly?"

"No. The anomaly is not your concern at this time."

"But it will be."

"I can say no more."

"Can't or won't?"

"Cannot. I have bread rising as we speak. If left too long, it will be ruined."

There was no rising bread. Not here anyway. "What bread? Is it sourdough? Sourdough is seriously popular right now."

He hefted the sack of salt. "You cannot carry this home without assistance."

"I work out. Well, I jog up stairs and ride everywhere. Now that I think about it, I've been skipping arm day for years."

"On a normal day, perhaps. But today is not a normal day."

He was right, darn him. There was nothing normal about the wind and weather, and I'd be pushing myself and twenty-five extra kilos toward home. Lucky for me, Jack provided a solution. He scrounged up a dolly and loaded up the salt. He walked me back to the door.

"One more question," I said. "Where are the rest of the ghosts?"

"For that, you will have to ask someone more knowledgeable about this island and the dead than me."

I took a deep, grounding breath and seized control of the dolly's handle. "I know where I have to go."

Merope's public library is a charming white building with inviting yellow shutters and—probably—a locked door.

Wrong. The door wasn't locked. The librarian was in. Boy, today was full of surprises.

Behind the circulation desk, Popi Papadopoulou, librarian and avid reader, was shuffling through stacks of picture books. Popi is a ball of sunshine. She's short, fair, and she always has a smile to hand out to the library's patrons. Especially the tiny ones.

"You're open," Captain Obvious—me—said.

Popi smiled like the island wasn't taking a beating. "What better way to get through this than with a book?"

"Picture books?"

"Ready for deliveries. Merope's littlest people are scared right now, and they can't go outside to play. Books have been bringing them some comfort, so I fight the wind and hand-deliver them."

Popi is an angel, and nothing will ever convince me otherwise.

"Is it okay if I look around for a book?"

She laughed. "Of course. That's what the library is for. Let me know if you need help."

I hesitated. Were the old librarians here? If they weren't, what would I do? How well did Popi know the island? Did she have access to the old knowledge? I knew for a fact that previous librarians all contributed to a ledger, a repository of Merope's histories and secrets.

Cross that bridge when you come to it, I told myself.

I wandered to the back of the library, where the non-fiction books lived. The former librarians normally prowled through the stacks, tutting over books that had been incorrectly shelved by hasty browsers. Today there was no sign of the library's ghostly guardians. I was alone with their books. Something dramatic must have wrenched them from their beloved books.

What now?

Back to the circulation desk I went. I leaned with both elbows on the polished wood.

Popi looked up from organizing picture books. "Can't find what you're looking for?"

"I don't know what I'm looking for. Well, I do but also I don't."

A smile danced in her eyes. "I thought you could find anything."

"My Google-fu is strong, that's all."

"Oh, it's more than that. You have a knack." She set aside the picture books. "Can I help? I'm a librarian, so it's kind of my thing. At least when it comes to books. Fiction or non-fiction?"

I rocked my hand back and forth. "Non-fiction that sounds like fiction."

"Politics?"

"Cold."

She gave me a thoughtful look. "Paranormal?"

"Warmer."

"Ghosts?"

"Hot."

"You're not here for a book at all, are you?"

"Ehh …"

She sifted through the possibilities. "The former librarians?"

I choked. "Scorching hot."

"The library's former librarians are unavailable right now."

"So I discovered. I don't suppose you know where they are?"

She looked uncomfortable. "Safe."

"From the wind?"

Although we were alone, her voice dipped down low. "I overheard them talking. They don't believe it's wind. They are certain this a paranormal event. How is that possible? Wind doesn't come from nowhere."

Today was one for the books. Heavy on shock value. Light on coffee.

"You can see them?"

"Oh, only since I took the librarian's position. It comes with the job, along with a special library card. I can borrow as many books as I like at one time."

"That's a good perk," I admitted. "The books, I mean. So, can you see all ghosts?"

"Just the ones at the library. Our former librarians, and any stray spirits who wander in, looking for a book. I like to pretend I can't see or hear them." She smiled. Her whole face lit up. "They say the most interesting things about me. What about you?"

"Normally I can see all of them. Since I got back to the island, I can't see any." Well, except for three of them. "But all the others have vanished or I can't see them for some reason. I was hoping the ghosts of librarians past might have more information."

She gnawed on the edge of her lip for a moment, assessing the risk of telling me the truth. Popi had known me for years. Instincts told me I was on her good folks list, I hoped. You never really know with people.

"Please?"

She reached under the circulation desk and retrieved a white pottery urn with a ceramic stopper, reminiscent of the pink jar sitting on my coffee table. The jar on my table was originally a ghost prison. Yiayia had been its prisoner.

"Salt?"

That made sense. Salt keeps things in and out. The librarians wouldn't be able to exit the urn without an intervention, but they'd be protected from roaming dead dictators and equally dead Russians.

She nodded once. "They will not be happy about this. Their plan was to stay inside until this wind or whatever it is stops."

"If this wasn't important, I wouldn't ask."

She reached for the stopper.

"Wait," I said. "I can alleviate some of their worries."

Popi watched while I poured a salt circle. I sat the jar inside the circle. Popped out the stopper.

"Why the salt?" Popi asked.

"Salt keeps things in and out. They won't be able to leave the circle unless I break the line, but also nothing ghostly will be able to get in either. It's like a bunker, but see-through."

She blinked, probably filing away the information for later.

"Kyria Chrysanthi?" I called out. "It's Aliki Callas. I need your help."

Nothing.

The jar didn't so much as rock.

Time to bring out the big guns.

"Sure, random person, you can shelve Stephen King next to Omeros. No one will notice *The Iliad* schmoozing with *Cujo*."

First there was nothing. Then the urn listed slightly. It began to rattle.

Score.

It rocked back and forth, then colors shot up and out of the jar. When they landed, the misty form of Kyria Chrysanthi, Popi's predecessor, materialized.

The previous librarian is a wafting, talking stereotype, right down to the glass, bun, and buttoned-up shirt. Even in death, she never misses an opportunity to stare down the length of her nose, the command to "be quiet" balanced on her tongue.

"King, Stephen, belongs in Fiction. Omeros belongs in Epic Poetry, 883." She shoved her glasses up her nose and peered at me. "You."

"It's me again," I said. "Don't panic. You're safe. Look, I drew a cool circle."

She sniffed. "More like an oval."

"Geometry wasn't my best subject."

"I remember."

Ouch.

Before I could formulate a witty reply that concealed my wounded feelings, she launched her next question. "Why have you disturbed our hiding place and put us in immortal peril?"

"I need your help. The island's ghosts are all missing."

"Hiding," she said. "We are hiding from what lies out there."

"The wind?"

"You, Aliki Callas, know better."

She was right, I did. "I have a plan," I said, lying through my teeth. I had pieces of a plan and a huge sack of salt. Apart from that, I was winging it. "I just want to make sure the ghosts are all okay."

"We who are formerly living are well, and we will remain that way as long as you do not expose us." She stuck one foot out, on the brink of leaping back into her cozy jar.

"Wait!"

She paused.

"What can you tell me about Mehmed II, Xerxes the Great, and some Russian guy called Vladimir?"

"Conquerors. Madmen. Foreigners whose egos were bigger than the backend of an elephant. But who is this Vladimir?" She closed her eyes. "Describe him for me."

"Blond, a watermelon with feet, basement dweller, Russian. Died in the 1990s, or thereabouts."

"His wardrobe?"

"Tracksuit."

"Slavs love their athleisure wear." She opened her eyes. "Your Vladimir does not match any description in the library's knowledge base."

"And the others?"

"Mehmed enjoyed men and poetry. He was published his poems as an individual named Avni. Some were inspired by Christian men, and quite sexual. He conquered Constantinople by being a source of irritation for fifty-five days."

"And Xerxes?"

"Greece was the beginning of his end. Did you know he was considered by many not to be the rightful heir to his father's throne? His half-brother was the eldest son, but his mother was a commoner. Xerxes' mother was the daughter of Cyrus the Great, the one who founded the Achaemenid

Empire. Darius choosing his younger son over his elder to rule was a political move. Xerxes spent his life trying to complete his father's works and wasting money on building projects. In the end, his own hubris killed him."

"I thought it was one of his own advisors and a eunuch?"

"They killed him because of his hubris."

None of this information was really new, just reframed. I gnawed on it a moment.

"If you had to defeat these guys, what would you do?"

The librarian peered down her nose at me. "Be clever. Be Greek."

CHAPTER SEVEN

AFTER THE LIBRARY I went home. Someone had left a sack of salt at my door. A twenty-five kilo bag, identical to the one I'd scored at the Cake Emporium. Weird.

I ripped the top of the bag a fraction and dipped my pinkie in.

Definitely salt. The taste-test said so.

I dragged the second bag inside, along with the first.

Even though I had a half-assed plan, which was more assed than half of anything, I felt good about things. The ghosts were fine; they were just hiding like everyone else. Now I knew exactly where Yiayia was weathering the gale force weather.

The whipping winds had deposited dirt in places that weren't supposed to have dirt, so I showered until I squeaked, wriggled into clean sweat pants and a cozy hoodie, and plopped down on the couch. Everything was quiet, except for the howling outside. Occasionally a flowerpot flew down the street and shattered against a white stucco wall.

Yiayia's jar sat on the table in front of me. I wiggled the stopper out. "I know you're in there," I told the jar.

Yiayia's voice filtered out. "There is nobody home. Take your watermelons and chairs and leave."

"You've lived on Merope your whole life and death. What could you possibly know about shooing away Romany people? None of them live here."

"I know I am safe in this jar."

"With the lid off?"

"That is a good point. Can you put it back in for me?"

"How about I make a salt circle around the sofa and you can come out?"

There was a pause, then: "That is a good plan. We will wait."

We? Dead Cat must be safe and sound in there with her.

I grabbed my saltshaker from the kitchen and sprinkled a large circle in the living room that included the couch and coffee table. Look at me, helping the dead all over the place.

I set the salt on the table and peered into the jar.

"Done. Come on out."

The jar rocked from side to side slightly, then cold air gushed out of the open mouth.

Dead Cat shot out first. He leaped smoothly from the jar to the sofa and immediately got to work using my furniture as a scratching post. No big deal. The nice thing about ghost pets is that they're low maintenance and inexpensive. No litter box to clean. No vet bills. No shedding.

Yiayia was next. First thing she did was check out my circle, then she aimed a complex series of obscene gestures at my windows, most of them inviting the Mehmed, Xerxes, and Vladimir to suck an appendage nature hadn't given her—although Yiayia would say nurture had scored her a lot of them over the years. In life, Yiayia was a woman of voracious appetites, especially for sausage.

My paternal grandmother is short, skinny, with chicken legs and what used to be a magnificent rack. Nowadays the rack was scheduled for demolition but was temporarily held in place with a 1950s cone bra. Today, for whatever reason, she was dressed up as a goat.

"Why are you a goat?"

She winked. "Better if I do not tell you."

The jar shuddered again, and out popped a walker, followed by a senior citizen in pajamas. The front of the pajamas was gaping open. I averted my eyes to avoid damage, including but not limited to blindness.

"Your grandmother knows I like goats," Vasili Moustakas told me.

My eye jumped. I poked it with my finger. The nerve didn't take a hint. It kept on dancing under my fingertip.

"Please stop talking," I told him. I addressed my grandmother. "Why was Kyrios Moustakas in the jar with you?"

"Do not get excited, it was just a fling," she said. "What else was I supposed to do while you were away?"

"Read a few books, watch TV, take some classes up in the Afterlife?"

"It was too dark to read in the jar. We had to dig deep down and explore our creativity."

Before my head exploded, I changed the subject. "Why are all the ghosts hiding?"

"Formerly living is the term we prefer," Yiayia said.

Twitch, twitch. "Why are all the formerly living folks hiding?"

"From the wind, of course."

"Dead people hiding from weather? Doesn't wind go right through you?"

Vasili Moustakas and his walker were pacing the width of the circle. "Do you want to see something?"

"I already saw it," Yiayia told him. "That wind is—" She stopped. There was a noise coming from my kitchen. An eerie rattling.

What now? Hopefully not another ghost-in-the-toilet thing.

"What is that?" I asked the ghosts. "Go take a look."

"Why us?" Yiayia wanted to know.

"Because you're already dead and I don't want to get off the couch. My everything hurts. I've been fighting wind all over the island."

She gestured at the floor. "Who poured salt all over the floor, eh?"

My Virgin Mary, she was right. Darn it. As the only living person in my apartment, it was up to me to check out the noise.

You've got this, I told myself. It's probably just a serial killer. Or rats. Or serial-killing rats. Nothing to freak out about.

I inched toward my bag. Felt around for the pepper spray. I was a human. I had thumbs. If someone was in my kitchen, I could blast them before they attacked.

I experienced a stomach-boiling moment of panic that whatever was in my kitchen couldn't be stopped with pepper spray. As if everything with eyes didn't immediately claw at their faces when blasted in the face with pepper.

You're being ridiculous, I told myself.

Prudence is good, I also said to me. This is how you made it to thirty-one. Ignore all the times you almost died in recent history.

One slipper-clad footstep at a time, I crept to the kitchen. With the pepper spray stuck out in front of me, I scanned the room.

Empty.

Huh.

Mice infestation? Big bugs? Neither thrilled me. I'd rather take my chances with a serial killer. Or even a regular, non-serial killer.

There it went again. A rattling. Rustling. A plastic sound.

From where?

Trashcan.

Now that I was out of serial killer territory, I was feeling more confident about my chances of survival. Even Jimmy Kontos couldn't squeeze himself into my trash receptacle.

I let my toes down easy on the pedal. The lid slowly rose. The pepper spray went in first, followed by my face.

Hmm …

Nothing inside except the Merope's Best cup with its soggy fruitcake crumbs.

The cup jumped. The bag rustled.

I leaped back. "MEEP!"

The lid slowly fell back into place.

"Is it a serial killer?" Yiayia called out.

"Coffee cup."

"From Merope's Best? Do not touch it if you value your health. Their coffee is not coffee. I heard their beans are uranium nuggets that travel through the digestive systems of weasels before being collected in a dead man's *archidia* bag and sold to Merope's Best. There is a man whose job it is to pick through weasel *kaka*."

I was sure that probably—maybe—wasn't a hundred percent true. But Merope's Best coffee always did have a distinctive toxic flavor, so who knows? The point was, the cup was rattling in my garbage.

"It's fine. Probably."

"If you have to touch it, use a wooden spoon. That advice works for many situations in life. Rabid animal? Hit it and run. Thieves stealing your firewood? Hit them until they run. Strange *poutsa*? Hit it with a wooden spoon until it cries."

Given that I didn't have strange garbage penis, I didn't hit anything. But I did locate my wooden spoon. I pressed the pedal. I poked the cup's lid until it popped off.

Huh. No mouse. No bugs. Just sad scraps of fruitcake.

"I told you to we had to go right!" a voice said behind me. I whipped around to see the squat misty form of Maria Zerva slapping her husband's arm.

"We did go right," he said. "And look, we are home."

She glanced around. "We are?" She crossed herself. "Thank the Virgin Mary. I have to *kaka*! It must have been all that *revithia*!" Kyria Zerva dropped her pants and sat on the trashcan.

For crying out loud.

The recently deceased Zervases were back and they were in my kitchen. All I could figure was that they'd hijacked my cup when I was busy with the police in the alley. Sam had come this close to eating a pair of ghosts when I took the cup to his place.

I backed away slowly and returned to the living room.

Yiayia's over-plucked brows jumped. "What is it?"

"More ghosts. Do you remember Maria and Stathis Zervas?"

"Of course. I remember when Stathis wanted to put a cucumber in my—"

"No! No cucumber. Bad."

"That is what I told him. But we were young and he had a lot of cucumbers."

Sounded to me like a Gwyneth Paltrow GOOP thing. Stick a cucumber up your hoo-ha to reduce puffiness.

The dead man shuffled into the living room. He gawped at us. Rubbed his eyes. Stared some more.

"Maria," he said over his shoulder. "There are strangers in our house."

"What strangers?"

"They look like *tsiganes*."

"*Gamo ton maimou*, Stathis!" Yiayia said. "It is me, Foutoula."

He squinted. "Foutoula? Is that really you? Why do you look like you were painted on a window?"

"Because we are dead, *malaka*."

He shook his head slowly. "Maria? Where are you? This is very strange. I do not like it. I can see through my hands." He tugged on his waistband, stared at his junk. "And I can see through my *poutsa*. Do you think I have the cancer?"

"If you did, you do not have it now," Vasili Moustakas added.

"Get out," I told the dead flasher

He shimmied his hips at me. Things flopped and bounced. Eww.

Stathis Zervas didn't look happy about any of this. "Vre, Maria?"

"What?" Maria Zerva yelled from the kitchen. "I am trying to *kaka*."

"This woman says we are dead."

"How can I be going *kaka* if we are dead?"

"I'm not some woman," Yiayia said. "It is me, Foutoula."

"Foutoula, is that you?" Maria Zerva called out.

My grandmother shifted into conversation mode. "What are you doing?"

"We are well. Our daughter is starting school next week."

The Zervases' daughter was not starting school next week. Eleni Zerva's forty-something daughter lived at home with her parents and served as their caretaker. She spent most of her time running around the island, hunting for her parents when they wandered off. She'd tried padlocking the gate and they broke free anyway, like a pair of enterprising dogs.

"How can we be dead?" Stathis Zervas was saying, his voice bewildered. "We were on our way to the festival. Nobody dies on the way to a festival."

"Vre, what festival?" his wife called out. "That old *booboona* has no idea what day it is. He is losing his eggs and basket."

Somebody had to break the bad news to them, and that someone was me—although I had doubts about whether the news would stick. Their grasp on reality was on par with an oil-dunked monkey grabbing at a banana. Still, I had to try.

"Kyria Zerva, Kyrios Zervas," I said with what I hoped was a calm, reassuring tone, "it's true, you both passed away this week. I found you myself in an alley."

That got me a pair of shaggy raised eyebrows from the male half of the married couple. "Found us? Did you lose us?" He laughed at his own joke.

There was noise in the kitchen, then Maria Zerva appeared. "Stathis, the toilet is broken again. Fix it"

"How is it broken?"

"There is no water."

I rubbed my forehead. Pressure was building up behind my eyes.

"That's my trashcan," I said.

Maria Zerva crossed herself. "You keep a trashcan in your bathroom?"

Every home in Greece comes with a trashcan in the

bathroom, directly next to the toilet. For the paper. Greek plumbing gags if you feed it a diet of butt wipes. If you're lucky, the trashcan has a lid. If not … all I'm saying is it's best to avoid eye contact with the can's contents.

"It's in my *kitchen*," I said, "but that's not the point. At the moment your bodies are in Merope's morgue, waiting for the coroner to do his thing."

Maria Zerva stared at me like I'd been punched in the face with compacted dirt. Which I had. I touched my nose and winced.

Eventually she came to a conclusion. "I know you."

"We've met lots of times," I said. "Allie Callas? I've done some work for Eleni before. I located you both on Mykonos, remember? We rode back on the ferry together."

She wagged her finger at me. "You are that *putana* Foutoula's granddaughter. Not the one with a husband and family. The sad, single girl. No children. No husband. What do your parents think about that? The grief they must feel … *po-po-po* …"

She made me sound like a failure.

"My life isn't *that* hollow," I said.

"Wait a minute. I have never charged for sex," Yiayia said. "Although there were times I was happy to role play. It can be fun to switch things up. Give a man a twenty before he touches the *mouni* and steal it back before he leaves."

Maria Zerva squinted at Yiayia. "Foutoula? What happened to your face? You look old."

Mt grandmother bared her teeth. "Have you looked in the mirror lately, Maria?"

"Okay," I said, cutting in. "Why were you both in the cup?"

"What cup?" Maria Zerva asked.

"You were hiding in a cup."

"You mean the hotel," she said.

Stathis Zervas was wrestling with existential angst. "How can we be dead?"

"You are older than Greece's *kolos*," Vasili Moustakas said.

"Not helping," I told him.

He grinned and continued stumping across my living room.

There was a knock on my door. I peered out to see Leo standing in the hallway, forehead bunched up. Exasperated with the dead, I flung the door open.

He smiled at me like I was the best thing about today. My stomach flip-flopped.

"What are you doing?" I asked him.

"Just got back from questioning Eleni Zerva."

I stepped aside to let him through. He dropped a kiss on my forehead on the way past.

"How did it go?"

"She was upset. But she was okay with us searching the premises for poison."

"Find any?"

"Not yet."

"So they were definitely poisoned?"

"I know an Eleni Zerva," Maria Zerva said. "That was my mother-in-law. The old *skeela*."

"You cannot call my mother a *skeela*," her husband said.

"I can and I did—to her face."

My eyelid fluttered. The twitching was out of control. Probably I had a neurological problem. Maybe a tumor.

Leo zeroed in on the fluttering. "Everything okay?"

"The Zervases are bickering. I knew they were suffering from dementia when they were alive, but I figured being dead would fix that. Apparently not."

"They're here?"

"If they're here, than that means they were murdered, right?"

"Afraid so. They hitched a ride from the alley in a Merope's Best cup."

He shook his head and laughed. "Of course they did. Do they know who killed them?"

"They don't even know that my trashcan isn't a toilet."

His eyebrows rose. "I'm afraid to ask."

"I'm afraid and I was a witness. Doubt they know anything, though. That's how post-murder memory loss goes. And these two didn't bring all their sandwiches to the picnic anyway. The best I can hope for is that you wrap it up fast and they move on."

"Be nice if we had any clues or suspects. Senior citizens with dementia don't tend to have a lot of enemies."

Across the room, Yiayia laughed. "Has that man of yours even met people? They do not need a good reason to kill, only one that makes sense to them. Tell him that."

My eyelid fluttered frantically.

"What?" Leo asked.

"Yiayia is trying to do your job for you."

He grinned. "Oh yeah? What did she say?"

I passed on my grandmother's words. Leo nodded once.

"That's true. But I was hoping for someone more obvi-ous. Investigating a murder with all that wind is a pain. For all I know, the evidence is bobbing around in the sea."

"Can I do anything to help?"

He blew out a sigh. "If those ghosts of yours come up a name, let me know." He nodded to the salt on the floor. "Redecorating?"

"It's the cool, new thing. Don't you read home furnishing magazines?"

"I shove everything under my bed and hope for the best."

Not true. Leo's place wasn't all gussied up with cutesy platitudes on the walls or fine art, but it was clean and tidy. Like Leo; although I suspected parts of him weren't entirely clean. His mind, for one.

"Want to make out?"

"Yeah, I want." He hooked his finger in the top of my sweatpants, pulled me up against him. He was hot and hard, all the way down. He blew out a long, sexually frustrated sigh. "But I can't. I was on my way to check on my parents. They're expecting me for dinner. It was supposed to be lunch but I got caught up at work."

"How are they?"

"You know, the usual Greek parents: 'When are you getting married?' 'Where are our grandchildren?' 'Do you want us to die without grandchildren like Kyria Varvara?'"

"That sounds like Greek parents."

"They want you to come over."

"Tonight?" I asked, faintly alarmed.

He grinned. "Soon. Baba said he'll cook a lamb."

I froze. It wasn't the lamb. More like a memory. Or another out-of-place thing. I needed to test a theory.

Leo shot me a concerned look. "What?"

"Have you got five minutes?"

"To make out?"

"For a snack."

"Depends on the snack."

I grabbed his hand and pulled him into my kitchen.

What did I have in the way of snacks? Not much. There was stale cereal from the More Super Market. Oregano and garlic chips. A sliver of cheese in the fridge.

I ripped open the bag of chips and thrust them at him. "Eat."

"Okay …"

He munched on a couple of chips. "Is this a fetish thing? No judgment. I'm on board if you get off on me eating. Feed me, woman."

"Not *my* fetish." I wandered around my apartment while he ate, checking the nooks and crannies. When I found nothing, I returned to the kitchen. "They're not here?"

"Who?"

"Your fan club. The succubi."

Jezebel and Tiffany are a couple of succubi who have claimed Leo as part of their fun, fancy, man collection. Pop culture has the she-demons all wrong. They're not blood-suckers, out to bleed men dry. They're collectors. To them, Leo is another Pokémon. And these two particular succubi get their kicks watching Leo eat. To be fair, I get it. Leo is a dish.

Except today they weren't hanging around, flipping through magazines and making pithy comments. They weren't lurking this morning either, when we were drinking coffee and kissing.

Were they hiding out in their pocket dimension, avoiding the weather? Why would a couple of demons be scared of a ghost trio that got their jollies making wind? I'd caught a glimpse of Tiffany and Jezebel's real faces. They had no business shivering in their bodycon dresses. Cthulu had nothing on those two.

"Isn't that good?"

"Yes, but also maybe no. I get twitchy when it's not business as usual."

He kissed me and sealed up the chips before placing them back in the cupboard. "I'll leave the weird stuff to you. Right now I've got to go get ready for dinner. Can I see you when I get home?"

"My place or yours?"

"Mine. Yours is full of ghosts."

His kiss melted me on the spot. Wasn't fair that he had to go eat with his parents.

"Kiss me like that later and I'll do anything you want."

"*Putana*," Maria Zerva muttered. Yiayia went to slap her into silence, but her arm bounced back when it struck the salt barrier.

He laughed, low and sexy. "Anything?"

"Not your laundry, so don't get too excited."

"That's too bad. I was saving it for you."

I shoved him out the door.

CHAPTER EIGHT

"Get in the circle," I told Maria and Stathis Zervas.

"No."

"Just get in it."

"No."

"Please?"

Maria Zerva jammed her hands down on her hips. "Oh, now you discover your manners, eh? Where were they before? Where is my *pandofla*?"

Missing, along with my patience. I was trying to herd the Zervases into a second salt circle for their own protection against whatever it was that had the island's ghosts— sorry, *formerly living*—spooked. Pun totally intended. They were resisting all efforts. I'd even placed my kitchen trashcan in the center, in case Maria Zerva needed to use the facilities.

"*Vre*, it is for your own safety," Yiayia told them.

"Why should we listen to you?" Maria Zerva demanded. "I know what you did with my husband's cucumbers."

"It was one time, and it was before you were married."

I gawped at Yiayia, horrified. "I thought you didn't do the cucumber thing."

"I never said that. What I told you is that he wanted to stick a cucumber up my—"

Maria Zerva stuck her fingers in her ears and screeched. Dead Cat raised his head and hissed at her. My clever little snookum.

I waved my arms. "Just. Get. In. The. Circle."

They didn't get in the circle.

A raging gust of wind slammed into the apartment building. Glass rattled in the frames. Like most of Greece, the island's newer structures were built to withstand earthquakes, but could they stand up to howling ghosts?

The Zervases scrambled into the circle. I closed the salt gap.

Finally.

"If those three weren't already dead, I'd kill them myself," I muttered.

"They will destroy this island," Yiayia said, "unless somebody stops them."

She was right. That somebody, I already knew, was me. I had this big bag of salt. What was I waiting for?

The final part of my plan. It was still eluding me. But maybe I could get started on the first part.

First, I had questions. Lucky for me, I had a houseful of ghosts who could answer those questions.

"Why were you ghosts—"

"Formerly living," Yiayia said.

"Why were all you formerly living ghosts hiding? This crazy wind is just three ghosts throwing a tantrum to get their way. Why are the, uh, formerly living scared of the formerly living? It's not like they can kill you."

"That does not mean they cannot hurt us," Yiayia said.

"How can they hurt you?"

She shrugged. "What is a ghost?"

"The soul of a dead person?"

"Shows what you know," she said. "We are more than the soul of the dead. We have form. We have bodies."

"Bodies? Really?"

"What do you feel when you touch a ghost?"

I thought about it. "Cold and clammy."

She waved her ghost hands at the ceiling. "That is our bodies. Anything that has a body can be hurt by a violent wind. If anything, the formerly living are in bigger danger. We could end up at sea, untethered from our haunting grounds. The living have more for gravity to grab."

"What about fans?"

She stared at me.

"What? I'm just wondering if I could use fans to, say, keep someone from using my kitchen's trashcan as a ghost toilet."

She pinched my cheeks with her ghost fingers. "You are my little *mounaki*."

I'd take that as a maybe, yes, I could experiment with fans.

"Okay, so when you're a ghost—"

"Formerly living," Yiayia said.

"When you're formerly living, can you see everything? Is it like omniscience?"

"No, you have to have a direct line of sight. It is like being alive but walls are less of an obstacle."

"So I could set up a salt circle somewhere private without the ghosts seeing, unless they were in the room with me?"

"Theoretically, yes."

"Next question. Can ghosts choose to remain invisible from somebody like me who can see them?"

"Not at my skill level. But older? Perhaps."

"Could you find out for me?"

"Not without popping back to the Afterlife. Right now I cannot do that."

"Because of the salt?"

"Because I am scared of those three *malakes*. Who do they think they are, coming to my island with their wind? I would *hezo* on them, but I think that Turk would enjoy it. He has that look about him."

"What look is that?"

"Turkish."

"Conquerors aren't really big on waiting for invitations," I told her. "That's kind of their shtick. They go where they want, when they want, and do whatever they want to do. Ride tanks. Eat meat with their fingers. Steal Poland."

"In the old days I would have hidden a knife in my underwear and stabbed them in the *poutsa*."

"That sounds like you," Maria Zerva said.

Yiayia threw her a rude hand gesture. Maria Zerva tossed one back. Before I knew it, I was in the middle of an obscenity-off. I wheeled the salt-bearing dolly out of my apartment before they ran out of gestures and switched to words.

Down in the stairwell, Jimmy Kontos was back to his usual tricks, being a gawking weirdo.

"Nice sack," he said. "What's in it?"

"Salt. I'd give you some but you're already salty enough."

"*Skata na fas*. You would be too if you couldn't get a coffee."

I peered out the door. Merope's Best was definitely open for business.

"Is this some kind of riddle? Okay, I'll play. Why can't you get coffee?"

"Do you know how much I weigh?"

I picked him up under the armpits. He had the heft of a medium-sized child.

"What the—put me down!"

"Okay," I said, dropping him on the marble tile. "Worried you'll blow away?"

"You think I want to do cartwheels down the street? What if Lydia sees me?"

"I feel like she's done a few cartwheels in her time." Probably without underwear, but I didn't say that.

"Woman, if I do any cartwheels I want it to be intentional, not because of the wind."

"Didn't you two go for coffee earlier? How did you manage then? Concrete boots?"

His cheeks flushed. "She was holding onto me so I wouldn't blow away."

I laughed.

His red face purpled. "It's not funny!"

"It's a little bit funny." I went to open the door.

"Wait!"

"What?"

"Can you get me a coffee?"

"You want me to brave Merope's Best to get you a coffee?"

"You're a lot bigger than me."

Why, the little twerp! "Forget it."

"Okay, sorry I said you're big. I meant taller. Oooh, you're a lovely tall person and not at all big. Especially not in the hips."

"Got cash?" I stuck my hand out. "I'm not buying."

He slapped some euros in my hand and gave me his order.

"Guard my salt, okay? Or else the coffee gets it, along with your change."

I struggled across the street, slapping aside the wind. The door closed behind me. Panting, I sagged against the reinforced glass.

Merope's Best's baristas were a different pair this afternoon. The staff featured a rotating cast of teenagers and twenty-somethings that enjoyed shitty pay and sarcasm.

"You again," the guy at the counter said.

"Me again? I haven't been in since yesterday, and you weren't even here!"

He rolled his eyes. "What do you want?"

"A decent cup of coffee, but since you don't sell those, give me a medium latte with three shots of raspberry syrup and two shots of almond."

That perked him up. "Is this for Jimmy Kontos?"

"Yes, why?"

"I love that guy. Have you seen his movies? He knows how to use those tools, too. It's not just an act. He built a doghouse in one of his movies, and then used it as a prop. When you bend a—"

"How about that haunted grave water," I said quickly before he could finish his sentence. He didn't contradict me about the grave water.

While the coffee substance was brewing, I glanced around the coffee shop. Still no sign of the usual cluster of ghosts that made the cafe their home base. Were they hiding in the store somewhere? Any of the For Sale flasks, bottles, and cups could be full of ghosts.

When it was ready, I grabbed Jimmy's order and karate-chopped my way back across the street. Night was rushing toward the island fast. I wanted to get to where I was going and get back as soon as possible. Yes, mostly because I was eager to make out with Leo, but also because I wanted the ghosts gone or at least contained.

After swapping the coffee for my salt, I rolled the dolly

to Ayios Konstantinos—Saint Constantine. It's not that I'm super religious, but if I was playing around with ghosts and their spooky allies, I figured why not a church? If God were real, maybe He'd have my back if my half-assed plan backfired.

Ayios Konstantinos is the island's largest church. The outside has graced many a calendar, with its brilliant blue dome and stained glass windows. The interior is more decorative. Everything that hasn't been jabbed by Midas is dark, polished wood. It's a typical Greek church. Light on seating. Heavy on the candles. Incense fills the air whether a service is ongoing or not. Near the sand-filled candle-holder, there's a large, ornate wooden box for donations. I have my suspicions about where the money ends up. Father Spiros, the priest and his sister love money almost as much as they love themselves. God, if He's on the list, is a significantly lower bullet point below schmoozing and sinning.

The church was empty. No priest. No priest's sister. No Kyria Aspasia, the church's custodian. It was just me and the eye-rolling Jesus up front.

With cupped hands, I poured the perimeter of the salt circle, leaving a small notch I could easily close with a foot swipe. There was sufficient room in the circle for three ghosts and their elbows. Now it was all over except the summoning. Hopefully I could herd the three dead dudes into the circle without them realizing they were sheep.

I whistled. "Vladimir, Mehmet, Xerxes!"

The church shuddered and groaned. Jesus rolled his eyes harder. Three figures appeared out of the ether, directly in the center of my circle.

Swipe!

The salty prison door slammed shut.

The wind died instantly. All of it. The whole island fell silent.

I slumped against the church wall. Sweet relief.

"That worked out well," I said to nobody in particular.

The ghosts started to ghost-sweat. Mehmet tugged at his robe's neck. Xerxes fanned his pits. Good thing I couldn't smell them. Only Vladimir was calm. He folded his arms over his ample stomach, squishing his man-boobs. Cleavage appeared over his tracksuit jacket's zipper.

"What sorcery is this?" Mehmed demanded.

"It's less sorcery, more culinary."

He jabbed me in the face with his stink-eye.

"Salt," I said. "It's a natural oogie-boogie barrier. Keeps them out and keeps them in."

Xerxes poked the air. His finger bounced back. He hip-booped the barrier.

Bounce.

"You have imprisoned me, Xerxes the Great!"

Aww, someone was in a tizzy.

"Relax," I said. "It's just temporary. You want off this island? I can't do it with a bunch of wind flying around. Do you know how long it takes to walk everywhere, fighting the wind? Not to mention that you've cut me off from almost all the ways I can access information. You want help? You have to help me first."

"Send messengers! That is what I do," Mehmed said.

"It's the 2020s. We've moved on from messengers."

"That is not my problem," he said.

"It's absolutely your problem. If you want my help, the wind needs to stop. Or you stay in the circle."

No chance I'd let them out. Not until the Afterlife's garbage truck showed up to collect their trash.

Mehmed's withering gaze turned to one of disturbing appreciation. "Have you ever considered marrying a dead man? Maybe one with four previous wives and a strong preference for slender young men?"

"Never."

"That is too bad. You would make a good fifth wife."

"You want a good wife, find a Persian," Xerxes said. "They are obedient and do not mind if you mate with your brother's daughter. Okay, yes, my wife cut up my sister-in-law's face because she blamed the mother for her daughter's actions, but … look! A squirrel!"

Yikes.

"Okay." I rubbed my hands together, hoping the friction would generate ideas. "You're going to stay here while I go do research."

"Here?" Mehmed was aghast. He did a lap of the circle, taking in the overblown decor. "In this Christian church?"

"Do you have a problem with Christianity?"

"No, no, no! I have known some very nice Christian men. Intimately. Man-on-man if you know what I mean." One at a time, he looked at us. "We touched penises together."

"She knows what you mean because you said it," Xerxes said. "What is a Christian?"

"More than two billion people follow that one," Vladimir said, releasing his cleavage long enough to waft a hand at Christ. Ayios Konstantinos's Jesus could teach Greek mothers and grandmothers a thing or two about eye rolling. His eye roll was epic. I could only assume he'd been listening to Kyria Sofia—the priest's sister—pretending her claws weren't hooked into the social ladder when the wind changed direction. The weather shift froze his expression until the paint and lacquer set.

"Christianity boils down to 'don't be a jerk,'" I told him. "Or at least it's supposed to. Your experiences may vary."

"That sounds like my religion," Xerxes said. "But it does not apply to people named Xerxes."

I checked my phone. The network was back up. Wi-Fi routers in the vicinity were popping up. *Skata Na Fas. Malakismeni Maimou. Iloveanimals.*

That last one was probably the church Wi-Fi. Kyria Sofia had a thing for animals. The sedately dressed priest's sister was the owner of the largest human-on-animal porn collection in both hemispheres. She kept everything hidden away in a computer folder labeled Sewing. Whether she could sew or not, I wasn't sure.

Dozens of text messages flooded my phone. Then it rang. Betty Honeychurch's voice came through, clear and delighted. "You did it!"

"Phase One is complete," I told her. "Phase Two is still up in the air. I have to get them from the circle to a container for transport."

I'm not transporting them anywhere, I thought as loudly as possible, hoping Betty would pluck that thought right out of my head.

"I understand," she said. Her voice had a wink in it.

The trick now was getting this done before Kyria Sofia showed up to inventory the gold and count the money in the donation box. Whether they liked it or not, I was going to send these three on a one-way trip to the Afterlife, where they belonged. They wanted off this island? How about way, way off?

"You'll need an emissary," Betty said, listening in on my thoughts. "Someone who can run an errand for you."

She was right. I needed a ghost to jog up to the After-life and have the Powers That Be come and collect their pests. If this didn't qualify for a sucky hole to hoover them up, I don't know what did. They were conquerors. These weren't nice old grandmothers or regular people. They had killed, they had maimed, and they had knocked out our Wi-Fi for days.

I wandered toward the door. My brain was kicking the plan around, testing it for flaws. "I'll be back," I told the three ghosts.

"You cannot leave us here like this!" Mehmed said.

"Stop. Vait. Do not leaf," Vladimir said in his bored, Russian accent.

"Relax," I said. "No one can see you. I'll be back soon with transport. Then you can be on your merry way."

Probably there would be nothing merry about it.

"You better not double cross us," Mehmed said.

"I will cut off your face if you do," Xerxes added.

"Not a problem." Definitely a problem. "I just want you off my island."

He gave me a satisfied smile. "You think like a conqueror."

My eyes rolled skyward. "Sit. Stay."

Now that the wind was dead, jogging home wasn't a hardship. Debris didn't fly into my eyes. I wasn't half blind by the time I stumbled into the lobby. Only the cold was out to get me, and I was dressed for that. The night felt relatively normal again.

I scrambled upstairs and threw myself into my apartment.

Dead Cat purred his approval. The Zervases were bickering about politics from thirty years ago. Yiayia and Vasili Moustakas—

I averted my eyes. Probably the damage was done anyway. There are things in this world you can never unsee.

"Yiayia?" I aimed my words at the ceiling. "I need your help."

"Mmmph mmph mpph."

"Let her finish," Vasili Moustakas said.

He would say that, wouldn't he?

"I need someone to go up to the Afterlife and give the Powers That Be a poke. There are three ghosts in a salt circle at Ayios Konstantinos that need the ol' black hole treatment. Or a bus. Or something that will get them off the island. Now or faster would be nice."

"We can go," Stathis Zervas said. For some reason he was wearing his Greek underpants on his head. "A vacation would be nice."

"Er, no thanks. I need somebody who … uh."

His wife stared at me with her hawkish eyes. "Somebody what?"

Yiayia forged onwards, undaunted. "Somebody who will not forget what they are doing halfway there, messing up the whole thing. Your husband cannot even remember his underpants go on his *kolos*. He looks like the Mickey Mouse if Mickey got his head stuck in a *faka*."

Probably that's what the mouse said when it realized the cheese was a trap.

Kyria Zerva was staring at me, swaying. "I know you. You look like that *putana* Foutoula. I can smell the cucumbers on you."

For crying out loud. "Yiayia! You're my assistant. Assist me."

My grandmother looked worried.

"I can break the circle," I said. "The wind is gone and the responsible parties are busy trying to figure out what to do about salt. They can't blow you out to sea or whatever now."

"I suppose I can help you. It might be difficult, though."

"Do that thing you just did," Vasili Moustakas said.

Yiayia ignored him. "Okay. Break the circle."

I scuffed the salt enough to make a gap.

Yiayia winked and vanished. Vasili Moustakas and his walker stumped away, taking the shortcut through the wall. He didn't scream, so I guess it worked out okay.

Before I could open my laptop and check email, there was a *pop*. Yiayia was back. She looked even more bedraggled than before and her bra was on backwards, leaving a dire gravity situation at the front.

"Ask me no questions and I will tell you no lies," she said.

"Did you relay my message?"

"Okay, that question I can answer. Yes."

"Are they going to scoop up the ghosts?"

"They said help would arrive soon."

Excellent.

"Can you put me back in the circle?" Yiayia asked.

"Are you sure? There's no more storm."

"Something still feels strange."

I closed the circle and hoofed it to the lobby, where my bicycle was patiently waiting. Although it was late evening, Merope's people were starting to poke their noses out. A few shops were flinging their doors for customers who needed to replenish food stocks. Crusty Dimitri's had a sign up that said they were open for business again.

Hopefully Kyria Sofia wasn't sniffing around her church. If I was lucky she was at home with her creepy brother, perusing the internet for more *Sewing* fodder.

I kicked down the stand on my bicycle. Pushed the church's door open.

Huh. The three dead men were still hanging out in their protective circle. The woo-woo cavalry hadn't arrived yet.

Mehmed spoke first. "Did you find us transport to this … Germany or China or … what was it?"

"USA," Vladimir said with a tone of disgust.

I looked up at the ceiling. Down at the floor. Nothing. No swirling, ghost-sucking hole. Did I need to break the salt line?

I crouched down. My fingers reached for the salty ring.

A hand snapped out of nowhere and closed around my wrist.

"Stop," Kyria Aspasia said.

Kyria Aspasia is the church's custodian. She's responsible for the gleaming gold and the slippery-when-wet marble floors. She's been around since dirt was new, and the hump on her back is filled with secrets and possibly fats like a camel. I also get the feeling she can see dead people as easily as I can.

She hoisted me up off the floor. For an ancient relic, Kyria Aspasia was strong. Probably from mopping these floors.

"What are you doing?" she said in my ear.

"I'll clean up the salt, I promise."

"Leave it there. I want to see if Sofia dries up like a slug. But I am not talking about the salt. Salt is salt."

I felt around tentatively. "Do you mean what's in the salt ring?"

"What else, eh?"

"You can see them?"

"Of course I can see them. Just because I am old does not mean my eyes do not work."

"It's just three ghosts. They'll be gone soon, I promise."

Mehmed cupped his hand around his ear. "What are you two talking about?"

"Cleaning products," I said over my shoulder.

"What three ghosts?" Kyria Aspasia said. "You have two regular ghosts and one problem. A big problem. That is more than a ghost. That is a ghost plus more ghost."

My blood ran cold. I closed my eyes and tried to think. "Which two are regular ghosts?"

I already knew the answer. I needed to hear it anyway.

"The men in the robes. The other one, I cannot say what that is but it has issues, looking at the size of it."

I turned around slowly.

Vladimir pouted. "The old woman is wrong, I am not problem. I only vant what to collect what is mine and go home."

"Vladimir?" Mehmed looked confused. "What is going on?"

The Russian scoffed. "Vladimir, Vladimir, Vladimir! Do this, Vladimir. Do that, Vladimir. Hey, Vladimir, come to Perseeah and peek up robes from cleaners. Vladimir spits on robes."

"What are you?" I asked him.

Vladimir sniffed. "The closest thing this world has to God."

Fear clutched my throat. Ghosts were one thing. Weirdo magicians were also one thing. Succubi, also a thing. But this was a whole other ocean in which I didn't want to dip my toes.

Vladimir belly-laughed. He had a lot of belly. "Okay, I exaggerate leetle. I am ghost. Boo!"

Well, that saved my underwear from an embarrassing pants-wetting incident. "You're still in my salt circle."

He pointed. "This circle?"

"Do you see another one?"

"This leetle salt is nothing. I luff salt. I vas born in the Yekaterinburg Salts Mine in Russia."

Okay, now I was panicking. If salt couldn't keep a ghost in or out, I was out of ideas. I hadn't tested the fan theory yet.

Vladimir stuck his foot out, gave it a theatrical wiggle. "You dare me?"

"No."

"Okay." He shrugged. "I do anyway. Is science experiment."

Like a sunburned leg through a vat of butter, he let his foot down on the far side of my circle.

"Huh. I didn't expect that," I said.

"I am surprising man, da? I haff meny surprises."

"I am surprised," Mehmed said. "Are you surprised, Xerxes?"

Xerxes sniffed. "Surprises are for common people, like this Greek woman with the dull wits."

Hey now, that wasn't nice. I wasn't dim-witted. My wits were sharp and pointy. It's just that when it looks like a ghost, and talks like a ghost, you expect it to be a ghost, not a ghost on steroids like ol' Vladimir here.

I raised my brows at Vladimir. "What do you want, and why are you enabling these two?"

"Because they are fun. Vell, not fun. Entertaining, like little bugs that live on rats."

"Fleas?"

"*Da*. Fleas."

"Are fleas entertaining?"

He shrugged. "If you watch them under microscope."

This. This was why the island's ghosts were terrified. They didn't care about a pair of tin-pot, long-dead conquerors. It was all about Vladimir. Whatever he was—he had to be more than a ghost—he'd also sent Leo's succubi scrambling for a hiding place.

"Did you mess with the weather?" I asked.

Xerxes raised his hand. "We did that."

"You did nothink," Vladimir told him. "I let you believe you had small amount of power left."

"Why?" I asked.

"You would like to know, da?"

"Yes, that is why I asked."

"Because they had leetle power and I took it for good reason."

Mehmed was aghast. "Thief!"

"Vhy? It vas being vasted on you two. All you vant is to take country, and another country, and then the vorld. You are wery bed mens."

"Spoken like a man who has never crossed the Helle-spont with five million men," Xerxes said.

"Three hundred thousand," Mehmed said, correcting him.

Instead of replying, Vladimir scuffed the salt with a breeze, breaking the line.

"I grow tired of these bed mens. Vatch vhat heppens now. This vill be comedy."

Mehmed glanced around. When a whole lot of nothing happened, he got smug fast. Xerxes was just as cocky. The two of them were on the verge of preening, the pompous pair of overblown peacocks. They strutted out of the broken circle.

Immediately, a swirling circle opened up in the church's gilt ceiling. Black. Eternal. Utterly terrifying, even though I knew it wasn't here for me.

"What is that?" Mehmed wanted to know.

"It is an ill omen," Xerxes said. "I know this because it looks like an upside down Spartan well. Nothing good even happens to Persians when there are Spartans and wells around."

Their heads went wonky first. Stretched like the hole was pulling ghost taffy. Then they were sucked up into the black void.

The hole disappeared. The gilt-and painted ceiling

returned. It was just me and Vladimir and Kyria Aspasia, who was crossing herself again for good luck.

Huh. So sending Yiayia as a messenger had worked. That seemed useful to know, for future reference. If there was a future. Toula's predictions were gaily ringing in my head right now.

"You're still here," I said to Vladimir."

"*Da.*"

"Why?"

"I heff business."

"What business?"

"That same business as all spirits that will not leave," Kyria Aspasia said. She spat a couple of times and crossed herself some more. Her hump jiggled. Secrets didn't spill out of the fleshly lump. Vladimir flinched at the spit but he was unharmed.

"Yeah, but what is that?" I asked. "To terrorize everyone, drag them to hell, and then what? Where's the fun in having everything capitulate to you?"

"What is it you Americans say? Do not knock until you haff tried."

I eyed him suspiciously. "Are you really a ghost?"

"I am dead, da."

"So what, you're just gassy? Is that what all the wind was about? Are you going to tell me what you want? I have a certain knack for finding things, which you probably already know."

"*Da,* I hear this. That is why I look for you here. They say you are woman who can find solutions to problems."

Okay. I'd play. Up to a point. The point being me finding a way to send him on the express train to the Afterlife, where he belonged. "What's your problem?"

"Hmm …" He tried lacing his hands behind his back. When that didn't work out, he settled for letting them dangle at his sides as he paced the length of the church. "What I vant is what those two vanted in a vey. I vant to get off thees island."

"Are you trapped here?"

"In manner of speaking, da. Ve are all prisoners of somethink. Even you. Live is prison. Death is prison. Everythink is prison."

"Is prison prison?"

He was unamused. "Everythink."

"Well, I think you're wrong. I'm not a prisoner. At least not that I know of."

"Some of us are prisoners of luff, or the past, or ourselves. Only you know which one are you."

Russian ghosts. Insufferable.

Kyria Aspasia rifled around her in pocket. She pulled out a glass bottle with a cork stopper. She yanked out the stopper and flicked the contents at Vladimir. "Be gone, *malaka*!"

The water went right through him. He glanced down at his tracksuit. "Vater?"

Kyria Aspasia inspected the bottle for defects. She gave it a little shake. "Holy water, blessed by our priest."

"*T-foo!*" Vladimir snorted. "That was vater from tep."

Of course it was. How completely unsurprising. I already suspected Father Spiros was a charlatan, at the best of times. It would be on-brand for he and his sister to fill the font from the nearest faucet without bothering to bless a drop of it. If his blessing was even worth spit.

"If people on this island find out, this will be a big scandal," Kyria Aspasia said. "I cannot wait until they do." She fanned herself. "Oh-la-la, all this anticipation."

"Find out what?" Kyria Sofia said behind us.

Several things happened at once. Kyria Aspasia cackled. My jaw dropped, and I was sure I got a guilty look on my face like a dog that stole and ate the remote control. A text leapt onto my phone's screen from Toula.

Duck.

What did she mean "*duck*"? Was this an autocorrect issue? Had it corrected my sister when she typed—

Vladimir reached out and touched my shoulder.

ZAP.

CHAPTER NINE

"I'M FINE," I said finely.

Leo's face said I wasn't any definition of "fine" that he was okay with. Normally he was the color of golden caramels. Leaning over the ER's bed, his complexion was the off-white of goat milk.

"You got zapped with I don't know how many volts of electricity."

"That's explains the smell of burning hair. How bad is it?"

He made a face. "Your eyelashes and brows will grow back."

I winced. My skin hurt. Everything felt pink and raw like I'd tussled with sandpaper. "How is Kyria Aspasia?"

"Unharmed. The lightning didn't get her."

The lightning wasn't lightning. Not directly from the sky, anyway. Vladimir zapped me with some kind of inbuilt stun gun. Definitely not a regular ghost. The average ghost had to work at being able to sit on a couch without falling through. Although sometimes outright denial helped. Case in point: Maria Zerva and my trashcan. She had no problems using my garbage as a potty because most of the time she had no clue she was dead.

"And Kyria Sofia?"

"Did somebody say my name?"

In sashayed the woman herself. Saccharine twinset. Omnipresent sensible heels and ladybug brooch. Handbag dangling from one wrist. Venomous bite.

"Allie Callas," she said in a sticky sweet voice. "Thank the Virgin Mary that you are alive. God Himself must have been watching over you."

That or Vladimir hadn't intended to kill me. Something told me if the Russian had wanted me dead I'd be a grease stain on the church's marble tile right now.

"What are you doing?"

Her eyes widened. "I came with the paramedics, of course. You *did* sustain injuries in my brother's church, after all. How could I sleep tonight if you were seriously hurt? I do worry about our flock, even when they do not come to regular services. Or any."

More like she wanted to make sure I wouldn't sue. Not that Greece was a sue-happy country. But Kyria Sofia tended to think with her purse. Bonus: now she was a woman in possession of a story. Knowledge and juicy new tidbits about people were a form of currency around here.

But then I was also a woman with a hip pocket full of information, wasn't I? And that was the main reason Kyria Sofia was in the ER right now instead of counting the gold at Ayios Konstantinos to make sure Kyria Aspasia and I hadn't pinched anything. She didn't want me to blab about her brother's fake-o holy water. One word and the siblings would be dunked in olive oil and chased off the island.

"I'm okay," I assured her. "Sorry about the salt on the floor."

She wafted her hand through the air. "Does not matter.

That is what Kyria Aspasia is for." She gave me a pointed look. "Were you there to give a donation to my brother's church?"

My look was equally pointy. "Oh, I think I've given the church plenty of donations already, don't you?"

Her smile was all teeth and no humor. I'd bested her— this time. "You have always been so generous to us. Will we see you in church soon?"

Leo frowned. The man knew something was up, but couldn't put his finger on what.

"If I feel a burst of philanthropy coming on."

The priest's sister nodded once and sashayed out of the room on her low, sensible heels.

"What was that all about?" Leo wanted to know.

No reason to keep it a secret from him. "Ayios Konstantinos's holy water is plain old unblessed tap water."

He laughed. "I'd be shocked if all that gold was real, too. I wouldn't put it past either of them to swap it out for shiny paper." He turned serious again. "This wasn't how I expected date night to go."

"I'm fine now."

"Fine enough to come home with me?"

"Why not? I already shaved. It was lightning fast."

"Let's see what the doctor says first."

The doctor chose that moment to swing back in. "You need to rest for a few days. Any chest pain, fluttering, arrhythmia, dizziness, I want you back here."

"Doctor's orders," Leo said.

"I hate your orders," I told the doctor.

"Perspective is everything. Be glad I didn't prescribe a suppository."

Leo took me home. The dolly and salt were back at the church, so I'd have to go back for them in the morning when I was less crispy.

Vasili Moustakas hadn't returned. He'd taken his dangling member and fled for good, by the looks of it. Only Yiayia was home. She zeroed in on my new Kentucky Fried look.

"My love! What happened to you?"

"Is it bad?"

"Not if you are bacon and eggs."

"I got electric shocked by a crazy Russian ghost. At least he says he's a ghost. I'm not convinced." I glanced around. "Where are the Zervases?"

"They found a baby, so they are reading it stories and singing it to sleep?"

An alarm went off in my head. "A baby? What baby?"

She pointed up at Leo's apartment above us. "The *nanos* with the big *poutsa*. I guess they did not see that part of him yet."

I looked at Leo. "Jimmy's getting story time from Kyria and Kyrios Zervas."

He shook his head and vanished into the kitchen. I heard the sounds of tea being made.

While Leo was making tea, I surveyed the damage in my bathroom mirror. My eyelashes were sizzled stumps. Ditto my eyebrows. My skin was lightly fried, and the tips of my finger and toenails were black. Good thing I'd gone with a leggings and sweatshirt combo instead of my usual jeans, otherwise I'd be sporting a burn mark on my belly from the backside of the button.

I eased into a tepid shower, wincing as the water struck my skin. Vladimir packed a punch for someone who had been dead for a quarter or so of a century.

As I rinsed off the stink of burning keratin, I contemplated what was next. With the dead conquerors sucked up by the black hole of judgment, I was down two problems. But in their place I had an even bigger issue. Vladimir was no regular spirit. A saltshaker wouldn't hold him still until the black hole vanquished him. Clearly he had unfinished business, and he wanted me to help. Thus far he'd been evasive about how, precisely, I could assist him.

Generally speaking, people—and, uh, other things— tended to avoid specifics when they were concerned about the truth. And they were concerned about the truth because where there was truth there was weakness. Therefore Vladimir had a weakness I could exploit. I just had to find it.

But not tonight.

What I needed now was tea and sympathy. Good thing Leo was on hand to provide both. He carried tea to the bedroom and tucked me into bed. Then he climbed in next to me.

"Finally, we're sleeping together," I said.

He grinned. "Sleeping is the operative word. You heard what the doctor said."

"You don't have to stay."

"Yeah, I do. I want to make sure you're okay."

Leo gently gathered me up in his arms. His body was warm and strong, and he felt like home.

"This is nice," I said.

"Very nice." There was a "but" in his voice.

"But?"

"I want to get you naked so bad it hurts."

Oh boy.

Toula called early the next morning. "You didn't duck."

Leo kissed me on the forehead and went to make coffee.

"I didn't have time."

"You never listen to me, Allie."

"What?"

My joke landed like a flaming turd. "Not funny."

"If it's not funny, then why am I laughing?"

She blew out a frustrated sigh. "At least you're okay."

"Totally fine, apart from the missing brows and lashes."

"I guess you could go see Stephanie Dolas for makeup tips."

We both laughed. Stephanie had plucked her brows down to narrow brackets, believing they'd grow back when fashion changed its volatile mind. Now she spent half the workday atoning for her sins with a brow pencil.

"I don't suppose you know if the world is still ending?"

"It's still a goner."

"Damn it."

Toula turned serious. "What's going to happen, Allie? Milos and Patra are supposed to have their whole lives ahead of them. My children can't die. Nobody's kids can. It's not right."

Fear punched me in the gut and throat. My own death wasn't that scary. Not when I knew the Afterlife provided a bounty of amenities and services. But the idea of my nephew and niece passing on was unbearable. They had to live. All kids did.

"I'm working on it," I said.

"Allie …"

"I find things. That's what I do. If there's a way to stop it, I'll find that way. Have some faith in me, okay?"

Her goodbye sounded damp.

I wouldn't let my sister down. I couldn't. And now that the lines of communication were back up again, I intended to march over to the Cake Emporium to brainstorm with Betty and her brother.

Okay, instead of marching, I'd ride my bike. If my fleece-covered backside could stand to touch the seat.

Leo grabbed his coffee to go. He returned twenty minutes later wheeling the dolly and salt sack.

"You left this at the church last night."

"Thanks."

"Should I ask why you need that much salt?"

"I have an electrolyte imbalance."

He laughed. "I guess I really don't need to know."

"It's for trapping ghosts. I didn't have enough salt, so I acquired some from the Cake Emporium."

"The shop I can't see?"

"The shop you can't see."

"Your life is weird."

"Parts of it. The rest is blissfully average. Are you okay with that?"

"I'm okay with all of you." He kissed me until I couldn't see straight. "Rest. Call me if there are any problems."

With my fingers crossed behind my back, I promised to do both. Sitting on the sidelines wasn't something I could afford to do right now. Not with Milos and Patra's lives on the line. I refused to fail them—or any one else on this island. This was my home. Nothing woo-woo was going to get past me if I could help it.

As soon as Leo was gone, I refilled my personal salt-shaker and showered gingerly. Dead Cat sat on the toilet seat, purring as I eased into loose sweatpants and an equally floppy sweatshirt. Even the soft cotton was abrasive on my poached skin.

The Zervases were sitting on the couch, staring at nothing. Yiayia looked bored. She lit up when she saw I was dressed.

"Are we going somewhere?"

"Cake Emporium."

"I like cake. Or I used to. Now when I eat, food falls right through my *kolos*. Is this a job?"

"Not really. More of a fact-finding mission. Could be we create a war room."

"That sounds boring." Her gaze slid to the inert Zervases. "But more exciting than whatever this is. Are they zombies now? Who can say?"

Yiayia rode in the basket.

We were halfway to the Cake Emporium when my phone pinged. Funeral arrangements for the Zervases were underway, and Eleni Zerva needed my services to locate her mother's old wedding dress. She asked if I could come over, and I promised I'd see her later this morning.

"Want to swing by the Zervas house with me later? Eleni wants me to find her mother's wedding dress."

"Probably for the burial," Yiayia said. "I was at their wedding, you know."

I didn't know. "What did her dress look like?"

"Boring. No style. No taste. No decoration. Not like my wedding dress. Now that was stylish. Gina Lollobrigida herself wanted to know where I got my dress. She wanted one just like it. I told her I made it with my own hands, and that was the truth."

"Gina Lollobrigida saw your wedding dress?"

"She was vacationing on Merope that summer."

I wondered if Eleni was hell-bent on finding her mother's original dress or if she'd settle for a replica. I also wondered what had happened to the dress in the first place.

The island was hopping today. Now that they could go out, everyone was bustling around, cleaning and fixing damage from the high winds. Everything else on the island was open, so I had high hopes that that my favorite sugar shop would be flashing its OPEN sign.

It was not.

The Cake Emporium's sign read CLOSED and the door was firmly locked. I cupped my hands against the glass and peered through. The shop was dark and the front window was empty. Still. Now that the freaky weather was over, shouldn't the shop be open?

Alarm bells tinkled in my chest. The genuine article, or lingering effects from the gazillion volts of electricity that had arced through my body, hunting for ground?

"What do you see here?" I asked Yiayia, who was adjusting her boob cones.

"A cake shop, but without cakes."

Probably all ghosts could see the shop. They were all woo-woo touched. They couldn't help it.

"Okay. Stand, levitate, whatever, but do it right there. I have to do a thing"

With a few shakes, I formed a protective semi-circle that butted up seamlessly with the shop's foundation. Salt wouldn't keep Vladimir out if he made a run for it, but it made me feel better to have a bit of completely useless protection.

I knocked on the door.

Nothing.

"Knock again," Yiayia said. "Maybe they are out the back, making cakes. Seems like that would be a normal thing to do at a bakery."

I knocked again.

More nothing.

"Can you poke your head in and see if anyone is around?"

Yiayia cupped a hand to her ear. "What was that?"

Very funny. "Come on. Please? You're the one that wanted to work for me."

"I expected to wear a trench coat and a fedora on the job."

"You can still do that."

"Let me see what the costume department has."

Pop. Yiayia vanished.

Too late I realized it wouldn't work. Not with all the salt in the foundation. Yiayia would never be able to cross the line. Oh well. She'd figure it out after a wardrobe change.

The door opened. A short man with hair ripped right off the rump of a poodle filled the gap, his smile merry like he was genuinely glad I'd knocked on the door. He wiped his hands on the white apron tied around his waist and nudged the door open wider with one hip. Flour sifted off him in pale clouds as he moved.

"Allie Callas! Finally I get to meet you. Betty keeps me so busy out back that I rarely get a chance to leave my kitchen. Ah well, keeps me out of trouble, doesn't it? Come in, come in. My sister will be here any minute now. She's just putting on her face, isn't she?"

I hoped he wasn't being literal. "Betty has another brother?"

"Just the one."

"And you're …"

"Jack, of course. Jack Honeychurch."

CHAPTER TEN

Wait, what?

Bewildered, I followed him into the Cake Emporium. He couldn't be Jack Honeychurch, could he? The Man in Black was Jack. He had said so himself. The Man in Black had opened the door, invited me in, and gave me salt on a dolly to haul the sack around town.

Surely the most circumspect and evasive man on the planet hadn't deceived me.

And yet, I felt like I'd been hoodwinked. Probably because I had. I figured it was healthy that I recognized I'd been conned. That meant I was halfway to recovery.

Although the lights were off and the cabinets sat empty, the fireplace inside the Cake Emporium was blazing again, singlehandedly trying to fight back winter. The space glowed, back to its warm and inviting self.

"Come on out back," he said. "Or you can make yourself comfortable in here, if you prefer. But out back is where all the magic happens. Did your friend—Sam, isn't it?—enjoy my pie?"

I shook off the vague feeling of being outside my own body. "He said it was just like his grandmother's."

Jack beamed. Exact same smile as his sister's. Warm, inviting, down to earth. "I love it when I hit a recipe right on the noggin."

"How did you manage to replicate his grandmother's pie?"

"Got the recipe from the woman herself. Lovely woman. Lovely. Some people won't give up their recipes, even after they go to the grave, you know. Mrs. Washington was overjoyed when I said I was making pie for her grandson, so she handed over her recipe, right down to the little tweaks that made it all hers."

My mind kept on spinning, thoughts sticking to the wall, riding the Rotor at the fair. Yes, it made much more sense that this was Betty's cake-baking brother—they did look alike—but then who was the Man in Black, and why had he been impersonating a baker?

Virgin Mary, I *knew* he wasn't a baker. Not with that black wardrobe. Should have listened to my instincts. Ungh!

"I'm really confused," I said.

"About pumpkin pie? I'm not surprised. Is pumpkin a fruit or a vegetable? It's quite American blending it up and pouring it into a pie shell. In merry old England you see it roasted, more often than not. Goes down a treat with some roast beef and potatoes."

The kitchen had undergone a transformation. Pristine both times when I'd been in this space before, today every surface was covered with ingredients and sweets at various stages of preparedness. Naked cakes waiting to be frosted. Layers of puff pastry cooling on trays. Custard simmering in a pot. A mixer whipping cream into soft peaks.

Jack turned off the mixer and dipped in a spoon. He

offered me a heaping blob of fluffy, whipped goodness. "It's honey whipped cream. What do you think?"

The taste of smooth, sweet cream filled my mouth, followed by a gentle hint of clover honey.

"Can I eat it like that, or do you have to put it on cake?"

The twinkle danced in his eyes. "As soon as Betty gets here, I'll have her box some up for you. Now what was it you were confused about?"

"Have we met before?"

His button nose wrinkled up. "I'd remember if we had. I don't meet a lot of people these days. Betty is the people person. I'm happier pottering around in my kitchen."

"The other day, I was supposed to meet you here to pick up a sack of salt."

"That's right! I'm so sorry," he said. "I was regrettably detained. But I did arrange for it to be delivered to your home. Did it reach you? I hope so."

That explained the mysterious bag of salt that had arrived outside my apartment.

"It did—thank you—but that's the problem. When I knocked on the door the other day, a man let me in. He gave me a sack of salt and a dolly to wheel it home."

"So that's where the dolly went. I've been looking for it everywhere." He stopped. "Wait—a man? Here? Inside the shop?"

"Tall, dark, dresses in black. Possibly an escapee from a Jane Austen novel. He's brooding and he wears tall boots, like he left his horse tethered in the nearby stables. Likely has several hunting dogs. Pointers or spaniels. At least one retriever."

"Goodness," Betty Honeychurch said from behind me. "We don't know anything like that, do we, Jack?"

A shadow passed in front of his face. "Er, no. No, we don't. Sounds like a bit of a dodgy fellow to me."

Please, I wasn't buying it. "Who is he?"

He glanced at the watch he wasn't wearing. "Would you look at the time? You'll never be able to open the shop if I don't get these cakes decorated."

Betty hugged me. "I've missed seeing all our familiar faces. But thanks to you, those three mischief makers are gone and it's business as usual."

I raised my hand. "Two."

A small ditch appeared between her brows. "What do you mean?"

"Two ghosts. Mehmed and Xerxes were whisked off to wherever it is naughty ghosts go, while Vladimir stepped over the salt line, zapped my eyebrows off, and … I don't know what happened to him after that, but I do know salt is no obstacle."

"No wonder you look a little pink. Are you all right, love?"

"The prognosis is good. I'm not confident about my eyebrows though. They might not make it. I might have doomed myself to a lifetime of penciling them back on."

"Well, if you need anything, I'm just a phone call or a strong thought away," Betty said. "Jack? We need to lock up and get home."

He looked crestfallen. "My cakes!"

"There won't be any more cakes if our shop is open to whatever is still out there on Merope."

"Which one is Merope?" Jack asked.

"Oh, it's a little island in the Aegean."

"Between Greece and Turkey," I explained. "Wait, you're leaving?"

"We have to, love. If that Russian fellow helps himself to the shop … well, we can't let that happen."

"Please don't go. I need help. I was hoping we could brainstorm a plan."

Betty looked around. She shivered as though geese were marching across her grave. "Not here, love. Let's go into the house and have a cuppa."

It took a whopping thirty seconds to travel to England through one kitchen door and one set of French doors that had no business being in a kitchen—probably because they weren't in a kitchen at all. The French doors opened into an opulent English manor house filled with strange art that made no sense to the human brain. I did my best not to make eye contact with the paintings, on account of how they scrambled my senses.

As Jack shut the French doors, there was a bone-rattling crash on the other side.

Betty winced. "Just in the nick of time, I'd say.

"What was that?"

"Something that just discovered the Cake Emporium is closed for business until further notice. Don't worry, it can't break through."

"Vladimir?"

"Or whatever it is under that human name. Come on, love. The kitchen is down here."

We strode past more eye-straining art. I focused on the wooden floors with their fancy inlays and the ceilings' elegant moldings. The Honeychurches' kitchen was a cavernous room, perfectly capable of whipping up a banquet dinner for people who had inherited their parents' titles. Jack boiled water— "He won't let me use the kitchen, will he?" —while Betty and I sat at the table in the cozy nook. We were surrounded by homey knick-knacks, which were mostly chickens and other farm-friendly fowl. A wall hanging featuring the sun announced that sleepy-heads needed to rise and shine. I rose every morning. It was the shining part that was getting tougher the further I got from my childhood.

"What is Vladimir?" I asked. "He said he's a ghost, and he looks like a ghost, but if you ask me he's acting like a bit of a poltergeist. He told me he siphoned off some of the dead conquerors' power. Can a ghost do that?"

"We don't know, do we, Jack?"

"That we don't, Betty. That we don't."

The kettle whistled. Jack Honeychurch organized a tea set on a tray. Boiling water poured into the teapot with scoops of loose-leaf tea. He slid the tray onto the table and wandered off. When he returned it was with a three-tier serving stand laden with goodies.

"Well, I definitely don't know what he is. My experience is limited to ghosts and the two succubi that follow Leo around, and they're pretty passive. I guess they don't have magazines in the demon dimension, because they read a lot of magazines." I thought about it. "The paper probably burns in all that fire and brimstone."

Betty used a pair of tiny ornamental tongs to drop sugar lumps in her tea. "This creature crossed your salt line, you said, love?"

"Stepped right over it. Slowly. Although possibly that was for dramatic effect."

"A creature impervious to salt that consorts with the dead." Her curls bounced as she shook her head. "Are you sure he's not a living human?"

"He can come and go like a ghost, and he's transparent. I genuinely believed he was a regular ghost right up until he stepped over that line like it was nothing." My brain went to work, twisting and turning the scant amount of information in my possession. "If he—it—is powerful enough to rattle doors, dodge salt, and stir up a violent amount of wind, why hang out with a pair of ghosts— even if they are long-dead conquerors? Surely not just for the power."

"Did this being solidify at any point?"

Good question. I felt fairly confident about my "no."

All this time, I'd been visually perusing the serving tray. So many options, so little room in my stomach.

"Go ahead and pick something," Betty said. "Anything you don't eat now, we can box up for you to take home and share with your policeman."

Pretty optimistic of her to assume I'd share. When I looked up, Betty was suppressing a giggle. I selected a napoleon with pale yellow custard between layers of crisp pastry. The pastry crackled as my fork attacked it.

"You said all three men plotted this in your shop while they were still alive, right?"

Betty's curls bounced. She stirred her tea. "Saw them myself, huddled around a table."

I rarely saw other customers in the Cake Emporium. "When customers come in, do you know when and where they're from?"

"Always" Betty said. "And when they leave, they walk back into their own time and place. There are no detours without my say-so."

"Where and when did Vladimir come from?"

"Moscow, 1995," she said without pausing.

"And everyone who can see the Cake Emporium has a touch of the ol' woo-woo?"

"Indeed they do."

"What would a Russian from the 1990s want with Mehmed and Xerxes? And what would they want with *him*?"

"They're both conquerors, aren't they?" Jack offered. "Powerful people shed power. They can't help it. They're full of the stuff."

"And Vladimir, as far as we know, was a nobody," I said. "Was he a human nobody in 1995?"

"If he wasn't, he was hiding it well," Betty said.

"So two of them became ghosts, and Vladimir or whatever he is—and whomever he is—became a super ghost. A ghost-plus. Can that happen?"

"I don't know, love. If there's one thing I do know is that almost anything is possible."

"Except fixing a fallen soufflé," Jack said.

"He can fix a fallen soufflé," Betty told me. "I've seen it with my own eyes."

Jack wiggled his fingers. "Magic," he mouthed.

Betty laughed and slapped at his hands. "Ignore him. It's possible this individual made a bargain with something for temporary powers."

"That can happen?"

"How else do you think people rise to the top without apparent hard work? Bargains are made and broken all the time. If I were you, I'd start at the beginning. Figure out what this Russian wants."

"I can't imagine he'd want anything on Merope in wintertime."

"Don't sell your island short. It's quite charming."

I took a deep breath and let it out slowly. So far I'd eaten none of my pastry. That wasn't like me. Maybe Vlad's magic finger had zapped the appetite out of me.

"I need to find out who he really is—or was—and start there."

"I have complete faith in you," Betty said.

That made one of us. Betty was right, though: I needed to speak with Vladimir again, one-on-one, minus an audience. Maybe then he'd tell me exactly what he wanted. Once his business here was finished, if he was a ghost, the Afterlife would reach out and snatch him up.

"I should get moving," I said. "I have to see a woman about a wedding dress."

"I'll escort you back." Betty shoved her chair back. Before I could blink, Jack presented me with a Cake Emporium box loaded with goodies, including a jar of his honey whipped cream.

How?

The Honeychurch siblings were a strange pair, but their hearts were good and I adored Betty. If Jack kept feeding me, he'd scoot higher up my list of favorite people, too.

"Promise me you'll be careful, love," Betty said as we navigated the mansion's hallways. "You're more than a customer to me. You're a friend."

"I'll be careful. Is it safe to go back that way?"

"Oh, yes. The way is already closed. There's just enough juice in it to send you back home. Here we go." She opened the French doors, then the door to the Cake Emporium's kitchen. She didn't follow me through. "See you soon, I hope." She hugged me tight, engulfing me in the smell of fresh, baking cookies with a hint of molasses and ginger. "Go on now."

I turned around.

The shop was empty. No kitchen. No storefront. There was nothing behind me, not even a door.

The Cake Emporium was gone.

CHAPTER ELEVEN

Yiayia caught up with me on the way to Eleni Zerva's house. Right now I was more worried about Vladimir, but a promise was a promise. My grandmother had dredged up a trench coat. I suspected (and feared) there was nothing underneath except Yiayia herself.

"Did you learn anything at your cake shop?"

"That I'm not as hungry as I thought I was. Can you not get your ghost goop in my to-go box?"

"What goop? There is no goop. There has been no oozing since that time I had to take the antibiotics for my *mouni*."

"Can you ride on the back anyway?"

Ghosts didn't feel like anything except cool, clammy air, and they didn't normally ooze, drip, or expel any substances. I'd heard stories about how some worked their way up to producing ectoplasm but I'd never seen it in person. All the same, I didn't want Yiayia's butt in my sweets. They'd never taste the same.

"Okay, but only because you are my favorite grandchild."

"What about Toula?"

"She is my other favorite grandchild, even though she has a stick in her kolos."

She wasn't wrong. Toula was born with an immovable butt stick.

We rode over to Eleni Zerva's house. Technically the white stucco bungalow belonged to her parents, but now that they were gone and her siblings all lived on the mainland, she was the only living resident. Had her parents left her the house, or was it destined to become one of those bones relatives pick over once the body was dead? Probably Leo knew. Right now he'd be making it his business to know everything about the Zervas family.

Using my Greek outside voice—louder than a regular outside voice, and shrill enough to peel paint off a wall—I called out to Eleni from the yard's gate.

Eleni Zerva appeared from around the back of the house. She was holding a shattered pot that rained soil as she moved.

"Allie!" she called out. "Come in."

Sometime between the hour when I found her parents in the alley and this morning, the Zervases' daughter had either dyed her old wardrobe black or acquired all-black clothing. As their daughter, she was bound to wear the black for two years to show respect. Eleni Zerva was mid-forties on the inside, mid-thirties on the outside. One of those ageless faces. Today she looked even younger, as though she had finally swapped the boulder for feathers. She'd been caring for her parents since their marbles began rolling away, and now she only had to worry about siblings fighting her to the death for the house. Eleni was tiny. Bird-like bones. Brittle hair in need of a good cut that didn't take place in her bathroom. Kind eyes and a pinched mouth from keeping her thoughts buttoned up.

With Yiayia wafting along ahead of me, I unlatched the gate and stepped into the small yard. Like almost every other yard in the village, the dirt was hidden under the concrete slab. Weeds did their best to punch through, but even they couldn't compete with concrete. Years ago, when my family moved back to Merope to take care of Yiayia (who was allegedly dying from—in her words—*mouni* cancer) the Zervases' yard had been bursting with color, all of it exploding from flowerpots arranged artfully around the space. Those same plants were still in residence, but now they were droopier than half-cooked noodles. Some lay in pieces. Others were sad, exhausted, thirsty for a non-alcoholic, caffeine-free beverage. It wasn't that Eleni didn't care. The woman had been up to her eyeballs trying to be a caregiver to her parents and hold down a job.

She stopped in front of me. Smiled. Then tears burst out of her eyes like her face was a chest and the wet stuff was Xenomorphs.

I gave her a tissue and a hug. That seemed to do the trick.

"I'm supposed to be sad that my parents are dead. I'm supposed to be grieving. And I am, but I'm also happy that they're gone. Does that make me a terrible daughter?"

"No," I said.

"A little bit," Yiayia said. "But have you met your mama? *Po-po*, now that is a woman who does not know a trashcan from a toilet."

My eye twitched. Good thing my grandmother was dead and nobody but me could hear her.

Eleni righted a chair that had toppled over during the paranormal temper tantrum. She sat and buried her face in her hands. "I'm relieved. Mama and Baba had not been themselves for so long. I had to quit my job, did you know?"

"I hadn't heard that."

"It's true. There was no other choice. I had to resign so I could be here full time to make sure they didn't wander off or hurt themselves. And it happened anyway. All that worrying, all that anxiety, all the effort I put into keeping them safe, and I failed them anyway."

I scrounged up a second chair, rescuing it from the fence. "How did they get out?"

Yes, I was veering into Leo's lane, but also I was just making conversation, wasn't I? Eleni Zerva started it. My goal in coming here was to find out about a dress. If she wanted to talk about how her parents managed to break out of the house and wound up murdered in an alley, I couldn't turn her down.

People love to tell me things. It goes with the job.

"I was in the bathroom. Before I went, I made sure everything was locked. They ate most of the soup I'd cooked for lunch, busted through the window, and left."

"Which window?"

"Around the side."

I followed her pointing finger. The window had been patched with plywood and the glass swept away. It was low enough to the ground that an elderly man and woman could have escaped without breaking a hip.

"Is this how they usually make their escapes?"

She indicated "no" with an up-down chin tilt. "It has been a while since they managed a successful getaway. I have been extra careful lately, since I realized how bad their memories had become. Recently I had to throw out dinner because Mama dumped a whole jar of salt in the pot. Allie …" Her face was fearful "… I think the police believe I killed them."

"Did you?"

"No! I did everything I could to protect my parents. Why would I kill them?"

"Then you don't have anything to worry about. That's what the police do: everyone is a suspect until evidence says they're not. Where does the dress fit into all this?"

She looked at me tearfully. "I should show you a picture of Mama's dress so you know what you will be looking for. Come inside."

I followed her into the house. The hallway was filled with the requisite religious icons. The Virgin Mary's portrait on the wall. A lighted nativity scene. Candles in glasses painted with saints and apostles. The walls were a violent mint green. Typical for the older set. How long until Eleni repainted and reimagined the house in her image? Soon, I hoped.

The picture she was looking for was sitting on a shallow shelf in the living room. Maria and Stathis Zervas on their wedding day, their expressions vaguely shell-shocked, as if they couldn't quite believe their parents really went through with arranging their children's nuptials. Arranged marriages were all the rage back in those days.

"This is Mama's dress. She wanted to be buried in it, but it vanished from her chest."

"When?"

"I don't know. It was there a year ago. Now … gone."

"Do you think someone came into your home and stole it?"

She indicated *no*. "I believe Mama gave it away, but to whom? I think she forgot her burial wishes. She forgot a lot of things. Both of my parents did. Some days, some moments, they even forgot me."

Yiayia was right about the dress, but she was also wrong. Kyria Zerva's wedding gown was a perfectly lovely tea-length dress. Lots of delicate lace and embroidery work. Not a bombshell frock; more girl-next-door.

"It's lovely," I said truthfully.

"Boring," Yiayia said, sticking her head through the wall.

My eye twitched.

Eleni looked concerned. "What are you doing?"

I poked my eye, held the nerve still. "I'm okay. Are you looking for this exact dress or a replacement?"

"It has to be this exact dress. I need you to find it, please, if you can."

I opened the camera app on my phone. "Do you mind?"

She waved a "go ahead" hand at the photograph.

It was difficult to reconcile the two nervous young people in the photograph with the two ghosts on my couch. Nowadays, Kyria Zerva used my trash as a litter box, and her husband wore his pants as a hat. Also, they were dead. The people in the picture were petrified but they looked alive.

"Depending on where the dress is, I might have to pay to get it back."

"No problem. I have not run out of money yet. My old employer even says my job will be waiting when I am ready."

We wandered back outside. "What am I going to do with my time now, besides work? I have been caring for them in one way or another almost my whole life." Her smile was tight and resentful. "I never married. All my siblings have husbands and wives and children. But Mama and Baba refused to let me go. Now it is too late."

"It's never too late," I told her.

She swallowed hard. Like she was clearing a wad of bread lodged in the pipe. "For me, yes. There was someone once. My parents sent him away because they needed me here. He swore he would not leave the island until I came with him. But then he went back on his word. He left without me. I never heard from him again."

"I'm sorry."

"*Ach*, it is in the past now, and the past never returns. Let me know if you find the dress, yes?"

"Not if—when."

Her smile was small and damp. "That's why I called you."

I called Leo. "How much time do I have before Maria Zerva can be released to the mortician?"

"You'll have to ask Panos to be sure, but I'm guessing twenty-four hours at the most. I think he's run all the tests. Why?"

"Eleni Zerva hired me to locate her mother's wedding dress."

"Isn't it in the wardrobe, or wherever it is women keep their old wedding dresses?"

"Apparently the dress vanished. Probably Kyria Zerva gave her dress away but never mentioned to whom."

"Good luck," he said.

Luck would be nice. So would ghosts without memory leaks. Now that they'd passed on, you'd think the Zervases would be free from their earthly dementia. But no. The condition had followed them right up to the grave. Chances were high Maria Zerva wouldn't remember the dress, let alone the recipient of her generosity. If that's how the dress wandered out of the house.

"There are currently about twenty thousand people on

Merope. I can question them all within twenty-four hours if I have to."

He whistled, low and impressed. "I wish I had your skills.

"It's less about my skills and more about talking to the right person. From that point on, the island grapevine does the rest. Eventually you get a gossip ping."

"People hate talking to the police."

"Because sometimes the police lock them up and feed them rats and make them wipe with their hands because toilet paper isn't in the budget."

"I've never made anyone eat rats or wipe with their own hands."

"Oh, you have. Not directly, but that's what happens when people are shipped off to Korydallos."

"So what do they get if they talk to you?"

"Not rats. I offer the promise of soft, quilted toilet paper, and they get to be useful. Never underestimate how much people want to be useful and appreciated."

"I appreciate you," he said with a smile in his voice.

"Same. I'll appreciate you even more if you call Panos Grekos to find out when he's releasing the Zervases to the funeral home."

"Anything for you," he said and ended the call.

On Merope, gossip passes through hubs. Sometimes the hub is a person. Sometimes it's a place. One of those places was the More Super Market, where people talked freely while shopping and Stephanie listened. She did her share of talking, too, which I was counting on.

I rode over to the More Super Market. The door was unlocked this time, and Stephanie was no longer playing butler. Instead, she was back behind her counter, performing feets of self-care. Literal feets. Grater in hand, she had her foot up on the stool, preparing to shave off several months' worth of hard skin.

"Is that a cheese grater?"

"It was cheaper than a foot file. What happened to your face? Was it a peel?"

"Electricity."

She set aside the grater to tap words into her phone. "That must be new. Where can I get it done? How much does it cost?"

The shop had gotten an upgrade. Everything looked clean. Someone had dusted the shelves and products. The windows were completely see-thru for the first time in years.

"Wow, did you clean?"

"No."

I raised both eyebrows.

"It was him," she went on. "The new boss. He told me to clean and I laughed at him, so he did it himself."

Funny. He didn't look like a guy that cleaned. Adonis Diplas struck me as a man who expected women to wait on him while he played king.

"I might be impressed," I said, "and also less likely to contract listeria."

She scraped the grater across her foot. Fine dust drifted to the floor.

Doing my best not to inhale, I wandered over to the deli and perused the small selection of cheese and cold cuts. But we all knew I was going to buy my usual mortadella and kaseri cheese.

"How is your family?" I asked Stephanie. "Are they okay after the wind storm?"

"My cousin is telling everyone that the wind blew her into the sea and that is why her lips are now four times their original size. I know she is lying. She got fillers. Cheap fillers. Now she looks like a duck that has been punched in the beak. Once she can talk properly again I am going to make an appointment with her doctor."

"You want to look like a duck?"

"A duck face is a money-making face on the internet."

I was sure that wasn't true, but who was I to stand between Stephanie and her waterfowl goals? "I'm on my way back from Eleni Zerva's house."

The grater's zester rasped across her heel. "They say she murdered her parents. Is it true, do you think?"

I sidestepped the question. "She asked me to find her mother's wedding dress. It's missing."

Her answer bounced right back. The trusty gossip ping. "Kyria Zerva gave the dress to Kyria Yiota. Her daughter is getting married soon and she is too cheap to spend money on a new dress, so she made Kyria Zerva give up her dress."

"How?"

"How does Kyria Yiota do anything? Nagging, screeching, and torture."

Crap. Worst-case scenario. I struggled to keep the grimace off my face and lost. Kyria Yiota was a pill, and her daughter was a poor henpecked creature that did whatever her mother told her to keep the peace. She was scheduled to be married this spring to a man her had mother picked out. Like many a dutiful Greek daughter, she and her husband were expected to live with her dear *mama* after the wedding and produce offspring as soon as humanly possible. Given Kyria Yiota's penchant for high maintenance, I wondered if she had thought things through. Grandchildren would draw attention and time away from her petty needs.

"Ugh," I groaned. "Are you sure it wasn't someone else? Anyone else? Maybe a nice serial killer? A shiver of sharks? Could she have dropped the dress into a storm drain with a red balloon floating above it?"

Stephanie shrugged. Foot dust drifted through the air, undoing her boss's handiwork. "I know what I know. Why does Eleni Zerva want the dress?"

"Her mother wanted to be buried in the dress."

"Are you going to steal it back?"

"What? No."

"Kyria Yiota will never give it up, especially if she got it for free. There is nothing she loves more in this world than herself and free things."

CHAPTER TWELVE

To DEAL WITH KYRIA YIOTA, I was going to need backup. Going alone and unarmed was foolhardy.

"Yiayia?"

Pop.

My grandmother materialized. She'd had a wardrobe change. Again. This time it was a bandage dress from some overpriced designer's collection. It emphasized her cones and made a crepe out of her pancake butt. Her legs looked like they belonged on a turkey. To finish off the outfit, she was wearing fluffy slippers.

"Slippers?"

"I want to be comfortable."

That made sense. "Can you ride on the bike in that dress?"

"Sit in this dress? Ha. That will never happen." She looked down. "I did not think this through, did I?"

"What do you know about Kyria Yiota?"

She made a face. "She has the personality of a wolverine, and I'm not talking that hunky Australian man with knife fingers."

I winced. "If she had something I wanted, how would I get it from her?"

"Without a human sacrifice? Money, maybe. But I would use tongs and a flameproof mask."

"That's what I figured." I girded my sweats-covered loins. "Okay, I'm going in. Cover me."

"I will sit on the sidelines and yell encouraging platitudes. Wait." She vanished. Almost immediately, she reappeared wearing a cheerleader outfit, complete with pompoms. I averted my eyes. Somewhere a Dallas Cowboys cheerleader was missing her booty shorts.

With Yiayia practicing her cheers behind me, I peddled over to Kyria Yiota's house. Rumor had it that Kyria Yiota was loaded, but you'd never know it to look at her home or her life. She lived like a pauper, right down to the absence of running water. I wondered how her daughter's fiancé felt about moving into a house with one bedroom, an outhouse, and a water pump in the yard.

"I don't want to do this," I said, kicking the stand on my bicycle.

"Turn around and go home."

"But I have to do this."

Yiayia patted my cheek. Cool, damp air brushed the skin. "Stay and face the gorgon."

How badly did Eleni need this dress? Her mother was dead, she'd never know. Although, yes, she was a ghost, so that might be a problem. Ghosts tend to have a lot of opinions, seeing as how they don't have much else. And don't get me started on the grudges. Nothing is more eternal than a well-loved grudge

That was it, then. Acquiring the wedding dress was a must. No other choice, unless I wanted to be haunted for all eternity by Maria Zerva.

Deep breath. I could do this. I had to.

I stood at the gate and said, "Kyria Yiota?"

Nothing.

Which wasn't surprising, given that I'd whispered her name. Maybe if I said it three times, she'd appear like Bloody Mary.

Louder this time: "Kyria Yiota?"

Yiayia shook her pompoms. Her hands went one way, her loose skin went the other. "Yiota, Yiota, is a *kota*. Once shoved a broom handle up her—"

"Please don't finish that," I said. "Honestly, I'd like her a whole lot more if she really was a hen. At least then we could throw her in an oven with potatoes."

An earsplitting screech pierced the cold air. "Who is that calling me?"

"Aliki Callas," I called out.

"Who?"

There was silence for a moment. Then the front door opened and a thin, pale woman about my age peered out and beckoned to me. Kyria Yiota's daughter Irini.

"Mama wants to know what you want."

Yiayia swiveled her hips and leaped in the air. One of her boob cones popped out of the cheerleader top. She jumped again. The other one popped out.

"I'm here about a wedding dress that belonged to Maria Zerva."

Her forehead crumpled up. "My wedding dress?"

"If it's the one your mother got for free, then yes."

"What about it?"

I explained the situation. "Eleni Zerva needs it back. The dress was never intended to be given away. Her mother stipulated that she had to be buried in her wedding dress, and now she's dead, so …."

Irini nodded once. "I will be back."

The door closed. While I waited, Yiayia performed

several jumping jacks and landed in the splits.

"I think my *mouni* is stuck to the ground."

I closed my eyes. "This isn't happening."

"No problem! It is okay! I can get unstuck with one good *mouni klasimo*." There was an obnoxious sound, and then Yiayia said, "See? Told you."

My eye twitched. "Why me?"

The door open and Irini emerged. "Mama says no."

"Is she open to negotiation?"

"No."

"I can offer her some money."

"She says no, the dress belongs to her. Maria Zerva gave it to her because she wanted Mama to have it, otherwise why would she give it away?"

Oh, oh, oh. I knew the answer. "Because she had dementia and didn't realize she was working contrary to her own wishes?"

"Mama does not care." She beckoned me closer. "I am sorry. I would give you the dress if I could, but she keeps it on a dressmaker's dummy in the kitchen."

Then her eyelid fluttered. Seizure or wink?

Wink, I decided when she repeated the gesture more pointedly.

Given that many of these old houses had two rooms and an outhouse, I wasn't surprised Kyria Yiota was keeping a dummy in the kitchen. But what did shock me was that Irini appeared to be helping me. Boy, her mother must have finally added one too many straws to that camel's back.

"Well, that's too bad," I said in a nice, loud voice. "I'll tell Eleni she can't bury her dead mother in her wedding dress, like Kyria Zerva requested. Be careful, okay? That dress could be cursed. Probably is, now that I think about it. I'm pretty sure defying a dead person's wishes is a sure-fire way to end up cursed. I wonder what horrors will befall your mother now?"

There was a cackle inside the house.

The door flew open all the way, bouncing off the exterior wall. Malevolence radiated from the woman filling the space. Kyria Yiota shoved her daughter back inside the house with a snarl.

If someone told me Kyria Yiota was three honey badgers in a navy blue housedress, I'd believe them. Long, pointy nose (perfect for poking into other people's business), no lips, hooded eyes, shrouded by a shallow nest of wrinkles and folds. Kyria Yiota is whippet thin because she believes eating anything more than cheese and bread is overindulgence and a sin. But I have it on good authority —well, goodish because my source is Stephanie Dolas— that she shovels candy into her face when no one is looking.

"You think I am afraid of curses?"

"Obviously not, with that face," Yiayia muttered.

Where were my grandmother's helpful affirmations now? I could really use some encouragement, something to help bring out my inner sass. Instead, being in the presence of human evil made me squeak, "Maybe?"

She pointed a bony finger at her chest, what was possibly the middle honey badger. "Curses are afraid of me, *vromoskeela*!" Then she clacked her teeth together and vanished back in her house, dragging her daughter along with her.

I stood there blinking for several seconds before Yiayia said, "We should get out of here."

Good idea.

I jumped on my bike and peddled away before Yiayia had a chance to fasten her pompoms. "Wait for me," she called out.

I stopped. She and her pompoms settled on back, although why a ghost needed to ride a bicycle was beyond me. Maybe Yiayia considered it bonding time.

"What are we going to do now?" she asked me.

"I guess I go back to Eleni and tell her Kyria Yiota won't give up the dress."

"Eleni is a good girl. She will understand."

Eleni did not understand.

"Kyria Yiota … that is bad. You offered her money?"

"She refused to even consider payment."

She took five steps, turned, and walked five steps in the opposite direction. The Zervases' living room wasn't made for pacing. As she added another twenty-five steps to her daily step count, serving suggestions sprayed out of her mouth. Kyria Yiota was somehow supposed to make a watermelon fit in a very tight hole while she was on fire. To complicate matters, several prominent religious figures would simultaneously be making sweet monkey love to a cactus.

"You can do anything with enough olive oil," Yiayia said knowingly.

Eleni couldn't hear her, and I wasn't about to pass on that message. I had my doubts. There were some things even a barrel of oil couldn't fix.

"It's not all doom and gloom," I said. "Irini told me where she's keeping the dress."

Eleni stopped. "That is good, yes? You can steal it back."

I winced. If I took the dress and Kyria Yiota discovered I was the culprit, which she would because I'd already revealed my hand by asking for the wedding dress, she'd unleash her scream. Goodbye eardrums. Animals all over the island would perish. Things would get apocalyptic. A warm-up act for the real punishment.

"I don't know about that."

"Please, you have to try. It was Mama's final wish."

Against my better judgment, I nodded once. "Okay."

She exhaled. "Good. Thank you. I don't want to have to—" She stopped, shook her head, regrouped. "I just want this to be over. I want my parents to rest peacefully and for the police to find out who killed them."

"They will."

"Or will they?" Yiayia asked. "I love murder mysteries."

My eye twitched.

A hollow widened in my heart and in my stomach. I'd been hoping to stuff the void with cake, but the Cake Emporium was still an empty storefront. My reflection looked as bummed out as I felt. Now I had no choice except to slum it at one of Merope's other *zacharoplasteios*—sugar shops.

Instead, I found myself at Merope's Best, ordering a cup of sadness and shame with a side of something that looked like a brownie but probably wasn't. Who knew I had a self-destructive side?

I didn't want to go home yet. The Zervases were there. Maybe Maria Zerva couldn't recall giving up her dress, but seeing her would only remind me that I needed to make a plan. Probably I needed a good *Mission Impossible* marathon with an *Ocean's Eight* thru *Thirteen* chaser.

I carried my cup and plate to the corner table and sat with my back to the wall. For a place that sold toxic waste by the cup, Merope's Best did brisk business, especially amongst young, trendy Greeks with strong immune systems.

I checked my email.

To my surprise, I had a message from Angela's new and oblivious love interest: George Diplas, daredevil meteorologist. He said intel from the island had already put us on his radar. George had done some digging and explained that although we'd experienced freak weather, there was no actual scientific date to validate those claims. The whole thing sounded like he was keen, but desperate to downplay his curiosity.

Ignore the email, I told myself. Let Angela be single for a while. Give Alfred a chance to make his move.

But it wasn't my business, was it? Last time I checked, Angela Zouboulaki was woman of fifty-something pretending we ticked the same age boxes on forms. If she wanted to find love, who was I to stop her?

I shot back a reply and suggested maybe he could swing by Merope, just in case the freak weather freakishly reappeared. Angela had given me the go-ahead to dangle free transport and accommodation under his nose, so I made sure he knew the island would roll out its red carpet and treat him like a king. Hopefully he had forgotten that Greece's king had been in exile since the late sixties, although now he was back and living as a commoner.

There was movement out of the corner of my eye. The Man in Black pulled out a chair and planted his proud, moody butt beside me. I hadn't seen him come in, and I should know. I'd purposely positioned myself so the whole store was visible. As always, he was dressed in black. His long coat fanned out behind him so he wasn't sitting on its length. He sat with his knees apart, one hand resting on his knee, simultaneously uncomfortable and at ease. He pushed the other hand back through his slightly too-long hair as if he were on the verge of saying something.

Not surprising, given that he'd approached me. People didn't normally sidle up to others just to sit.

I decided to get the first word in. "You're not Jack Honeychurch. I met the real Jack Honeychurch and you're definitely not him."

"I never claimed to be Jack Honeychurch. You assumed."

I opened my mouth. Closed it again. He was right, damn him. I'd assigned a name to him—a name he never offered as his own.

"But you said you had bread rising."

"Professional bakers are not the only people in this world who make bread."

"Virgin Mary. You're right."

His tilted nod said he was moving on from the name snafu. "I understand you discovered who or what was assisting your ghosts."

"Can we really call them *my* ghosts? The only reason I stumbled across them was because I could see them."

His mouth was a grim line. "You are correct that they were not your spirits. Nevertheless, they became your problem when this … *being* singled you out to assist them."

"And I kept my word. I said I'd find them a way off the island, and that's exactly what happened."

"Two, yes, but not the third. He is still on this island somewhere."

"Is he, though? Since his minor hissy fit at the Cake Emporium, I haven't heard a peep out of him. Even the weather is back to normal. Barely a sea breeze."

"The Russian cannot leave this island on his own."

"Why not?"

"He is trapped."

"How? What's keeping him here?"

"A compact, perhaps. Or old, unfinished business. He alone can tell you what it is he wants and how he can move on."

"He did say he had business. I haven't had a chance to determine what yet. Do you know why the others couldn't leave the island? They wanted to conquer the world, which wasn't exactly unfinished business. More like never-going-to-happen business."

"Think, Allie Callas, and the answer will come to you."

"Here and now? Because I kind of came here to do the opposite of thinking. I've been hired to do a thing I don't want to have to do."

"Perhaps the problem will solve itself."

"Am I still supposed to be thinking?"

His eyebrows rose. He nodded slightly. So that was a "yes" then. Figures.

"Okay." I picked at my brown lump of whatever this was. "Three ghosts arrived on Merope via the Cake Emporium. They became stuck, unable to backtrack because the Honeychurches closed the shop. They couldn't cross the salt line. So they came to me because they thought I could get them off the island. But why couldn't they—"

The answer slapped me upside the head.

"Salt water. They couldn't cross the sea on their own because it's too salty. So they needed me to either carry them across the sea or secure passage for them via the Cake Emporium."

He inclined his head. "Indeed."

"But the third one, Vladimir, isn't fazed by salt."

"Not all things can be penned in by a few grains of salt. When you want to keep something strong in or out, you have to build a more sturdy fence or cell."

"Are you saying if I want to trap Vladimir, I need to use more salt next time?"

His lips quirked upward. Not quite a smile. But it had promise. "Soon you will not need me anymore."

"I don't need you now."

"Au contraire. I have saved you more than once."

"Sure. But last time it was my dead grandmother who saved me, while you were nowhere to be found."

He bowed his head. "Forgive me, I was detained."

"Who are you?"

"A friend."

"What are you?"

"A friend."

"Is the world about to end?"

The Man in Black's expression shuttered. Silence reigned for a moment, about as well as it could in a coffee shop playing maudlin hard rock songs rearranged and set to a lone flute.

I poked the brownie. "Don't give me that. Answer the question."

"Some outcomes are constantly in flux, while others are set in concrete."

"Well, which one is it? Is the fate of the world in flux or wearing concrete boots?"

"You want certainty where there is none."

I slapped the table gently. "So it's in flux. Which means something can stop it."

Yes. This was great news. The world's march towards destruction wasn't inevitable. Which meant there might be a way for me to intervene, if I could find that way. If only I was less of a Frodo and more of a Captain Marvel. "I don't suppose you could be my Samwise Gangee?" I said to the Man in Black.

He raised his eyebrows at me.

"No, probably my grandmother is my Sam. That's a problem. She's much more of a Merry and Pippin."

The coffee shop's door opened. My gaze cut to the swaggering figure decked out in sweatpants, coat, and a ball cap over hair I knew was sandy blond. When he caught me staring, he grinned his crooked grin.

"The coffee must be good," Adonis Diplas called out.

The whole coffee shop fell into a shocked, horrified, and outraged hush, except for the flutist piping out Black Sabbath's *Heaven and Hell*. The silence held for several seconds.

Until it shattered.

Everybody laughed, including me. The baristas put their foreheads on the counter and shuddered from the giant guffaws. I glanced over to see if the Man in Black was laughing. He didn't look like the type.

He was gone. Again.

Darn it. And just when the conversation was getting confusing yet informative.

"Okay," Adonis said with a good-natured grin. "I'm a brave guy. I'll try it anyway. Give me what you've got."

Everyone eventually tired of mocking the More Super Market's new owner. They went back to trying to survive their own personal cups of taste bud hell. Adonis Diplas— bravely or stupidly—put in his own order then wended through the tables to get to me.

"Where did your friend go?"

"Can you describe him?"

He thought about a moment, then frowned. "No. For some reason I can't."

"Probably it's the flute music. It has a strange numbing effect on the brain."

"Is that Black Sabbath?"

I nodded once. "Earlier it was Metallica."

"Who would do that to good music?"

"Merope's Best has no respect for the sanctity of music or coffee." I poked my brownie. "Or whatever this is."

"Looks like a brownie."

"It does, doesn't it? But don't be fooled by its tender crumbs and its gentle browns."

He reached over and broke off the corner. Very presumptuous of him. The brown thing vanished into his mouth. He made a face. "Carob."

"See?"

"What about the coffee?"

"Worse."

He grinned. "Can't wait to try it."

Over at the counter, the barista raised a cup. "For the man that thinks he is a god."

"That's you," I told him.

He winked and stood. "Not the first time I've heard that." Off he went to collect his coffee. But wait, there was more. Instead of leaving like a normal person, he returned to the table like we were friends.

For crying out loud. "Can't find the door?"

"Company is better in here."

"It's really not."

"Putting yourself down?"

"I'm working. You're interrupting."

His eyes cut from my cup to the plate. "What are you working on? An eating gig? How do I sign up?"

"Multiple problems and their solutions."

"Tell me about them. Maybe I can help."

What could it hurt? "Okay. I need to acquire something for a client—something that rightfully belongs to the client, or so they believe. Ownership is hazy because it was given away by someone without all their faculties. The new owner won't give it up for anything."

"This about that wedding dress?"

Ungh. Nothing was a secret on this island. "Stephanie?"

"She talks a lot. Half the time I don't think she realizes she's doing it. Her mouth goes on autopilot while she's painting her nails or whatever other inappropriate things she's doing on the job."

"She gets the work done."

Could be that was true. Stephanie was competent at accepting cash and making change. Things got weird when you waved plastic at her. But Adonis Diplas couldn't come to my island and sort-of insult my people.

"You're loyal, aren't you?"

"Aren't you?"

"Sure." He shrugged. "If they're worth it. Talk to me about the wedding dress situation."

I told him about Kyria Yiota and her daughter, including the wink and nod from the bride-to-be. While I was doing that, Adonis took several swigs of his coffee without puking, retching, or glowing the dark. What was wrong with him?

"You offered her financial compensation, right?"

One nod. "I also suggested that the dress was cursed."

"Extortion?"

"Do I look like a woman that does extortion?"

"You look like a cupcake, which means you could definitely do extortion and get away with it."

"Flattery will get you nowhere."

He fiddled with the cup. Nothing exploded—this time. "Okay, okay. Real talk. Looks to me like the only options on the table are giving up the dress, or stealing it back. That or locating a convincing replica. I bet someone out there could makc one for your client."

"She wants the original."

"Get the replica and tell her it's the real thing."

"Which would be fine, right up until Kyria Yiota's daughter walks into the church in Maria Zerva's dress. Everybody on the island talks and shows off photos. Plus we regularly flock to the churches if there's a wedding, even when we're not invited. There's no way to keep the real dress a secret."

"Big problem."

"Are you mocking me?"

"No." He reached for this coffee again. "What if I could get you the dress?"

"You mean steal it?"

"I mean repossessing it." He made a face. "Yes, steal it."

"I'd say 'no thank you,' because that's wrong and I'm dating a policeman."

He laughed. "I know. That's why I'm offering to do the stealing instead of putting you on the spot."

"Knowledge of crime is a crime." I shook my head. He had some nerve. "What's in it for you?"

"Your business is finding things. Could be someday I need something found."

"So this is what, payment in advance?"

He splayed his hands on the table. "Bartering system, like the old days before money."

"I don't think so." With one finger, I pushed the carob brownie across the table to him and grabbed my coffee. "I'll figure something out."

"You know where to find me if you change your mind."

"I won't."

"You might."

"I won't."

"Are you trying to get the last word in?"

I left him to dangle on his own question mark.

CHAPTER THIRTEEN

Boots off. Coat and bag swinging from the coatrack. Phone on my desk. Ignoring my coffee, I got to work checking over my email and messages from the past few days. Merope's people had lost things this past week, and a lot of them were hoping I could help find them.

I couldn't do much about chickens that had been cast out to sea—poor birdies—but I could help people book a general contractor.

I called Filip Filipou, the island's most reliable general contractor. That meant he answered his phone half the time and showed up to work within a week of when he promised he'd be there "this afternoon."

"It's Allie Callas," I said when he picked up.

"Hold, please."

Filip made beat box noises with his mouth and hummed *rembetika* tunes. In the background, cups clinked and men cackled.

"If you don't stop that right now, I'll help your wife find that thing she wants found."

The sound stopped. There was swearing as he told his

pals what would happen if they didn't quit hee-hawing like a drove of donkeys. No donkey I knew would ever hold still for any of that. One swift kick and the culprit would be shopping for a new knee.

"My wife can never get it."

"Then you'd better quit swilling coffee and help me out."

He sounded surprised. "How did you know I was drinking coffee?"

"I have eyes everywhere."

Also I knew how to listen—*really* listen.

"Okay, okay, what do you want?"

I gave him a list of my clients and the repairs they needed for their homes before the rain started up again.

"Okay. Tomorrow."

He ended the call.

Unsatisfied and not remotely reassured, I rode over to the waterfront *kafeneio*, where he was arguing about politics with his buddies. When he spotted me, he turned white and dived under the table.

I nudged his backside with my boot's toe. "I can see you. Get up."

"Is she still there?" he asked his coffee-drinking buddies.

I hooked my finger through his empty belt loop and hauled him up off the ground. Easy, given that he was built like a loop of wire. Filip was a couple of years ahead of me in school, which put him in Toula and Leo's class. He came from a long line of general contractors, all of them unmotivated craftsmen. They were excellent at what they did, when they could be bothered doing it. Other contractors around the island were even less reliable. They promised the moon and delivered moon dust.

"In case you hadn't noticed, the island is in disarray.

My clients need help today, now. Not tomorrow or however you interpret time."

"I am busy!"

"*Vre*, the *malakas* is busy," one of his friends told me.

Give me a break. "What are you, the Greek chorus?"

They cackled. I ignored them.

"Busy doing what? Drinking coffee with these women?"

The hyenas stopped.

"I work hard, I need coffee," he whined.

I marched inside the *kafeneio*, a small, dark place that smelled like old people who hadn't taken their winter baths. I swiped a to-go cup off the counter. Outside again, I grabbed Filip's cup and dumped the contents in the paper cup and slapped it into his hand.

"Saddle up," I told him. "First job is the Papadopoulos house. A hole in their roof needs patching so their rooster doesn't escape."

"They keep their rooster in the house?" he asked.

"He's a house rooster. His name is *Ftero*."

"*Ftero* is what you pull out of a bird before you eat it."

"Touch him and they'll be using you to stuff a pillow."

Now that Filip Filipou was up and moving, I moved to the next item on my list. I was procrastinating on the whole wedding dress thing. I didn't want to steal it back, but no other plans had leaped into the fray to wrestle theft out of the ring.

"What possessed you to give Kyria Yiota your wedding dress?" Yiayia was asking as I opened the door.

Blind panic stabbed me in adrenal glands. "What are you doing?"

"A little ghost humor," Yiayia said.

"I thought you were formerly living."

"I keep forgetting to be politically correct."

My eye twitched frantically. I waved her over. "You're not supposed to mention the you-know-what."

"Why not?"

"She might get upset?"

My grandmother snorted at the idea. "*Vre*, Maria, are you upset?"

"I am going to do *kaka* in Yiota's soup."

Yiayia turned back around. "See? She is fine."

"She just said she was going to *kaka* in Kyria Yiota's soup. How is that fine?"

"If you ask me, someone should have gone *kaka* in Yiota's soup years ago."

Yiayia had a point. Or maybe someone did poop in Kyria Yiota's soup and that was the origin of her malfunction.

"You're still my employee, right?" I asked my grandmother.

"Only if I do not have to do anything gross or scary."

"Your mission, should you choose to accept it, is to spy on Kyria Yiota."

"You said nothing gross or scary! Wait—why?" Yiayia's watery eyes glittered. "Do you think she is hiding state secrets?"

"Like most human beings, she has a routine—a routine that means she leaves her house predictably at certain times."

"I like it." Yiayia changed her tune. "You want me to do a thing that is like a stakeout."

"That's exactly what it is."

"Can I have snacks?"

"You can't eat snacks. You're dead."

"Why do you keep saying that?"

"Because it's true?"

"It is hurtful, that is what it is." She grinned. "Relax, my love. I am joking. Being a ghost is amazing. I can do anything except change the channel on the television. The best part is I can go through walls. Do you know what I saw the other day?"

"Was it a sex thing?"

"How did you guess?"

"I know you."

"Sofia Douka was wearing a strap-on *poutsa* and her brother Spiros was dressed up like a Great Dane."

Something told me that by "Great Dane" she didn't mean Viggo Mortensen. "You mean *Kyria* Sofia and *Father* Spiros?"

"It was a big one, too. The deluxe model. Very expensive."

My voice squeaked out. "Her brother?"

Yiayia tapped a finger on her chin. "Is he her brother? They were not raised here, you know. We only have their word for it that they are siblings."

"Wait—they're not from Merope?"

"They have been here so long that only the old ones remember that the Doukases adopted Spiros and Sofia from the mainland."

Maria Zerva stuck her head between us. "I remember."

"See?" Yiayia said.

"Do you remember how you ate poison?" I asked Maria Zerva.

"Poison? What poison? Everything is poison if you eat enough of it. Especially hamburgers and cake." She hobbled over to the window, where her husband had his nose pressed to the glass. Death couldn't keep a good

Greek from watching all the comings and goings in the neighborhood.

"Okay, so now that I'm horrified while simultaneously being more informed, can you go over to Kyria Yiota's house for that stakeout?"

Yiayia vanished and instantly returned with a new wardrobe change. This time she was in full cat burglar regalia. Although if you asked me, she was likely to hook a pointy boob on something. Good thing she went through objects these days.

"Any advice?" she asked me. "I want this to be the best stakeout in the history of stakeouts."

"Stay out of sight."

The rest of the morning was me reaching out and touching the internet on behalf of clients. I ordered building supplies, replacement furniture for outdoor furniture that had been damaged by the wind, and agreed to hunt for a dog. Cerberus had last been seen chasing a cat toward the far end of Merope, where the cliffs were high and the bones of Ayia Paraskevi—Saint Friday—lay broken on the ground after a bone-busting quake. Other structures on the island survived. Newer construction and building codes saved their skins. The only serious casualties were plates and vases that nose-dived off shelves.

Nowadays the old church was a maze of stone walls in varying degrees of disrepair. The domed roof bore a gaping hole, like Zeus had swung past and punched it in the eye.

Given that his owners were north of ninety, I'd promised Cerberus's family I'd go find him—yes, right now

—and bought a quick *tiropita* before hitting the cobbled streets of Merope again on my bicycle.

Cerberus was a dog of dubious genetic origins, although I figured at least one Newfoundland and one bear figured into his mix. The sweet pup was black, friendly, and the size of a small planet with a Velcro temperament. Usually he was content to watch over his yard like store-owner watching for shoplifters. The cat thing wasn't his usual MO. Must have been some cat.

I left the village's only town behind me, along with the cobbled roads. Out here, the paths were all dirt, worn down by those who lived on farmlets and those whose business took them into town regularly. I rode on and up until the Ayios Paraskevi—Saint Friday—appeared through a break in the orchards. Olives and citrus fruits were king here, but the church itself was surrounded by neglected fruit trees that no one wanted to love.

I kicked the bicycle stand not too far away from the dilapidated corpse of the old church. A few walls remained mostly upright, leaning together like drunk girls at a bar. Some formed a loose room at the back of the church. Ayia Paraskevi is popular amongst tourists, who come here to take selfies with broken bits of Greece as the backdrop. Locals partake of the church's hospitality, too. Certain locals. Especially folks that dabble in secret sex and collect meth recipes.

Oh look. There was a wild used condom, right now, languishing in the raggedy weeds punching up between the remnants of the marble floor.

I used my best outside voice to call the to the missing dog.

"Cerberus! Who's a good boy? Where's my ickle bickle puppy-boo?"

I scanned the area, searching for signs of the humongous canine. Tracks. Mountains of poop. Any indication of something outside the normal wildlife.

"Cerberus! Puppy wuppy want a treat?" I rattled the paper bag with the corner of cheese pie I'd saved for him.

I rounded the back of the church. Nothing there except weeds and dirt and cliffs. No poop. No cat. No—

Movement behind me.

No, not movement. Huffing. The wheezing chuckle of someone who found this oh-so amusing. Vladimir's ghost stepped out of the shadow.

"Today is wery lucky day."

"For me, I hope. For you, not so much."

"You vant me to stand here so you ken try your salt again?"

"I'm not here for you."

"Mebee I am here for you, da?"

"What do you want?"

He brushed the ground with his toe. The dirt moved as if pushed by a breeze.

"I vant to go beck."

"So go back. I'm not stopping you. You're a fully-grown whatever you are. Go buy a ticket or fly or whatever it is you do to get around."

"If it vas that easy, I vould have done it already. I need your heelp. You will do this think for me. Tell your friend to open her shop so I ken go."

"I can't do that."

"Pick up phone. Call her. Phone today go everywhere. In my day, vas stuck to wall like sticker."

"Won't make any difference. The shop is gone. Betty won't bring it back just because you made poor choices. You should have stayed in your time and place."

"I made mistake."

"We all make mistakes. Then we get to live with the consequences. That's life."

"Vhat if you did not heff to liff with them?"

I suddenly became aware the Russian was moving closer, centimeter by incremental centimeter. Playing Ginger Rogers to his Rasputin, I was steadily scooting backwards. There was a narrow band of land left between me and the rocks and the swirling water below. I scooted sideways. The Russian spirit moved with me, sweating in his tracksuit.

"You mean die?"

"*Nyet*. Go back. Make different choice. Maybe thees time not die."

"Impossible."

"With cake shop, all thinks are possible. You heff to make them open it."

"I can't help you if I'm dead," I told him.

He stopped. His tiny blue eyes blazed as he gawped at the rapidly approaching edge. "That is problem. Do not move. I do not vant you to die." He drifted backward, signaling to me with a 'come, come' hand wave. "Moof closer. I vill not hurt."

"Last time you zapped me! My eyebrows sizzled off. I have nubs for eyelashes."

"That vas accident. Sometimes I do not know own strength because I took power from those two idiots."

My feet refused to move.

"Come." Vladimir waved his hand in a rolling motion again.

There was a low growling emanating from one of the church's busted walls. A black behemoth leaped from the stones and landed on Vladimir. The ghost popped like the world's biggest bubble.

I fell forward, onto my knees. Relief swept through me.

Cerberus sat back on his haunches, grinning as if he'd had a marvelous time taking out the trash.

"Who's a good boy?"

He lifted his leg, peed on a tree.

Cerberus loped alongside me as I rode back to his family's house. He whined when I stopped at the gate. His ears, normally tall, perky triangles, drooped. He gave me a worried look.

"What is it?"

He nudged the gate with his nose.

"It's okay. They asked me to come find you."

I called out to his owners and waited.

Silence.

Maybe they went shopping.

"I'm going to check on them, okay, sweet boy?"

His tail slapped my thigh.

With a feeling of impending doom settling heavy in my stomach, I pushed through the gate and knocked on the door. The yard was tidy. The more fragile plants were covered with cheesecloth to protect them from the frost. Despite their ages, Cerberus's family made their place spotless after the windstorm. I wished I had their energy and motivation.

Nobody answered.

Weird.

I jiggled the handle. The door swung open. At the gate, Cerberus was panting and pacing. Pale sunlight filtered around me, lighting up the tiny living room. Cerberus's people were on the floor, gone and never coming back. Holding hands. Smiling.

My heart cracked.

How was I supposed to break the news to Cerberus? Poor pup was orphaned.

At the gate, the dog's sounds changed. He made happy chuffing sounds.

"Good dog," Kyria Vretto said, petting her dog with a newly transparent hand, "Who is a good boy?"

Me, Cerberus's expression said. He sniffed at his *mama*, then pulled away, confused by her lack of scent.

"What happened?" I asked Kyria Vretto. "Were you murdered?"

"*Po-po*, no. It was our time," she said. "But I have unfinished business. Can you help me one more time?"

"I'll do my best."

She smiled. "You are a good girl. Find a good home for Cerberus, yes? He is a clever boy, and he will help you choose his new family."

Cerberus whined. The poor boy looked miserable. My heart hurt for the poor baby.

"I can do that. I promise to find him a loving home."

She went to squeeze my hands in hers but they wafted straight through. "Dead people problems," she said. Then she turned around and walked into a light only she could see.

I called Panos Grekos, the coroner. Cerberus and I waited together for him to arrive.

"I'll fine you the best home on Merope," I told the dog.

He raised his nose and howled.

When life gives you lemons, take the dog home. I'd made a promise I intended to keep. After the coroner carried Cerberus's family away, I located his things: bed, food, bowl, brush, toys. No way could I carry everything home on my bicycle, so I called Leo for backup.

"What's the biggest thing you've ever had in your back-seat?" I asked him.

"Why?"

"Humor me."

He thought about it a moment. "Just after I moved back to Merope, I arrested a German woman on the beach. She took up the whole seat."

"What did she do?"

"She wanted to ride a donkey. When the operator refused, she clubbed the man with her ice cream."

"Great. This should work, then. Can you meet me?"

"Where? What's going on? Wait—does this have anything to do with the call you made earlier to Panos Grekos?"

"Most definitely."

"I'm on my way."

Leo arrived ten minutes later. The car approached slower, slower, until it stopped. He stuck his head out the window, gawked at Cerberus.

"Is that thing real?"

"Shh. You'll hurt his feelings. He's not a thing, he's a dog."

"At least one of his parents was a bear."

I rubbed Cerberus's ears. "Don't listen to the man. You're all dog. Can you take us home?"

Leo gave the dog a dubious glance. "Can't you ride him?"

"He'll probably be the best behaved passenger you've had in the backseat."

Leo didn't look convinced. But he loaded Cerberus's things in the trunk while I ushered the massive dog into the back. He sat in the middle of the seat, his nose resting in one of the metal mesh loops.

"Poor baby just lost his family."

"So what, you're taking him home?"

"Kyria Vretto asked me to find him a new home?"

"Before she died?"

"After."

He tapped the brake. "They were murdered?"

"Keep driving. No, regular death. She had unfinished business so she came right back. Once I agreed to find Cerberus here a new home, she toddled off to the Afterlife. Know anyone that wants a dog?"

He glanced back at Cerberus, who was slurping my hair through the mesh. "You, by the looks of it."

"A dog in *my* place? Are you kidding?"

"I've heard of worse ideas."

I snorted. "I haven't."

Cerberus whined.

"You hurt his feelings," Leo said.

I gave Leo the side-eye. "Any breaks on the Zervas case?"

"From what I can tell, they ingested rat poison and then took themselves out for a walk while their daughter was in the bathroom."

"But who poisoned them?"

"No idea yet. We haven't found the poison. Panos said the only other stomach contents were chickpeas and bread."

I gagged

Leo's eyebrow jumped.

"I'm a mess, I know," I said. "I hate chickpeas."

"It's good Greek food."

"It's definitely Greek, but can we really call it food? Did Panos say when he's sending them to the funeral home?"

"Tomorrow."

Time was running out. I needed to get my mitts on that dress. The way things were going I'd be forced to grovel to Adonis for help.

Instead of heading directly back to our apartment building, Leo jagged right toward the main road, sticking to the marginally wider streets that could accommodate cars. He stopped outside a nameless hole-in-the-wall shop that sold souvlaki and gyros.

"Want to come with me?"

"Probably better if I wait with Cerberus. He's still grieving."

Leo eyed the dog, who was licking my cheek. "He doesn't look like he's grieving."

"Maybe not on the outside …"

Cerberus did a better job of waiting patiently than I did. Now that I was getting a whiff of the sizzling meats, my stomach was threatening to mutiny if it didn't get fed.

"I'll find you a good home," I promised the dog. He gave a sad whine and leaned against the mesh, as close as he could get, under the circumstances. I shoved my fingers through and did my best to pet him. That seemed to make him happy.

While I was waiting, I checked my email. George Diplas wanted that ticket. He was intrigued by our recent spate of weird weather. I called Alfred to get the ball rolling.

"Mrs. Angela will be pleased," Alfred said in a tone that indicated only one of them was destined to be happy about this.

"I'm sorry."

"Your efforts will be rewarded, as always."

"Alfred, tell her how you feel."

"Impossible, I'm afraid. By the way, Mrs. Angela

requested that you be at the dock to meet Mr. Diplas's ferry when he arrives."

"She doesn't want to do it herself?"

"Mrs. Angela is not one to wait at docks."

He had a point. Angela had been raised on a diet of dirt and weeds; then she had the bright idea to marry money—twice. One husband died and the other may as well be dead after she took his money, too. She'd spun her fortune into an even bigger fortune, and along the way had developed a hatred of dirt and bumping up against the masses, unwashed or not. Given that she owned her own luxury yacht, I couldn't picture her waiting for the common ferry, even for her potential third husband.

"Let me know when he's scheduled to arrive and I'll be there."

Leo opened the car door and swung a bag of gyros into my lap. They were hot, fresh, and I was tempted to abscond with the whole bag. The only things stopping me were Leo's badge and handcuffs. I had no doubt he'd wrestle me to the ground and tie me up to reclaim his fair share.

Which sounded like fun, come to think of it.

"I know what you're thinking," he said.

"You really don't."

"I bought one for the dog, too."

My heart turned gooey over Leo's sweetness. "Really?"

"He looks hungry."

A thick thread of drool unspooled from Cerberus's mouth. "He does look hungry," I admitted.

"Did I get it right?"

"Not even close."

"Going to tell me what it was?"

"Not if you don't let me eat this gyro."

He grinned and hit the gas.

CHAPTER FOURTEEN

WE ATE OUR GYROS. Cerberus looked at his gryo—no onions, no *tzatziki*—and inhaled. The gyro vanished, fries and all.

"He's looking at mine now, isn't he?" Leo asked.

"Yes."

"He can't have it." Leo tossed him a strip of shaved meat anyway. "Do we have company?"

I glanced around. "Besides the drooling dog? No."

The air rippled slightly. A pair of supermodels teetered out of the nothing, stumbling on their skyscraper heels.

"He's eating," Jezebel said.

"Without us!" Tiffany added.

"Ugh. You weren't invited," I said, although secretly I was sort-of glad to see them. Well, *glad* was a stretch. But their arrival meant things were as back to normal as my life got. Maybe the Cake Emporium would return soon, too. "Where have you been?"

"I take it they're back?" Leo muttered.

"Apparently."

"Around," Jezebel said.

"Hiding out in our pocket dimension," Tiffany said.

Jezebel ripped off Tiffany's head, bounced it around the room, and somehow the head ended seamlessly in its original position. Tiffany went, "Ouch!"

"You're not supposed to say we were hiding," Jezebel told her.

"Why not? We were."

I waved my gyro at them. "Why were a pair of demons hiding anyway? Aren't you sort of invincible?"

"You have been watching too many movies."

The last of my gyro disappeared into my mouth. Now that it was gone, Cerberus unglued his eyes from my food and acknowledged the succubi with a swish-thump of his tail. Everything flew off the coffee table. He had no tail awareness.

"Sure you don't want a dog?" I asked Leo.

"It's bigger than my cousin."

"Maybe Jimmy could ride him around town. We can get Cerberus a little saddle …"

"Never let Jimmy hear you say that." He chucked his chin at the dog. "What's he so happy about?"

"Apparently he likes demons."

"Weird," he said.

"I still want to know why a couple of she-demons were hiding from a trio of ghosts."

"Ghosts." Tiffany sniffed. "Nobody is scared of ghosts. They are toothless and see-through. They have no real power over the physical world. And they play a sad amount of Bingo."

"My best friend used to play a lot of Bingo," I said.

She gave me a pointed look. "Exactly."

"So why hide?"

"Because one of them was stealing power, and we have

a lot of power to steal. Do you know what happens to a demon that gets its power stolen?"

"What?"

"Nothing. Nothing happens to us," Tiffany said. "Ever. We have to stay in our dimension and go nowhere, and do nothing. Who can live like that?"

"Never underestimate the appeal of staying home, seeing no one, and eating your own snacks."

"Anyway," Jezebel said. "The ghosts are gone. Now we are back to gaze at our favorite Greek toy."

"Two of them," I said. "The third one, the one that was doing the weather stuff, is still here. Maybe he'll show up and suck up your power. That would be a shame."

They glanced at each other. Shrugged. Tripped on their heels before stumbling back into their pocket dimension.

Dang it. Me and my big mouth. I could have pumped them for information. I was locked out of my usual sources, and pretty much winging it where Vladimir was concerned. I still had no clue what kind of ghost he was. All I knew was that he could throw one heck of a temper tantrum and siphon power out of other oogie-boogies.

Out of nowhere, the building rattled.

Leo dropped his food. He grabbed my hand and pulled me over to the apartment doorway. We stood inside the frame with its thick overhead beams.

A voice filtered through the window. "Hello? Allie? You are home, *da*? Are you hidink from Vladimir? Come. Ve talk. Ve did not finish conversation. I vould come in but that vould be bed without invitation."

I relaxed and tensed at the same time. The contradiction manifested as a twitch. "Not an earthquake," I told Leo.

I marched over to the window and stuck my head out. Vladimir was pacing down below. When he saw me, he rose like a mighty blond blimp. Somewhere under the bloat, the man had killer Slavic cheekbones. He looked contrite.

"Sorry about cliff. Are you hidink from Vladimir?"

"Was I trying to?" This was news to me. "I was eating. People have to eat. Remember that?"

"If you are not hidink, come out. We talk business."

"You tried to push me off the cliff!"

"No! I vas trying to talk. Already I apologize, *da*?"

"So talk. What do you want?"

"To be Vladimir again."

"What do you mean?"

"Ask your friends to open their shop and I vill tell you."

"I couldn't even if I wanted to. The shop is gone. They won't give in."

"Bring it back and I vill leave your time."

Behind me, Cerberus growled. He lopped up next to me and leaned against my hip. He stuck his head out the window.

Vladimir clicked his fingers and vanished.

"What was that about?" Leo asked.

"More dead people problems. He wants help, but the help he wants is impossible. The local oogie-boogies are afraid of him and no one will give me a straight answer about how I can divert him to the Afterlife."

"Oogie-boogies? Is that an official word for them?"

"It's a catch-all. You're a living human or an oogie-boogie."

"I heard that," Yiayia said, her head appearing in the middle of Leo's living room floor.

"Quit eavesdropping."

"I wanted to see if you two were finally …" Her voice

trailed off. Somewhere below the floorboards, I had the feeling she was making an obscene hand gesture.

"Eating our dinner? Thanks, but we just finished."

"You mean the dog just finished," Leo said. He nodded to Cerberus, who was carrying Leo's gyro wrapper and circling the apartment as if looking for something.

"Trashcan is in the kitchen," I told the big pup. He blinked at me and carried the wrapper to the kitchen. When he returned, it was without the garbage.

Leo gawked. "Did he just take out the trash?" On his hip, his phone beeped. He glanced at the screen, made a face. "Does the More Super Market sell rat poison?"

"Sure. It's next to the cereal."

He stared at me.

"Hey, I don't stock the shelves. You got a problem with cereal schmoozing with poison, talk to Stephanie. Why?"

"Apparently she told Pappas she sold rat poison to Eleni Zerva recently. I have to go."

Home again. Cerberus stepped inside politely and took stock of the place. Dead Cat leaped off the couch and sauntered over to inspect the newcomer. Smart cat. He had enough self-awareness to know he was already dead and this dog couldn't hurt him. Cerberus did a loop of my place and helped himself to the couch.

Maria Zerva appeared. She crossed herself three times in a row and waved her ghost hands at the ceiling.

"*Ay-yi-yi*! What is that? You cannot have it in the house!"

"How do you know I can't have it in the house if you don't know what it is?"

"It looks like a … a … a funny looking donkey."

"Dog."

"No!"

"Still a dog, no matter what you believe. Also, this is my place! You don't get a say."

As if he knew I'd come to his defense, Cerberus left the couch and splatted down on my foot.

The dead woman made grumbling noises and went in search of my trashcan. Trying to stop her was futile.

"Do the police know who killed us yet?" her husband asked.

"The sexy policeman my granddaughter isn't sleeping with is going to arrest Eleni right now," Yiayia said. "She poisoned you! Your own daughter. Can you believe it?"

I gawked at her. "Yiayia!"

"What?"

"How do you know I'm not sleeping with him? Maybe I am."

"You would be happier if you were."

She had a point. "Still, you can't eavesdrop and you can't just blab about police business."

"Why not? What else do I have to do with my time?"

"Find some friends?"

"My friends all tried to resurrect my dead body. I need new friends."

"So go make some. Or go live in the Afterlife with the other formerly living folks. Or … aren't you supposed to be doing that thing I told you to do?"

"Already done," she announced proudly.

"It's a stakeout! It's not something you get done in a couple of hours!"

"It is when I am running the mission."

"Did you get anything?"

"Besides nauseated?"

"Anything helpful?"

"When Yiota goes to the outhouse and she takes her crochet, you know she will be in there for hours. That sounds like a perfect time to sneak in and steal the dress."

"*Po-po*, we thought you were a nice girl," Stathis Zervas said. "You come from a good family, except for your grandmother. Now you are doing the stealing?"

"I am standing right here." Yiayia looked down. "Well, levitating."

"How do you know?" I asked my grandmother. "Like I said, you were only gone a couple of hours."

She shrugged. "I have resources."

"What resources?"

"Other ghosts and ghouls that lurk around the area."

I blew out a sigh. How could I possibly fault her for using other sources of information? That was a regular day's work for me. "How many times a day does she do this?"

"Every day at 6:00 AM, 12:00 PM, and 9:00 PM."

"That seems like a lot," I said. "I bet she really enjoys crocheting."

"Or she needs more fiber," Yiayia said.

I performed the mental math. Given that it was midwinter, the early morning or night bathroom trips would be perfect. That way I could use the darkness to my advantage. Dawn didn't show up after 7:30 AM and the sun flitted off around 5:00 PM. Tonight was out. Waves of exhaustion were already slapping me upside the head. If I was going to outwit Kyria Yiota, I needed to be rested. She was wily.

"I need sleep," I told the ghosts.

"Shouldn't you take that dog out first?" Yiayia asked.

Cerberus had been so quiet all this time that I'd forgotten the big dog was leaning against my leg, his head using my foot as a pillow.

"Walkies?" I asked him. He leaped up. Good thing my place was newer, earthquake-proof construction.

My alarm went off at 5:00. I made coffee. I drank coffee. I dressed in black after a tepid shower that made my skin shriek. After Cerberus ate, I took him out for a potty break. He cast mournful glances at Merope's Best, which wasn't yet showing signs of life. Probably they were out scraping the roads for something to brew.

Upstairs, I patted the sofa. "I'll be back soon," I assured him.

He didn't look convinced.

"You can't come with me. Not to Kyria Yiota's. If she catches me, I can't be certain that she won't cook and eat dog."

That didn't cheer him up, but he did three circles and flopped on the ground.

"Yiayia?"

Despite no longer being a sleeper, Yiayia was in a bathrobe and fuzzy slippers.

"What?"

"You're with me."

"What? This is your quest! I already did the stakeout. Seems to me like you are asking me to do more than my share."

"Someone needs to keep a lookout. I don't have any other ghosts on the payroll."

She squinted at me. "Speaking of pay …"

"Moving on," I said quickly. How did one pay a ghost anyway?

Ten minutes later, I parked my bicycle far enough away from Kyria Yiota's house that I could sneak up in silence.

From a distance, the outhouse was dark blob on another, slightly less dark blob. The blobs were surrounded by other blobs. I crouched down in a patch of shadow and waited for a mobile blob with legs. At six on the dot, a familiar blob toddled out of her house with a bag under one arm, carrying a candle in her opposite hand. That made sense. You can't crochet in the dark. Well, Kyria Yiota couldn't. Out in the world somewhere, some brilliant visually impaired person could probably work wonders without a speck of light and a crochet hook.

As I waited, the outhouse door's hinges sang the song of their oil-deprived people. Kyria Yiota slammed the door shut behind her. Orange light peeked out from between the wooden slats.

"If she leaves that outhouse, do the signal," I told my grandmother.

"Okay. I will do that." She made a face. "What is the signal?"

"Yell, shriek, anything."

"Wait. I have advice. If she catches you, pretend you are selling something."

"Selling what?"

"Something. I do not have all the answers."

"Thanks for slightly more than nothing."

No sarcasm whatsoever: "You are welcome."

Time to move.

Avoiding the outhouse quadrant of Kyria Yiota's house, I sneaked around to the side where the kitchen was located. Easy enough to figure out once I spotted the wood-burning oven's vent jutting out from the wall like a bashed toe.

I peered through the grubby window.

Dark.

Of course. The house's owner didn't splurge on unnecessary electricity. She probably resented the refrigerator for guzzling watts.

Given that Yiayia hadn't yet erupted in a chorus of squeals and warnings, I decided to risk flicking on my flashlight. I aimed the beam through the window.

A-ha! Irini's intel was solid. Maria Zerva's wedding dress was standing in the gloomy kitchen, held up by a dressmaker's dummy.

That meant this mission was all over except the actual stealing.

I tried the window.

Unlocked. The two panels swung open slowly, mildly inconvenienced by a thick, sloppy paint job at some point. But they did open. Hooray.

That had to be a good omen, right?

My heart stumbled around in my chest. The little goober would give me away, making that much of a racket. Irini wouldn't say a peep, but her mother had the ears of a moth. According to scientists, moths had hearing superior to every other living creature, except maybe Kyria Yiota listening for gossip and other scandals. Still, I had a dead woman's wishes to honor. I didn't want Maria Zerva hanging around my apartment after Leo solved her murder, complaining about going to her grave in the wrong outfit.

In was the only way out.

I boosted myself up and managed to slither through the open window like a lumpy, oversized caterpillar. My stumbling heart found a slam-dancing rhythm that blocked out ambient noise.

Fabulous. I was doing this semi-deaf.

I scrambled to my feet. The dress was right there for the taking. Several steps across the floor and it would be mine. The pale cream fabric was wreathed in cold, soupy shadows.

I lifted my foot. Lowered it quietly.

SNAP.

What the—

I stumbled backwards, my other boot landing on something small and flat. That flat thing acted like a roller skate, throwing me in the other direction. The floor caught my head.

SNAP. SNAP. SNAP.

Metal bit into my fingers and face. Good thing I was wearing gloves. My nose and lips weren't as lucky. Pain jagged through my face. *Again*.

In the distance, a door slammed. Some primal part of me recognized the sound as the outhouse shuddering.

"Great evil is coming," Yiayia said, appearing through the wall.

"Yiota?"

"Yiota."

I rolled over.

SNAP.

"Yipes! Ouch! Make it stop."

Either Yiota was raising alligators or she had a serious problem with mice.

A dark malevolent force in a housedress moved into the kitchen. It laughed. "Look, I caught a big rat with my *faka*! I knew I would."

I heaved myself up off the floor. My nose and lips and ears were wet with blood. "I've been trying to reach you about your vehicle's extended warranty."

The light flicked on. A lone bulb that definitely wasn't an energy saver.

Kyria Yiota cackled her head off. She wagged a finger

in my face. "You came to steal my dress. Too bad. You cannot have it. Eat my *faka*!"

"Eleni Zerva is prepared to buy a replacement."

"Eleni Zerva is going to be in jail soon for poisoning her parents! What kind of child is this that poisons their parents, *vre*? My Irini would never do that, would you, Irini?"

Silence.

Kyria Yiota ramped her voice up to an ear-shattering pitch. "IRINI! *VRE*, IRINI, WHERE ARE YOU, MY LEAST FAVORITE *SKATOULA*?"

A shadow moved into the room. "Here, Mama."

"You would never poison me, would you?"

Irini flicked her gaze up at the ceiling. "Er, no?"

"See?"

Clearly we weren't seeing the same thing. Irini's face said now that her mother had brought it up, poison sounded like a pretty neat idea."

Yiayia was on the same page. "If you ask me, someone is about to eat poison. Maybe Eleni Zerva can give her some tips."

This conversation was careening off the rails. I did my best to salvage it. "So *I'll* buy you a dress. Any dress you want, except maybe not Vera Wang because my bank account isn't that healthy."

"No." Kyria Yiota reached sideways. A broom appeared in her hand. She struck me with the hairy end. Bristles slapped my face.

"Ouch. Stop. You can't do that. This is assault!"

"You broke into my home. *You* came to rob *me*. What would you policeman boyfriend say, eh? Get out, you big rat!"

She swept me out the door.

I skedaddled.

CHAPTER FIFTEEN

YIAYIA SLAPPED a piece of transparent ghost paper on my bathroom counter.

"What's this?"

"I need you to do a performance review. How am I doing at my job?"

I dabbed my face with antiseptic, yelping every time the cotton ball connected with my ouchies. An amateur dick would assume I'd been smacked in the face with a grill.

"You were supposed to do a proper stakeout! I should have known about the mouse traps!"

Glasses appeared on the tip of her nose. "So are you a five—completely satisfied with my performance, or a four —satisfied with my performance."

"What performance? Instead of doing the job, you consorted with ghouls and got lousy information!"

"You have to be sociable in this career to get ahead."

"I know what I have to be in this career because it's my career, my company! You're just my assistant!" I slapped the paper out of the way. My hand whooshed straight through it. "You're not an assistant if you're not assisting! It's right there in the name!"

"A three?"

"No, it's a 'get out of the way because my phone is ringing, and you can't do phones like a real assistant with real hands because you're dead!'"

With my wounds screeching, I snatched up my phone. Angela was on the other end, fizzing over because George Diplas was scheduled to arrive on this morning's ferry.

Just what I needed. "This morning? Are you serious? Can't you send a car?"

"You said you would do it."

"That was before I caught thirty mousetraps and a broom with my face."

That didn't slow Angela down. "A hat with a veil. That is the perfect solution. Come here first and I will give you one of mine."

Angela's hats weren't for funerals. They covered up the evidence after her refreshment appointments with cosmetic surgeons all over Europe—at least until the swelling went down.

"It's okay," I said. "I'll go au natural. So what if I look like Frankenstein's monster."

"I will send a hat with the driver anyway."

"You're sending a driver? Why do I need to go?"

"You are the one who has been corresponding with George, therefore you are the best one to be there to greet him." Her voice lowered. "Put in a good word for me, yes? Maybe tell him about my money and my charms. Tell him I almost became a lesbian, if you want. Men like that."

My eye twitched, which set off a fresh round of stinging. I glanced at the clock. I had thirty minutes before the morning ferry arrived. Long enough to grab a coffee and cry over my life choices—up to and including trying to slop makeup over my injuries. George Diplas wasn't here for me anyway, I reminded myself. He'd be completely disinterested unless I transformed myself into a medicane.

I grabbed my bicycle and wheeled it over to Merope's Best. The barista stared at my face.

"Did our coffee do that?" she asked.

Yikes. "No, but could it?"

"Our coffee is capable of anything," she said darkly.

"Better give me a decaf."

"Are you sure you hate yourself that much?"

"Okay, make it vanilla latte."

The other barista ripped the lid off a bottle of vanilla extract and poured it into my cup, maintaining eye contact the whole time. While I waited for him to work out his dominance issues, I checked out the clientele. Lydia was at one of the corner tables, tapping on her phone.

"Are you mad at yourself?"

She looked up. "Always. What's your excuse for being here?"

"Feeling sorry for myself. I got hit in the face with thirty mousetraps because I didn't have the heart to say 'no' to a client."

"You need to work on that."

"Got any tips."

"Whip them when they won't comply."

"I don't think that will work on my clients."

"It works on everyone."

Lydia's means of supporting herself was a mystery, I realized. Obviously she had money to spare or she wouldn't be wasting perfectly good funds on Merope's Best.

"What do you do, anyway?"

"I'm a consultant."

"That's vague."

"Very. That's what I love about it. I could be anything. Maybe even a spy."

"Are you a spy?"

"No, I'm a consultant."

The barista called my name. "I have to go," I told her, "before my brain breaks."

"Whip them," she reminded me. "Whip them hard."

My vanilla latte was terrible, which was a plus. Usually it was vile, bordering on toxic. By the time I reached the dock, the ferry was imminent and I had a serious caffeine buzz. My teeth chattered and I could smell colors. The omnipresent stink of fish was a dull green.

"We meet again," someone said. Good cologne. Recent shower. He smelled like a cornflower blue sky.

"What are _you_ doing here?"

"Meeting somebody." Adonis Diplas gestured at the ferry visible in the distance. "You?"

"Now? Slumming."

He laughed. "What did I do to earn your mistrust?"

"Besides hitching your wagon to the most inbred family on the island for the low cost of a small grocery store?"

"It made sense at the time."

"And now?"

"It makes even more sense. I get to stay single and run a grocery store on one of Greece's prettiest islands."

"Would you really have married Effie?"

"Sure, why not? I'm a man of my word."

He didn't look like he kept his word, especially if that word was "I'll call you" or "The check is in the mail."

"Hmm."

"I know that sound." He zeroed in on today's injuries. "What happened to your face?"

"Mousetraps."

"It's okay if you don't want to tell me."

"Seriously, mousetraps."

"Your life is strange." He grinned at me. "So who are you waiting on?"

"George Diplas. Any relation?"

"Cousin. Don't tell me you didn't know."

"Do you know how many Diplases live in Greece?"

"No." He grinned. "But I bet you do."

Smartass. "It's a lot. I couldn't possibly have known you were related."

"Well, we are. My aunt called this morning, said I had to be here if I love my family and don't want to spit on their name."

Greek families. I understood.

"I didn't need to be here," I muttered.

A white limo pulled up to the dock. The driver was Angela's usual guy. He wasn't from around here, although I supposed he was now. Either he didn't speak Greek or he didn't speak at all.

Adonis gave the limo an amused once-over. "Merope must be rolling out the red carpet for George. It's not necessary. He's not a red carpet kind of guy."

"That's one of Angela Zouboulaki's limos. She's funding your cousin's trip."

That got a brow-raise out of him. "You know Angela Zouboulaki?"

I shrugged. "She lives here. I do a lot of work for her. We're kind of like friends."

He whistled low. "She owns half of Greece."

More like a quarter, but I didn't tell him that. "Why do you care?"

"What does she want with George?"

Well see, Adonis, she wants to bang him like a storm door in hurricane season. But I didn't say that. Not just because I'd have to educate him about storm doors. Angela straddled the blurry line between being a friend and a client. Telling virtual strangers that she was hunting for her next ex-husband wasn't my place.

"She's somewhat of a weather enthusiast."

He didn't look convinced. "Really?"

"Why not? Weather is interesting. Your own cousin loves it so much he spun it into a career."

The ferry moved into position. With the elegance of an escapee wheel of cheese, the big boat butted up to the dock. Everyone leaped into action. Rolling out the foot-bridge. Securing the pathway so passengers wouldn't topple into the water. A couple of local widows flung elbows. One of them stuck out a foot, tripping an overenthusiastic tourist. A rare sight in winter. The tourist didn't care. She got up laughing. "Did you get that? It's true what they say about old Greek ladies!" she yelled at a friend in English. "They're vicious!"

The widows hobbled onto the dock with sacks of live chickens. Then the tourists. Finally, George Diplas stepped onto the footbridge, military duffel slung over one shoulder. In person he was a real beast. Chest like a superhero. Arms like a pair of cranes. They built them pretty and tough in the Diplas family. He was dressed in cargo pants, boots, and other winter accouterments designed to keep out the cold. He look like a man who was here to fight the weather and win, not cozy up to Angela.

His gaze fell on Adonis. He broke out in a grin. "Cousin! What are you doing here?"

"Your mama called me, *vre malaka*. She said to remind you to wear clean underwear."

"Underwear is for girls like you," he said. The men cheek-kissed, hugged, slapped each other on the back. Very Euro-caveman. Once they detached, his gaze slid to me. "The new bride?"

"Ha. If he wants to marry his fiancée, he'll have to wait until she's finished doing time for murder," I said.

George shook his head. "Nobody tells me anything."

"Allie Callas." I stuck out my hand. "We've talked over email."

"You're the reason I'm here," he said. He shook my hand with his bear paw. He nodded at the scenery. "Looks calm here now."

"At the moment. Could flare up again at any minute, though. There have been some localized problems."

"That doesn't sound like normal weather patterns."

"Do you have any experience with freak weather without any scientific explanation?"

"No such creature. There's always science behind it, even if we don't have answers. Yet."

Could be he was right. But this time the science, if it existed, was presented in a woo-woo box. I wasn't sure he was ready for that.

Oh well. All I had to do was accompany him to his hotel. Then my work here was done and I could go limping over to Eleni Zerva's to beg for a reprieve on the wedding dress gig. Tousling with Kyria Yiota was way out of my skillset. Eleni would have to compromise or yield.

As soon as we turned, Angela's chauffeur leaped out to open the door. Adonis waved me in, then clambered in behind me.

"What are you doing here?"

"He's *my* cousin."

I rolled my eyes. "To the accommodations, my good man," I told the chauffeur. The limo jerked slightly and began climbing the hill.

While the men chatted about family gossip, I messaged Eleni and told her we needed to talk. As soon as I was done with that, there was a telltale *pop* and Yiayia appeared. Of course *she* was wearing a broad brimmed hat with a dark veil, but the pointy boobs and chicken legs gave her identity away.

"I have never been in a limo before. Not while it was moving."

I couldn't ask why she was in one while it wasn't moving. Something told me I didn't want to know.

"Scratch your head if you heard me," she said.

I scratched my head.

She cackled. Then her attention turned to George Diplas. "I know him. He is that handsome man that does the weather. What is he doing on Merope? And the other one … *po-po* … if I were thirty years younger and not dead … Have you considered having some fun with them? Come, Allie, uncross your legs and live a little! Save a donkey, ride all the men you can before everything dries up and you have to buy stock in olive oil."

She had me. I couldn't protest. Not without the menfolk pegging me as a nut. I scratched my nose with my middle finger.

Didn't work.

"The other one looks like he would do that thing you like … and that thing you hate. But you would enjoy it because it is him doing it." She fanned herself. "Ooh-la-la, what I would not give to be alive."

The air beside her shimmered. When it stopped, Vladimir was there, oozing over the edges of his tracksuit. "Hello! It is me, Vladimir! We talk now, da?" He flicked the air and Yiayia flew out of the limo. He leaned back and smiled. "There vas bug. Have you negotiated my passage home?"

"Not yet," I muttered.

The Diplas men stopped talking. They stared at me.

"It's nothing," I said. "Just reorganizing my to-do list. I'm a busy businesswoman, I talk to myself a lot."

"Let me give you taste of vhat will happen if you do not heelp," Vladimir said. He snapped his fingers.

Slowly at first, with a great grinding sound, the limo began to spin in place. The chauffeur pounded the brake and accelerator. Nothing happened. We kept on spinning.

Adonis's knuckles glowed white as he grabbed at the handhold. "What's happening?"

"Weather," I said.

George perked up. "Open the sunroof!"

The chauffeur was too busy mashing pedals and not understanding Greek to follow his order. Normally I'd be freaking out, but this was all Vladimir's doing. And Vladimir wasn't anything more than someone else that wanted my help. He wasn't about to kill off his chances of escape. With the limo spinning and heading for centrifugal speeds, I located the button that made the sunroof open. The motor whirred. The sunroof slid back. George's top half slithered up and out the window.

"Hold on to me," he called out. "This is amazing! We're the only thing moving. Must be some kind of super-charged miniature whirlwind! I've never seen anything like it!"

His cousin held onto his legs. I leaned back. Raised an eyebrow at Vladimir. "Kind of busy," I told him.

George misunderstood. "That's okay. Adonis has got me. I want to take pictures but I'm afraid I'll lose the camera."

"Get not busy." Vladimir said. "Find time for me, Vladimir. Then all thees goes avay."

"I've been trying to communicate with you! You keep blowing me off, no pun intended."

"Vait," he said. "There is problem."

He vanished. The wind went with him. The limo hit the ground with a metallic thud. George fell back into the limo, landing on top of Adonis.

"I love this place!" he said. "I need a camera crew. Can I call my guys?"

"Let's get you situated first, then I'll talk to my, uh, client," I told him.

Now that we'd stopped spinning, the chauffeur was back in control.

Adonis raised his eyebrows at me. I gave him a "What?" look. His eyebrows hiked higher. I whatted harder. We did that until the limo stopped rolling.

I peered out the window.

Holy mother of goats.

"This has to be a mistake," I squeaked.

I excused myself and exited the limo. I called Alfred. He had to be responsible. Angela would have a fit if she knew this place even existed.

"I take it the eagle has landed," Alfred said. "Did he arrive intact or in little bite-sized pieces?"

"You booked him into the Hotel Hooray?" I hissed.

"Mrs. Angela requested that I find him a room. The Hotel Hooray—" his sour face bounced off the satellite and into my ear "—is the only hotel accepting reservations right now. It is winter, you know."

Petty, yet endearing.

"Tourists got off the ferry. Real hotels are open. They always have a few rooms."

"Huh," he said. "How strange. I must have been misinformed. Oh well. Moving on."

"Alfred, just tell Angela how you feel."

"That would be grossly inappropriate. Mrs. Angela relies upon me. Speaking of my employer, she has requested that you bring Mr. Diplas to the house for a luncheon today."

"Me? Why?"

"Because he knows you."

"Forget it," I said. "I find things. I'm not her personal assistant. I'll let him know that you'll be sending a car."

Alfred went quiet for a moment before asking: "What is he like?"

"The kind of man a lot of women would like to climb like a tree. Angela will be bored with him by the end of the week."

"After she has already climbed the tree."

I winced. Poor Alfred. But if he wouldn't make a move, there wasn't much I could do. He wasn't Jimmy. I couldn't just pick him up and drop him on Angela's doorstep. Not when his livelihood was on the line.

"I'm going to have to get him checked in, aren't I?"

"I'm afraid so."

I sighed. "Last time I was here, I made advances on the proprietor to get access to a room. I drove a minivan. I wore a tiny dress."

"I have confidence in you," Alfred said.

⸻

Hotel Hooray rented rooms by the however long you needed them. A week, fifteen minutes, no big deal. The owner, a gelatinous lump named Manolis, spent most of his waking hours with his hands in his pants, massaging the monkey. He touched money and keys and food with those same hands. Which was why I pushed through the door using my elbow.

The Hotel Hooray used to be a brothel in the old days. The building moved on, but some of the girls remained.

These days they got their jollies mocking Manolis and what little manhood he possessed.

"Here come people," the former women of rentable affections crowed. "Wait—it's Allie. Allie!" They shook their wares and waved.

I winked.

"Hey, she's with people, so she can't talk," one of the women said. "Tell your friends not to touch Manolis' hands. He just shoved a plug up his *kolos*. It's in there right now."

"Not for sex," the other one said. "He ate bad fruit."

"Maybe for sex," the first one said.

I gestured at Adonis. "Ring the bell."

"You ring the bell."

"I'm not getting paid to ring the bell."

"Neither am I."

"I'll ring the bell," George said.

I cringed as he pushed past us and pressed his naked finger on the bell. Probably now he had Manolis' butt cooties.

Note to self: don't touch George.

Something in the back room went, "*Och*!" The door slapped open. Manolis rolled out looking like at least one of his parents originated in a clogged sewer under London. His eyes grazed our clean (except for George's finger) group. They snapped back to me.

"You owe me sex," he said.

Laughter blasted out of Adonis. He swung around and gave me an are-you-kidding look. "You owe this guy sex?"

"I don't owe him anything!"

"You going to pay thc man?"

"I forgot to stop at the ATM. You pay him."

Amusement danced in Adonis' eyes. One of us was

having too good a time, and it was him. "Lady, I don't have the equipment."

"Why not? You have two holes. Manolis doesn't look picky. And from what I understand, you're not picky either."

Manolis was turning colors. He didn't know what to do about us. We weren't checking in and we weren't here to deliver anything.

"You don't know anything about me," Adonis said.

That sounded like a challenge. "I know you'd sell yourself to Greece's biggest bunch of inbreeds for the low, low price of a tiny grocery store. You didn't even hold out for anything good. I would have gone for a piece of the newspaper business. It's not growing but it has potential."

"I'm an entrepreneur."

"That's just a fancy word for someone who's unemployed most of the time."

Manolis held out a key. "Do you want a room?"

"No!" we both yelled.

This freakin' jerk was scabies. When his wedding fell through, why didn't he just sell the More Super Market and stay on the mainland, waiting on his next scam?

"George Diplas, checking in," George said.

Manolis made a big song and dance about whether or not George's room was ready, like the sheets were ever changed. If George was lucky his room would have toilet paper and an empty wastebasket.

I cleared my throat to get the innkeeper's attention. "The room is as ready as it's going to get, isn't it, Manolis?"

He stopped. "Yes."

"Hand over the key."

"Don't touch it with your bare hands," the two dead sex workers said.

"Don't touch it with your bare hands," I told George. "And wash your hands as soon as you get to your room. If there's soap." I glanced at Manolis. "Soap?"

He sighed like I was balancing on his crotch in high heels. "I will bring soap."

———

George Diplas wasn't my problem anymore. Neither was Adonis. I hoofed it back to the limo and had the driver pop the trunk so I could retrieve my bicycle. I needed the ride home to blow off steam.

There was no reply yet from Eleni, so I decided to stop at her place on the way.

My phone rang.

"Did you pick up my present?" Angela asked breathlessly.

"Yes, I picked up the weatherman."

"Is he at the resort?"

Yikes. I sidestepped that one. She and Alfred needed to work through their issues. "He's all checked in and he knows about the luncheon at your place."

She pounced on the next subject. "What does he smell like?"

"Was I supposed to sniff him? Because I didn't sniff him. People tend to be protective of their personal space."

"It's okay, I will find out myself. I cannot handle a man that does not smell good. My nose is very sensitive."

"He looks clean," I said.

"Looks can lie. My mama always made sure we looked clean for church, but under our clothes we had fleas."

I dodged a hole in the dirt road. "I didn't see George scratch, so that's a good sign."

"We will see," she said darkly.

She ended the call.

I stopped in front of the Zervas house. The gate was open. Everything was quiet. Too quiet.

"Eleni?"

Silence.

I went up and knocked on the door. A neighbor stuck her head out. She squinted at me.

"Who is that?"

"Allie Callas, Foutoula's granddaughter."

"I knew your grandmother."

Not a stretch on an island this small.

"We were friends at one time," she went on. "Special friends. *Very* special friends."

My eyelid fluttered. "I'm looking for Eleni."

"The police arrested her for Maria and Stathis' murders! *Ah-pa-pa*, what a child they brought into this world. After everything they did for her, this is how she repays them."

"They did stop her from getting married, so I wouldn't exactly call it a healthy relationship."

"He was a foreigner! Who lets their good Greek daughter marry a foreigner?"

"Lots of people?"

"You know nothing." The door slammed.

So this was it, then. Leo had evidence Eleni poisoned her parents. Enough to make an arrest. That didn't mean my business with Eleni was cancelled. I rode over to the police station to beg for some one-on-one time with Eleni. Even two-on-one would be fine if someone had to be in the room.

Leo lit up when I pushed through the door. He was leaning on the reception counter, his weight resting on his hands. It did things to his forearms that made me gooey.

His smile fell off once I moved closed and he got a load of my face.

"What happened?"

"With you being a policeman and all, it's better that you don't know."

"Did you commit a crime?"

"Little bit. But I got what was coming to me, so I'm already rehabilitated."

"Does this have anything to do with the big rat Kyria Yiota is telling people she caught in her mousetraps?"

"I can neither confirm nor deny."

He shook his head. "Allie."

"My job requires a certain amount of creativity sometimes. Anyway, I heard you arrested Eleni Zerva?"

He blew out a sigh. He didn't look happy. "We found proof that she murdered her parents—proof enough to make the arrest."

"What proof?"

"You know I can't tell you that."

"She bought rat poison from the More Super Market and then put it in their food—food she didn't eat?"

He swore softly. "How did you know?"

"I get around. Also, you already told me she bought the poison. The rest wasn't a leap. Can I talk to her?"

His face said "no." His mouth said, "What about?"

"Her mother's wedding dress."

He turned around. "Pappas? Go with her. Sorry," he told me. "I have to send someone with you. It's not that I don't trust you, but I'm building a case here."

I squeezed his forearm. I couldn't help myself. "No problem."

He made a low growling sound that I really wanted to hear again in a more private setting.

Pappas led me out back. Merope's lockup wasn't much

to look at, but for half the year it didn't need to be. The rest of the time all it needed was to be strong enough to hold a passel of drunken Germans or Brits, singing the songs of their people in alcohol-soaked gibberish.

Eleni had the place to herself. She was using her time to read. She jumped up when she saw me.

"Allie! Can you get me out of here?"

"Sure," Pappas said. "She can find you a time machine so you can go back and un-murder your parents."

She shot him with her stink-eye. "I didn't murder my parents."

"She keeps saying that," Pappas told me.

"Maybe she didn't murder her parents," I said.

"Maybe she did."

This conversation was circling the toilet bowl. "Sit in the corner and be quiet," I told Pappas.

"Nice leggings," he said. "What kind of underwear do you wear with those so the lines don't show?"

"Pappas."

"What?"

"Stop speaking or you'll get the pepper spray."

"I'll be quiet."

"Have you got an attorney yet?" I asked Eleni.

She bit her lip. "Do I need one if I'm innocent?"

My Virgin Mary, didn't she watch crime shows? "You need one."

"Who?"

"I'll make some calls for you."

My injuries suddenly registered. "What happened to you?"

"Kyria Yiota."

"She attacked you?"

"With about thirty or so mousetraps. She booby-trapped the dress. I'm sorry, but I don't think I can get your mama's wedding dress. I hate to give up, but Kyria Yiota is savage. She scares me."

"I knew we should have left her in that tree," Pappas muttered.

She burst out crying and flopped on the ground. "I can't do anything right. After everything I did to keep my parents safe, they still ran away and died. And now I can't get one stupid dress back so I can bury my mother."

My heart softened. But was it soft enough to take another run at Kyria Yiota and her mousetraps of death?

Eleni's nose blew a snot bubble. I passed a tissue through the bars.

"That better not be contraband," the constable said.

I mouthed a rude word at him.

Yes. The answer was yes. For Eleni, I'd take the risk. Kyria Yiota was just one fifty-something woman. There had to be a way. Maybe I could promise her an exclusive mansion in hell or her own personal iron maiden to sleep in.

"Fine. I'll try again."

"Thank you." Her face was blotchy. Her eyes were red. "I just want to go home, put my parents to rest, and live my life."

"And go back to work."

"Yes. Is that so bad?"

"Totally normal, I'd say. You've been your parents' keeper for a long time." I passed her a second tissue, this one to mop the tears. "What about your lost sweetheart?"

"Too late for us. He's probably married with a passel of children. If he really loved me he would not have left. He would have fought for me, you know?"

"Maybe he couldn't. Maybe he's still out there, single, thinking you're the one with a husband and children. If you give me his name, I can find out."

Her eyes widened. "You can find him?"

"Sure."

"Without him knowing?"

"Absolutely. All I need is some basic biographical information. If all you've got is a name, I can work with that, too."

She hesitated, then nodded. "Okay. His name is—"

Out of nowhere, the police station began to shake. Bars rattled. Glass tried shattering and gave up when it realized it was shatterproof. Overheard, the roof made a sound like an angry whale. Metal twisted as the roof peeled back, opening the sardine can.

The sky churned.

And then an invisible hand grabbed Eleni and ripped her out of the police station.

The roaring, the shaking, the rattling stopped. The world went quiet.

"Raise your hand if you just saw that," I said to Pappas.

His hand went up. His eyes went down.

"I wet my pants," he said.

CHAPTER SIXTEEN

CALLING THE POLICE WAS UNNECESSARY. So that was something.

Leo made us go over the details a dozen times. By the fifth time, Pappas and I were adding sound effects and a dash of interpretive dance. Pappas was naturally gifted at jazz hands, and I had spirit fingers nailed. Pappas made mouth noises uncannily similar to the wrenching roof.

Leo watched us with his arms folded, probably wondering who the heck we were and whether or not we needed to be heavily medicated.

"Someone needs to fix the roof," he said.

"This is a government building," I said. "Won't they organize repairs?"

We all looked at each other and laughed. Greece's government wouldn't be sending a repair crew. Merope's cops were on their own.

"I know a guy," I said.

"Filip Filipou?" Leo asked.

"Actually, yes."

"He's booked through next month. I already called him about fixing my parents' fence."

"Did you try threats? I find threatening Filip really motivates him. He'll be at your place at dawn, ready to build a new wing on if you threaten to tell people he supports the other sports team."

He rubbed his face. "I don't suppose you could …?"

"As a matter of fact, I can."

"What about the prisoner?" Pappas asked. "What do we do about her?"

"She flew away," I said. "Maybe she'll fly back when she's ready to nest."

"I've got people searching for her," Leo said. "What could have done this?"

"Aliens," Pappas said.

Leo looked at me.

"You heard the man," I said. "It was totally aliens. Haven't you ever seen that movie? Julianne Moore. *The Forgotten*. Whoosh! Sucked up into the sky."

"Aliens," Leo said in a flat voice. "You really think it was aliens?"

"It was that or more of the freak weather we've been having lately. There was an incident earlier in Angela's limo." I gave him a pointed look. "A small, personal-sized tornado."

A ditch appeared between his brows. He was really struggling with this. I wasn't sure which was worse in his mind: ghosts or aliens.

"I'm going to call Filip," I said. "Then I'm going to help look for Eleni. If you need anything …"

"Drinks. Lots of drinks. Meet me later?"

"The Good Time?"

The Good Time is the most decent bar in town for locals. Not too flashy. Normal prices, no gouging.

"I will be there," Pappas said eagerly.

"You're not invited," Leo said.

The constable made a face. "This is a free world."

"Is it, though?" I asked.

"Not if I lock him up," Leo said.

"Ha! There's no roof," Pappas pointed out.

"He's right," I said. "I guess you could cuff him to the bars."

Pappas bolted.

Vladimir had Eleni. Or rather, Vladimir took Eleni. Why and where? Those were the two questions burning a hole in my bottomless bucket of curiosity.

What business could a Russian who'd died in the 1990s want with a live Greek woman?

At the back of my mind, tiny hands waved. They wanted my attention. I'd missed something, but what?

Halfway home, it hit me. I skidded around a corner and almost slammed into a donkey. I jumped back on the bike and sped home. I had a specific question, and if I approached things the right way I might get my answer.

Yiayia was sprawled out on my couch with a cocktail in one hand.

"This is my medicine," she said. "I need it after getting kicked out of the limousine by that crazy Russian."

"Sorry," I said. "Are you okay?"

"A few more of these and I will be swinging from the chandelier."

"I don't have a chandelier."

"That will not stop me."

I dropped my things on the desk. "Where are my other guests?"

"In the bathroom, playing with the mirror."

"Really?"

It was a ghost thing. The dead had all kinds of fun with their newfound invisibility. I found the Zervases making faces at themselves in the bathroom. There was a lot of gum and very little dignity.

I leaned in the doorway. "The man Eleni wanted to marry, tell me about him."

"There was no man," Maria Zerva said.

"There was a man," I said. "Start talking or I'll trap you in a salt circle and you'll never be able to use my kitchen trashcan as a toilet ever again."

"You are so cruel. What did we ever do to you?"

"Besides haunt my apartment?"

She sniffed. "It is not as if we have a choice."

"I'm not going to solve your murder. The police are on it and they've already pegged Eleni."

"Eleni would never!"

"That's what she said, although to be honest I wouldn't blame her if what she said about her sweetheart was true."

"He was nobody!" Stathis Zervas said. "A Russian tourist who wanted to become a Greek and stay in Greece. Russia is very poor and there are few opportunities for unskilled *malakes* who want to steal good Greek girls like our Eleni and do crime here."

My cheeks froze up. "Russian?"

"Who is Russian?" he said. "We are Greeks!"

"You just said Eleni's man friend was Russian."

"Eleni?" he barked. "That is my mother's name. What about her?"

"They say you cannot take it with you," Yiayia said from beside me, cocktail in hand. "But it looks like these two took their dementia with them."

Stathis Zervas glanced around. "Does anyone else smell cucumbers?"

"Eleni is your daughter," I said, trying to get them back on track.

His forehead crinkled. "How can my mother be my daughter?"

I was going nowhere—and fast. "If you can't help me with your daughter, at least tell me how I can get your wife's wedding dress back from Kyria Yiota."

Maria Zerva snapped to attention. "Yiota has my wedding dress? How did she get that?"

"You gave it to her."

"I know that," she snapped. "Her daughter is getting married."

So it was true, Maria Zerva had handed over the dress on purpose. But was she herself when she did it? Hard to say.

"Speaking of marriage," I said, casually circling back around. "I heard your daughter wanted to marry a Russian?"

She made a face. "You should have seen him. Big. Fat. Pale. Eyes the blue of the evil eye. Hands like hams."

"Big hams," her husband said. "Like the *kolos* of a pig."

"He was good to Eleni but that was just for show. He wanted to be Greek, and he chose her to use."

I felt breathless, desperate to fill in more blanks. "What happened?"

"We pushed him off a cliff!" Kyrios Zervas said.

"You cannot say that," his wife said.

"But it is true."

"That is why you cannot say it," she said.

The older I got, the harder it became to be surprised by anything. Even shoving calculating lovers off a cliff.

"Really? You pushed him off a cliff because he was in love with your daughter? That seems harsh."

The Zervases laughed and laughed until they wheezed. "Push Vladimir off a cliff? Do I look like Hercules?" Stathis Zervas said. "We gave him a ferry ticket to the mainland and some money. He never came back."

CHAPTER SEVENTEEN

VLADIMIR WAS Eleni's banished honeybun. Eleni's banished honeybun was Vladimir.

My head spun.

"You're sure his name was Vladimir?"

"No. Sergei," Maria Zerva said with absolute certainty.

Oh, brother.

"No," her husband said. "It was Alexei."

"Sergei."

"Alexei."

"Ivan."

Stathis Zervas's whole face scrunched up. "Who is Ivan?"

"That Russian boy that was sniffing around Eleni."

"Eleni?"

"Your daughter," I said between gritted teeth.

"How can we have a daughter?" Maria Zerva said. "We were just married, and we did not make the sex before we were married. I was a virgin."

Yiayia raised her glass. "Not in every hole."

"Not helping," I said.

"Who said I was trying to help? I am enjoying the show and this drink."

"Anyone want a cucumber?" Stathis Zervas said, away with the fairies again.

My face hurt. My veins were doing a throbbing thing that I was sure wasn't normal. Probably I had high blood pressure. All that biking over the island and eating mostly, sort-of right, and I was going to be taken down by bickering ghosts.

"The Russian," I said. "Tell me more."

Maria Zerva's voice turned dreamy. "He wore a fluffy Russian hat, and he had a big mustache."

Vladimir didn't have a mustache or a hat. That didn't mean much. You can shave a face and remove a hat. "Anything else?"

"He wore a heavy gray coat to keep the cold out." She dabbed her eyes. "Their love was caught in the fire of revolution."

A light bulb flickered on, somewhere in one of the dustier corners of my mind. "Are you talking about … *Doctor Zhivago*?"

"Omar Sharif," Yiayia said.

"He *was* Doctor Zhivago," I said.

"Oh-la-la. I loved that man," Yiayia said. "I should see if I can find him in the Afterlife."

Her and a billion other horny old dead women.

Squeezing the Zervases was a dead end for now. Their memories were mashed potato. Nothing they said was reliable. One minute they murdered Vladimir. The next they gave him a one-way ticket home.

Bottom line: somehow, sometime, he died, and now he was haunting my island. *If* this was the same man. If weather-weirdo Vladimir and Eleni's Vladimir weren't one and the same, it was one heck of a coincidence.

I leashed Cerberus and took him downstairs to do his business. His business took a while. A lot of pee-mail to check. Also, I was pretty sure he was checking for crumbs from Merope's Best. Could be letting him scarf them was animal abuse. I didn't want to be an animal abuser, so I tried pulling him away. The big dog didn't budge. He wanted those crumbs and he wanted them bad.

"They'll give you the runs," I told him. "I know what I'm talking about."

Cerberus ate the crumbs anyway.

So far I'd had zero time to hunt for his new fur-ever home. But I'd have to, and soon. I couldn't keep a dog this size in my apartment. Or any dog. Dead Cat worked out fine because he was dead.

He jogged up the stairs alongside me. I looked at him. I looked at my apartment. My cozy, too-small-for-a-huge-mutt home. I didn't have the heart to leave him cooped up here.

"Want to come to work with me?"

His tail slapped the floor. I took that as a "yes."

Cerberus loped next to my bicycle as I set out for … I wasn't sure where. My to-do list read like a horror novel. Get the dress from Kyria Yiota. Find Eleni. The first item was terrifying. The second had the potential to be a disaster. I didn't know where to begin looking for Eleni, and her parents were no help.

I headed to a quiet spot on the island where I could call up the dead without people giving me serious side-eye.

"Hey, Vladimir?"

Vladimir didn't appear. No one did. But three goats did wander over to see if I was offering handouts. Their goatherd slouched over the hill to retrieve them. He shook his crook at me.

"They're goats," I said. "All I had to do was stand here and look like food."

"I know you," he said. "I had a good time once with your grandmother."

"You and everyone else."

He grinned a gold and gappy grin. "I know. I was there."

I watched him vanish over the hill with his goats, bells jangling at their throats.

"It seems you have your motive," the Man in Black said. He was petting my dog. Cerberus gazed up at him, a dog in love.

"C'mon. You're embarrassing yourself," I told the dog.

Cerberus kept on wagging.

"He likes you," I told the Man in Black.

"Animals usually do."

"Want a dog?"

"I would not take your pet from you, Allie Callas."

"He's not mine. His owners passed and their last wish was for me to find him a new home."

"And he has."

"No."

He looked at me. Cerberus looked at me.

My brain revved its engine. Synapses synapsed. Words processed. "Wait, what did you say about a motive?"

"The Russian. He is here for his lost love, is that not true?"

"I think so. I'm still piecing it together."

"What do you think will happen now that he has her?"

I pounced. "Do you know where they are?"

"No. The Russian is a being of incredible focus. He has maintained this one single goal, nursed it as though it is a beloved grudge. He cannot be allowed to fulfill the rest of his goal."

"You mean to use the Cake Emporium to go wherever it is he wants to go?"

"I am less concerned with the wherever, and more concerned with the whenever."

"He said he wants to go home. I assumed Russia."

"Russia, perhaps. But Russia when?"

"Are you saying he wants to time-travel back to his own time?" Thoughts tumbled in my head. "Can he do that?"

"Based on your brief experience with time travel, what do you think?"

I traveled back to that night in Ayios Konstantinos, when we took a peek at the past.

"We looked through a window, that's what you told me."

"A window, like a door, is an opening. One can wriggle through a window if they dare."

"I already tried that today. Things didn't work out how I planned."

"If you require assistance …"

"You're not the first man to ask if I need help stealing the wedding dress, but thanks. So I shouldn't help Vladimir?"

"Help? Yes. Help the man. Direct him to the Afterlife if you can. But you cannot send him back to his time for a … do-over. His time has been and gone. Sending him to the past would interfere with the established passage of time. What has happened has already happened. Do you understand?"

"Send him back, break time?"

"Correct."

"Big badda boom?"

"Yes."

"But I thought time wasn't exactly linear?"

"Everything in the cosmos has a time and place. Think

of them as apples. If you pull one apple from the bottom of the pile, the other apples fall. You cannot prevent the falling, even if you attempt to place the apple elsewhere."

"Would this, uh, apple-pulling be a world ending event?"

"The universe would do its best to compensate, but ultimately it would fail."

That was it then. Toula's big scary premonition. If Vladimir jumped back in time, the world would end.

"So what do I do with him? If I keep denying him what he wants, he's going to tear up my home and hurt my people."

"You care about them."

"I live here."

"Dwelling in a place does not automatically make people care. You are, in a way, this island's guardian."

"If that's true, I'm doing a lousy job."

"On the contrary." He looked at some point past my shoulder. "I must go."

"Can't you give me more answers?"

"I cannot interfere with the future or the past, only the present."

"Are you from another time? Maybe the Regency? Or is this" —I waved at his outfit— "all the rage in the future?"

He did his vanishing over the hill this time. I figured he was shy. Disappearance anxiety.

I rode around the edge of the island, periodically stopping to call out to Vladimir.

Nothing happened. Birds looked at me like I was nuts and that was it. Cerberus grinned up at me every time I stopped. Petting happened. Then we moved on to the next hollering spot.

My phone rang.

"The car just went to collect George," Angela said. "When will you be here? Everything is ready."

"Never? Does that sound good to you?"

My sarcasm flew over her perfectly coiffed head. "Terrible. I'll see you in twenty minutes."

"Can't. I'm on another job."

"What job?"

"Reclaiming a wedding dress from Kyria Yiota."

"Is that vile goat still alive?"

"Malice will keep her going forever."

"Get the dress later. My reception lunch is more important. George Diplas might be my next husband."

Alfred wiped me over with his disapproving gaze. "Is that what you're wearing?"

I looked down at my leggings and sweatshirt. They were both close enough to clean that I could pass as respectable. "It is when Angela calls me while I'm working and demands I get over here immediately."

"I suppose it will have to suffice."

"Is everyone else here?"

"In the dining room." His lips pursed.

"What?"

"Mrs. Angela is not quite herself."

"Not herself how?"

"Best if you see for yourself. You will help her, won't you?"

Didn't I always?

In slippers provided by Alfred, I scooted to the massive

dining room, which had been opened up for the occasion. The back of the room was all window. The protective barrier that rolled down in case of bad weather or zombie attacks were fully retracted, offering up an endless view of the sea. At this time of year, the Aegean was a blob of gray paint slopped below a lighter slap of thin, pale blue. The dining room was painted the same white as the others. The moldings were the same colorless hue. Ditto the enormous table that seated twenty. Besides the people, the only color came from the art, which was Nordic and featured an excess of icebergs.

The guest of honor was at the window, holding a meatball on a fork.

He was surrounded by dead men.

CHAPTER EIGHTEEN

"Here she is," Angela said, realizing I'd shuffled into her dining room. I performed a neck-jarring double take. Normally Angela was firmly in the "more is more" camp. More jewels, more makeup, bigger hair. Anything to detract from her age and origin story. Today she had swung the other way. Simple ponytail. Complicated and artful no-makeup makeup. Small jewelry. White jumpsuit. From a distance she could pass for forty.

"Here I am," I said.

Plate in hand, Adonis Diplas was circling the table like a Great White. Even in slacks and sweater, he managed to look like he'd spent time making license tags. He winked at me. "Here's my favorite snoop. Did you get that dress yet?"

"Not yet, but I will. What are you doing here? Get tired of huffing Stephanie's foot shavings?"

He grimaced.

We were a party of four, plus Alfred who came and went, and the twenty-seven dead men clustered around George. Everyone else was blissfully unaware. Lucky devils.

I avoided eye contact. Didn't want to involve myself in

their business. That didn't stop me from sneaking peeks at them. The ghosts were all twenty-somethings. Lower end of the decade. Lean. Cheekbones sharp enough to slice lamb. Mishmash of exteriors, but the builds and bones were the same. None of the dead men were locals. Not from my time here, anyway. George must have brought them with him, somehow.

Angela dragged me aside. "He is delicious, no?"

"I don't usually eat men. They give me indigestion. I think it's the aftershave."

"Do you think he likes me?"

"I think he likes the view."

"You mean me?"

"I mean the actual view. I haven't seen him look at you yet."

She stared at his back. "That is a problem."

Adonis moseyed on over with his plate in hand. The white ceramic square was loaded up with a pile of Greek *mezedes*. "Checking out the view?"

"She is," I said.

"Ha."

"What does he mean 'ha'?" Angela wanted to know. "What 'ha'?"

"I wondered why you two were scheming to bring my cousin to this island."

"I wasn't scheming," I said in my defense.

"Right. You're the rich woman's flunky though, doing her bidding, enacting her plan."

"I am not rich," Angela said. "I am wealthy. There is difference."

How dare he. "I'm not a flunky."

He waved the fork under my nose. "None of this will get you anywhere unless you're on the level about the weather thing."

"I always get my man," Angela said.

"Not George," Adonis said.

Angela's eyes made a good faith effort at narrowing. The fillers only let them go so far. "Why not?"

"Because he likes men," I said.

Adonis shot me a curious glance. "Yeah. How did you know?"

I eyed all the transparent plus-ones. "Lucky guess."

Had Angela not been Botoxed into a smooth, shiny shell, her face would have fallen. "He's a sister?"

"Look, you can't tell people he prefers men," Adonis said. "He has a reputation."

"He does?" I asked. "People that do weather have reputations?"

"He keeps it quiet because of our grandmother. She would have a heart attack if she knew he's never going to give him great-grandchildren."

Angela recovered. "I can buy him all the children he wants. They are cheap enough if you have the right connections, and I have the right connections. You can get a great deal on babies in Ukraine. I have been thinking about buying a child to inherit all this someday. Although, of course, if I fund enough science they could find me a way to live forever."

My eye twitched.

"What are you doing?" Adonis asked.

"You look as though a dog has been using your face as a chew toy," Angela said.

"I'm fine," I said. "Totally fine. I'll be back."

I went to find Alfred, who was sitting in the butler's pantry, staring at the wall. He maintained eye contact with the stark, white paint.

"Is everything to your satisfaction, Miss Allie?"

I leaned against the marble counter. "Want some good

news?"

"Did Mr. George fall off the cliff?"

"Cheer up. There's still hope for you. You're more likely to be George Diplas's type than Angela."

"But I don't want him." He thought about that for a moment. "Ah. I see." He sat there for a moment longer, then he seemed to come to a decision. He stood and shot his cuffs. "I must return to the dining room. Would you care to accompany me?"

"Do you have an aspirin?"

"Of course," he said. "Are you sure you wouldn't prefer something stronger? Mrs. Angela keeps a supply of every known analgesic, including the ones on the naughty list."

"Plain aspirin is fine."

"I must confess, I was sorely tempted to slip a little oxy into Mr. George's drink."

"Alfred?"

"Yes, Miss Allie?"

"That's illegal."

"Only if one gets caught, Miss Allie. Only if one gets caught."

Back in the dining room, Angela had made her move. George's arm was now tucked through hers, and she was walking him around the room as though he was a purebred dog. One of the smaller, fluffy ones, with an appetite for ankles.

Adonis gravitated to my side. He threw a few quiet words in my ear. "Nice work if you can get it."

"Jealous?"

"No."

"Are you sure? You got a tiny market. Your cousin could wind up owning a huge chunk of Greece."

"I'm satisfied with my choices. Do you think she is?"

I snorted. "They're each other's problem now, not mine."

"Thinking over the dress dilemma?"

"No." The ghosts swirled around George. Their mouths were moving but nothing was coming out. "Yes."

He turned serious. "Walk me through it."

"Through what?"

"Let's brainstorm the dress thing. You want the dress, you can't get the dress, and stealing it didn't work."

"I wasn't stealing it. I was trying to get it back."

He took a swig of his drink. "Sure. Call it that if it makes you feel better. Now let's figure out your next move. Sounds like this woman has her heels dug in hard. Any idea why?"

"Because she gets her kicks being an awful person."

"Probably something is missing in her life. Not money, obviously. She married?"

"Her husband ran off with a German woman when their daughter was a baby."

"So she's what? Middle-aged, cranky, and probably horny. Want me to seduce her while you go in and grab the dress?"

I stared at him. "What's wrong with you?"

"My parents have been asking me that same question for years. There's nothing wrong with me. I am who I am."

"Sounds to me like you'd be a more interesting match for Angela. She likes them criminal and unattainable."

"Oh, I'm attainable."

"For a price?"

He laughed. "Everyone has a price. If they say they

don't, they're not being offered enough. So what do you say: seduce this Kyria Yiota so you can get your dress?"

"No. I wouldn't inflict her on anyone, not even you."

"How bad can she be?"

"IRINI! IRINI! Where are you, *booboona*?"

A projectile hurtled across the yard.

We were near Kyria Yiota's house, hiding around a corner. Adonis needed to know how bad she was before he committed to helping me.

He raised an eyebrow. "*Pandofla*?"

"*Pandofla*," I confirmed. Definitely slip-on footwear. The day Greek mothers gave birth they bought their first pair of throwing shoes.

"IRINI!" Windows rattled in their frames. "I should have closed my legs instead of letting your father do that thing he liked! What a daughter I have. One child and she is not even *skata*! You are the reason I am *malakismeni*!"

"You" in this case was poor Irini, who sloped across the yard carrying a roll of toilet paper. The rough, one-ply butt scraping kind. No wonder Kyria Yiota was a grouch. Who wouldn't be with a raw butt?

"That's one of her better moods," I said.

"You've done a stakeout?"

I told him about the outhouse crochet-fests that occurred at regular intervals.

"Got an idea," he said. "Not the seduction. I couldn't do that to myself. But there's another way."

"What?"

"Be back here tonight."

"Can you give me a hint?"

"This time look out for traps."

At home, I called Leo to find out if they had found Eleni Zerva yet.

"Nothing so far. Merope's a small place until you launch a manhunt. We need more feet on the ground."

"How can I help?"

"Find me more feet?"

"I can do that."

He blew out a sigh. "It's okay, we've got this. Don't want any civilians getting hurt. That … that whatever it is … it's unpredictable."

Not entirely, but I didn't say that.

I gnawed on the problem. He was right about one thing. Mobilizing Merope's citizens to hunt for Eleni was potentially disastrous. If everything went well, we'd have bickering, skirmishes, and some wooden spoon-on-wooden spoon violence. People would be wounded, emotionally and physically. The folks on this island didn't need any new grudges. Not when they were already quietly seething.

Who could I get?

The answer whacked me over the head with a slipper.

"Got to go," I said.

"You're plotting."

"Am not."

"Honey, you can't fool me."

"Okay, just a tiny bit of plotting. But it's for your own good."

"Just don't do anything crazy. I don't want to find you in the ER again. It's no good for my blood pressure."

I made the promise with my fingers crossed. As soon as the call ended, I mobilized the about-to-be commander of my ghost army.

"Yiayia?"

POP.

Yiayia appeared. She was gripping a margarita glass, a thick layer of salt coating the rim.

"How would you like to be the commander of my ghost army?"

"Would I get to crack a whip and make them my *skeelas*?"

"Whatever gets the job done."

She vanished. When she popped back, she was wearing a skintight rubber cat suit and thigh-high boots. Very Madonna circa the early nineties. "Where are my soldiers?"

"Angela Zouboulaki's house, probably. They're following George Diplas."

"Why? What did he do?"

Good question. I had several more. The dead men weren't from Merope, and they were exclusively interested in the meteorologist. Ergo—in my mind, at least—they had either followed or accompanied him to Merope. Given that the island was surrounded by salt water, my money was on accompanying him. They couldn't cross on their own, so they'd hitched a ride in something George had one his person or luggage.

"I'm not sure. But I need you to go to Angela's house and convince them to help us search for Eleni Zerva. While that's happening, I'm going to do a thing."

"What thing?"

"Taking Cerberus out to see if he can sniff out Eleni."

I took Cerberus to the Zervas house first and helped myself to Eleni's scarf, which was hanging on a hook just inside the front door. Cerberus sniffed the item, then lost interest when he realized it wasn't food.

"Can you find her, boy? Who's the best dog? You are."

His tail flopped around. A small squeak leaked out of his butt. He spun around and bit the air.

I gave him the scarf again. This time he lurched away from the Zervas house. I let him lead the way. Through Merope's streets. Down steps. Up more steps. Along cobbled roads.

Until finally he stopped outside Crusty Dimitri's.

"She's not here. Nobody comes here on purpose, unless they're all out of other options."

He grinned up at me.

"Don't you know even the local animals avoid this place?"

Either he didn't know or didn't care.

"I'm not buying you souvlaki," I told the huge dog that definitely wasn't mine.

"Are you happy now?"

I'd watched Cerberus scoff down the souvlaki like it was good. It wasn't good. I knew that from experience. There would be poop soon. The kind that couldn't be contained in a bag.

"Now that you've stuffed yourself with mystery meat, can we focus?" I waved Eleni's scarf under his nose.

This time he led me to the Cake Emporium.

The storefront was empty. The sign was gone. My favorite place was husk. Still. Betty and Jack had pulled up stakes and moved on. Not forever, I hoped. I missed the cake. I missed my friend.

"She's not here, either."

I'd half expected Vladimir to bring Eleni to the shop, given that this was the only terminal leading to the past and future, in every inhabited location. Instead, the place was deserted.

Pop.

Yiayia and her leather cat suit shimmered into existence. "Good news. They are willing to help, for a price."

Figured. But under the circumstances I was okay-ish with indulging them. Quid pro quo, ghosties.

"What do they want?"

"For you to solve their murders."

I was mildly outraged. "What, all of them?"

"If you promise to find their killers later, they will help you right now."

At least they didn't want payment up front. "Okay."

"I'll tell them."

She vanished.

Having Yiayia in my life again was nice, and having her as my ghost assistant was a definite plus. Yes, she didn't like venturing into spooky basements, and yes, she'd forgotten some of her living values and had to occasionally be reminded not to do things like looking up priests' cassocks or watching men pee in public restrooms. But those incidents were rare.

My phone rang. Toula said, "The time 2:47 PM seems important. Whatever you have to do, do it before then."

Forty-five minutes from now.

"Can you be more specific?"

"No." She sounded huffy, like she was battling PMS. Or maybe she was just a mom.

"Okay."

"Whatever it is you're doing, be careful, okay?"

Cerberus barked.

That put Toula on alert. "What's that?"

"A dog. He could be your dog if you say the word."

"Wow," she said. "It's like you're trying to make my life harder."

"So that's a 'no' on the dog?"

Toula ended the call.

Forty-three minutes. What could I possibly accomplish in that narrow frame of time?

Yiayia reappeared with twenty-seven of her new pals, the slim young men that had swarmed George Diplas earlier, tracing his steps around Angela's dining room. Blandly attractive. Forgettable faces. Anonymous. You could see them in one moment and forget them in the next. All of them dead. All attracted to George Diplas.

"Thanks for coming." I described Eleni and Vladimir, told them what I needed. "When they're found, my grandmother—"

"I am her assistant!" Yiayia told them.

"—Will get in touch and we'll get started on your murders. Any and all details will be helpful."

They glanced at each other, then at me.

"Does that work for you?"

More silence. These guys weren't big talkers.

"Uh, how did you communicate with them?" I asked Yiayia.

"Ghost paper. They wrote notes on account of how they were murdered and cannot speak."

"You can't speak?" I asked them.

A sea of nods and chin chucks and other gestures that confirmed that none of them were capable of being chatty. Which was refreshing from a bunch of ghosts. Normally they suffer from verbal diarrhea and it's impossible to shut them up.

But how was I supposed to—

A light bulb flickered on.

I knew why they couldn't speak. My Spidey senses were pinging all over the place. I knew what I had to do.

"Where is George Diplas right now?" I asked my grandmother.

"The tasty weatherman? At the Zouboulaki house. Angela is about to show him her collection of money."

My client was bringing out the big guns. I addressed the dead men. "While you're hunting for Eleni and Vladimir, I'm going to do something bonkers that might solve your murders. Deal?" They nodded silently, then popped away, en masse.

My grandmother gave me a nervous, worried glance. "This thing you are going to do, is it dangerous?"

"Only if I get caught. Can you go back to Angela's place and keep an eye on George?"

"Both eyes, and my ghost hands."

"No hands, only eyes. Come find me at the Hotel Hooray if he leaves Angela's house."

She blew me a kiss, shimmied, and then vanished.

Now it was just me and Cerberus the homeless dog again.

"Too bad you can't fit in the basket," I said.

He eyed the back platform thingy. Well, why not?

"Okay, big boy. If you fits, you sits."

I steadied the bike. He carefully placed his front paws on the platform, followed by his back paws.

"I've got this. I can do this. We should get you a little doggie helmet. Wait, no, you'd need an extra-large."

I pushed off and we rode west, toward the Hotel Hooray, Cerberus doing his best balancing act while I worked on compensating for his mass.

Cerberus guarded my bicycle while I went inside to deal with the motel's gross owner.

"You again," Manolis grunted. "You going to pay up?"

"Forget it. You're going to help me." This time I didn't go the bimbo route. I told Manolis what I wanted.

His eyes fixated on my chest. Sad. Desperate. Pointless —given that I was wearing a puffy coat that turned my curves into boxes.

"What do I get out of it if I give you the key?"

"Self respect. You'll have done one decent thing in your life."

He wiped his nose with his forearm. "I've done good things."

"Name one."

"I pay for porn."

"How is that good?"

Big, oily smirk. "I am supporting young women's futures."

I rolled my eyes. "Just give me the key."

He inhaled. Puffed out his chest. Doing his level best to look bigger and more intimidating. I wasn't intimidated.

The clock behind his greasy head inched closer to Toula's deadline. The happy former hookers waited with bated breath to see how this would all shake out.

"Okay," he said. They exhaled. "But I want something. You find things and I want you to find something for me."

"What?"

A new smirk oozed across his face. "A doll. A special doll. One that will make *baba* happy." He grabbed his crotch and readjusted his goobers.

Ew. Gross. But better than inflicting himself on a female of the human species, I supposed. A doll wouldn't need antibiotics and a Silkwood shower. It could get by with bleach and a hose.

"Fine. Okay." I waggled my fingers at him. "Key."

With a porcine grunt, he reached over to pluck the

backup key off its hook. "The honeymoon suite," he told me.

Cerberus followed me to the so-called honeymoon suite, which was just a regular room but the pink sheets had been washed this year. The bed was made. George hadn't unpacked his bag. Nothing hung behind the curtain that served as a closet door. A miasma hung in the air: despair, drugs, rumpy-pumpy. The room begged for an open window.

I wasn't here to open windows.

My only interest was in George's duffel.

I checked my watch. Fifteen minutes until Toula's deadline. I crouched down by the duffel. Which, apparently had already been opened. George had taken something out. Clothes for the four-person reception at Angela's house?

Maybe that was it. But where had he put the old clothes? They weren't on the floor or in the flimsy closet. In the duffel? Not unless he'd buried them at the bottom.

Could be he ate them. Who knew? Whatever he'd done with the clothes, it wasn't relevant. I went back to digging gently through his bag. George was a pro packer. He knew how to maximize the space, turning his compact into an SUV. He was all about the cotton. No manmade fabrics. His underwear was all boxer briefs. Black. His toothbrush was electric, one of those buzzing brushes that slaps gunk off teeth using sound.

A-ha.

At the bottom was a gap. A box-shaped space where something had been and now wasn't. Everything was still packed neatly around it. There was no way George forgotten to fill the void. Something had been removed.

My gut told me that George Diplas had been a bad, bad boy.

Wow. Angela really knew how to pick 'em.

Whatever had been in this space had to be here some-where. But where? The Hotel Hooray didn't have heating or A/C. Staying here meant taking your chances with the seasons. Too hot? Open a window. Too cold? Close the window. That meant no vents to hide things. Safe? Forget it. The hotels amenities were things like running water and air. Room service was any bugs or rodents that showed up without being invited. The medicine cabinet wasn't a cabi-net, although some of the mold might be penicillin and therefore medicinal.

But the toilet cistern was an actual tank full of water, wasn't it?

Yes. Yes, it was.

Ten minutes to go. I opened the tank, careful not to splash water on the floor. The idea was not to let George know I'd been here, snooping through his belongings. Nestled inside the tank, sealed in a heavy-duty freezer bag, was a plastic container. White and opaque. Precisely the size of the gap in George's luggage.

"Interesting," Yiayia said, appearing with a *pop*. "What do you think is in the plastic box?"

"That's what I'm about to find out."

I stripped off my coat, pushed up my sleeves, and lifted the container out onto a towel.

"Do you think he is collecting trophies from the men he kills?" she asked in a breathless, excited voice.

"Wait, what?"

Yiayia shrugged. "All those young, pretty dead men hanging around a gay man who keeps his sexuality out of the public eye? They are not exactly swooning, are they? He killed them. On those true crimes shows, serial killers are always keeping trophies. They cannot help themselves.

I bet George keeps trophies, too. I bet they are in that box."

She was right. Probably about George, too. And she was reading my mind. I definitely pegged George as a killer.

I popped the lid on the container.

I peeked inside.

I closed the lid.

"What is it?" Yiayia wanted to know.

"Condoms."

She slapped the air. "*Po-po.* That is disappointing. I was hoping he was a serial killer. At least he is safe. You should grab a handful for you and Toula's yummy policeman."

That was a gut poke with a stick. "He wasn't a policeman when he was with Toula, and she's married now —with children."

She had a point, though. Leo was Toula's high school sweetheart, and he always would be. And someone— mostly Toula—would be there to remind me when I forgot.

Normally I wasn't the jealous type. Normally I didn't have to be. But I really liked Leo and I really didn't want Toula slapping me around the head with their past. No one wants to think about their boyfriend bonking their sister, even if it was more than a decade ago.

"Sometimes I do not think she knows that." She peered over my shoulder. "Take some anyway."

"I can't."

"Why not?"

I made a face. "They're all used."

True story. Every last condom in the box had been filled, removed, and a knot tied in the open end. The ghosts must have hitched a ride to the island in the container, bound to their, uh, leftovers.

"Definitely that is something a serial killer would do. Better put them back. George is on his way here."

"What?" I freaked. "Why didn't you lead with that?"

"I was caught up in the mystery. I could not help myself. Now that I am dead I am even more curious than before. It is like I am more Greek than Greek."

Angela's house wasn't far. Nothing on Merope was far. He'd be back within minutes.

Toula's warning flashed in my head. I glanced at my watch. I had two minutes and counting.

I zipped up the plastic bag and lowered the container back into the cistern and carefully replaced the lid. I folded the towel and sat it on the shelf.

The door rattled. Someone was jiggling a key in the lock. Already? It was too soon. I had nowhere to go. The bathroom window was a possibility but there wasn't time to shimmy through. I flew into the bedroom and dived under the bed. Cerberus followed me.

"Let's be quiet together," I told him.

The door opened. George Diplas's boots entered the room. Presumably with the rest of him. The door remained open. More footwear entered. Sneakers, this time. Clean, white, bright.

"What's it like being on TV?" a man asked. He sounded young. Like the dead men.

"It pays the bills," George said. "Amongst other things."

"I didn't know you were … you know."

"What?"

"That you like men."

"You're not going to tell anyone, are you?" George asked.

"Nobody knows about me either, so …"

"Perfect. Take your clothes off."

They kicked off shoes. Pants. The feet assumed a certain position at the edge of the bed, centimeters from my nose. The bed squeaked.

"The human body is so elastic," Yiayia said.

The bed squeaked some more.

Cerberus farted.

The squeaking stopped.

"Was that you?" George said.

"Not yet."

The men separated. There was a sticky, sloppy noise and the other guy went, "*Oof.*"

This was it. We were done for.

George crouched down. His gaze met mine. I waved as best I could under a cramped bed.

"Just checking for bedbugs," I said.

"With your … is that a bear?"

"Dog. And he's not mine. Say, do either of you want a dog?"

The other guy crouched down. I recognized him as one of the baristas from Merope's Best. "I know you," he said. "Somehow our coffee hasn't killed you yet."

"Is it even coffee?"

"I'll never tell."

"Did you find any bugs?" George asked.

"No, but I suspect there's something hibernating in the mattress."

I wriggled out. George and the barista were naked from the waist down. I averted my eyes. "I'll just be leaving now. I'll tell Manolis to give Angela a discount on the room, seeing as how there's something nefarious in the mattress."

George grabbed my arm. "Why are you here?"

Cerberus growled, low and threatening.

"I told you: bugs. I'd heard rumors, so Angela sent me over here to make sure the room was clean."

"Why don't I believe you?"

"Never trust anyone that drinks our coffee for years and doesn't die," the barista said.

"Okay, fine," I said. "For some reason you're being trailed by a couple of dozen ghosts. Young, cute men. I wanted to see if you're a serial killer."

Yiayia winced. "That was a bad idea."

I half expected George to flip out. This was definitely the part where killers switched to their murdering personas.

Not George.

He tipped back his head and laughed. "Serial killer. That's hilarious. I've never killed anything in my life. I'm a Jainist. We don't do any form of violence. Everything has a right to live. That way the universe remains in balance."

"Wait," the barista said. "Go back to the bit with the ghosts. That sounds cool."

"I was making that part up," I said.

"So funny," George said, his goobers wobbling as he escorted me to the door. I did my best to avoid eye contact with his one-eyed snake, but it kept looking at me.

"But ... wait ..."

He shut the door behind us.

"That was weird," I said to Yiayia. "What about the used condoms? They were all tied neatly on the ends so the goop wouldn't spill out. Who does that and collects them?"

"Maybe it's like notches on the headboard? Real notches are better. Less sticky. Smell better, too. Old semen smells like rotting ocean critters."

I stared at my grandmother. My eyelid twitched. She wasn't wrong, damn it.

Thump.

"Did you hear that?" I asked her.

"Probably the dead body hitting the floor."

That was quick, even if George was a serial killer.

The door flew open. George reappeared with his pants in hand. He threw the pants around my neck and pulled me in. The door slammed behind him. Cerberus was stuck outside. The big dog scratched frantically on the door. Panic rose up in me when I saw the barista lying on the ground, passed out or worse.

"You are a serial killer!" I said. "I knew it! I love being right, but sometimes I really hate being right."

George rolled his eyes at me. "You know nothing."

"I know you're a serial killer."

He thought about it. "That *is* a problem. Is that why you lured me to this zero of an island?"

The audacity of this butt-clown. "Hey, Merope isn't a zero. It looks pretty on postcards and it's hopping in summer."

"It's a dump."

"Is not."

"Why are you arguing with me?"

"I can't help myself. It's what I do when I get anxious, like people who need to pee when they're stressed."

George was stronger than he looked, and he looked like he could wrestle a tree and stand a chance of winning. He tightened his pants' legs around my throat. "How about my now?"

"Still feeling chatty."

The pants tightened some more. I gave him a thumbs-up.

Right about now would be a nice time for a rescue.

"He looks like he wants to kill you," Yiayia said, circling us.

I managed to squeeze some words out. "Can't you do that thing you did last time?" I said to her.

George misunderstood. "I didn't bring rope. I wasn't expecting to meet anyone."

"Impossible," Yiayia said. "Last time was a one-off, an anomaly. But I can make jokes about his *poutsa*, if that will help. It is very big. He should register that as a weapon."

Mocking his penis wasn't going to help anyone, least of all me.

Rope, eh? So that was it. His ghost entourage was quiet because he had strangled them—probably after sex, given that he was keeping a whole pile of gross trophies. Talk about taking a risk. Those prophylactics were either covered or filled with DNA, including George's. No wonder he traveled with them and hid them in toilet cisterns. Although what he did when flying was a mystery.

"Do you kill them all?" I rasped.

"Whom are you talking about?"

"The twenty-seven dead men. The used condoms."

He looked surprised. "Twenty-seven?"

"Please, like you don't know."

Cerberus was going berserk outside. Hopefully someone would hear him and come to my rescue. Sure enough, Cerberus's barks settled to whines, and then stopped altogether.

Someone knocked on the door.

"Your dog is barking," Manolis called out. "It is disturbing the other guests. The woman in 103 just had to extended her stay for another fifteen minutes because her customer could not finish with all that barking."

Manolis. Not my first choice, but okay. If I could just get to the door …

I scooted backwards. My fingers found the handle. I jiggled it. George twigged to what I was up to and jerked me forwards with his pants noose. Too late. One hard tug got the handle working. The door swung open. Cerberus lunged inside, all teeth and fury. Manolis grabbed him by the collar.

He smirked. "You should have come to *baba* if you wanted it rough."

Oh, puke.

"Just having some fun," George said.

"No problem." Manolis adjusted his frank and beans. "Call the front desk if you need a cameraman."

George kicked the door shut with his bare foot.

Several things happened at once.

I realized he had a bare foot. Meanwhile, I was in boots.

My boot found his foot—hard.

The door busted open. Cerberus surged forward and clamped his chompers down on George's wiener. In his defense, I can only assume he mistook it for a pork tenderloin.

George screamed.

The door tore off entirely, taking half the wall out with it. Vladimir was standing there with Eleni Zerva.

CHAPTER NINETEEN

Events kept unfolding simultaneously.

I fell on the floor, gasping.

George jumped around, clutching his crotch.

Cerberus howled. He wanted that pork tenderloin.

The barista snoozed through the whole thing. Probably he had a serious concussion.

Manolis shrieked about the damage to his crappy motel.

Eleni was glowing. (Not literally.) "He found me. Can you believe it? It's the most romantic thing ever. Like Dracula when he tells Mina he crossed oceans of time for her in that one movie."

"You can see him?" I asked.

"Well, no. But he can write, and I can see his writing."

"And you're okay with that."

"Romantic," she reiterated. "He says you can see him, that you can see all ghosts. How does he look?"

"Shh, not so loud." I glanced at Vladimir. "Transparent, and he's wearing a blue tracksuit."

She frowned. "Why is that man jumping around, grabbing his *poutsa*?"

"Cerberus mistook it for a tenderloin."

"It *is* big," she said. "He looks familiar."

"He's just got one of those faces."

"I am going to kill you!" George Diplas screeched. Tears poured down his cheeks.

Eleni turned. "Vladimir? I really don't want this person to hurt Allie. She has always been good to me."

There's no one more compliant or eager to impress than a man in love—even a dead man. He waved his hand. George rose up into the air and flew headfirst into a twisty olive tree several meters from the motel. The weatherman struck the ground with a sickening *thud*.

"He'll be fine?" I said. "Right?"

Eleni shrugged. "Maybe."

"I am going to call the police on all of you!" Manolis shrieked in a high girlish voice.

"He won't," I told Eleni and Vladimir. "They've rapped him over the knuckles too many times for weird sex crimes. Mostly exposing himself to tourists and peeking in windows."

"I will," Manolis said. "I am doing it right now." He held up his phone and stabbed numbers I knew would summon Leo.

"I have to go," Eleni said. "The police are looking for me."

"Did you kill your parents?"

"No. There were times I wished they were dead so they could be themselves again. But I did not hurt them. All I ever did was protect them."

That sounded like the Eleni Zerva I knew.

"Go," I said. "I'll make something up."

She hesitated. "Meet us at Ayia Paraskevi later, okay?"

"Last time I was there, Vladimir tried to throw me off a cliff."

He made a face. "It was mistake. Is frustrating when someone will not heelp."

"He will behave this time, yes, Vladimir?"

His ghost finger touched the air and drew words in dust. "Of course, my little *pusik*."

She giggled. "I love it when he writes Russian to me."

In the distance, police sirens were audible.

Eleni hurried away with Vladimir beside her.

"Where is she going?" Manolis shrieked. "She's a witness!"

I played dumb. "Who?"

"That woman. The Zervases' daughter."

"You're imagining things."

His eyes narrowed.

"Do you want that doll or not?" I asked him.

His eyes went all beady. Someone was calculating the euro value of his silence. "That price was for the key. For this … for this, I want more."

"How much more?"

"An hour with you."

"No."

"Half an hour."

"No."

He gave me a hopeful look. "Fifteen minutes?"

"No."

"What can you give me?"

"I won't kick you in the *archidia*."

"What if I want you to?"

"The best I can do is finding someone to belittle your manhood and maybe crush your nuts with high heels."

He thought about it for a moment. "Okay. We have a deal."

His expression mild and unreadable, Leo stared at the absent door and wall. Technically they were both over there, the door dangling by its hinges, and not missing at all.

"Looks like something tore the wall out."

"Looks like," Manolis said.

"The Feng Shui is better now," I told him.

Leo's face said it didn't know about Feng Shui. "Same thing happened at the police station, except it was the roof."

"Who cares? Not me. I have things to do." Manolis winked at me on the way past. My skin crawled.

Leo had more questions. He swung around to inspect George Diplas groaning under the tree. "Why is that weather guy sitting under the tree with no pants? And why is he here on Merope?"

"It's a very funny story."

He waited.

"Angela had me bring him here to investigate the weird weather."

"The weather that wasn't weather?"

"Exactly."

"And why did he kiss a tree?"

"This is the bit where you thank me. I caught you a serial killer. Happy Birthday in advance. Or Merry Late Christmas."

Leo blinked. It was a lot, I knew.

Okay, probably I should explain better. I mentally rewound and took another shot at storytelling.

He made a face when I got to the bit with the used condoms. "If you cross reference his travel plans with missing men, you'll find his victims' names. I'd ask their ghosts, but he strangled them. None of them can speak. Maybe they can write them on ghost paper …"

"Ghost paper." Leo swallowed. "What about the guy on the floor? Who is he?"

"Barista from Merope's Best. One of the Papadopoulos kids. He's alive, but he needs medical help."

Leo didn't waste time. He made the call. By the time he was done, an ambulance was on its way.

"How did the door and—" he gestured at everything "—come off? I mean really."

"A stiff breeze and shoddy construction."

He didn't buy it. The wind was having some quiet time, and the Hotel Hooray was built for all kinds of banging. Even acts of God hadn't done more than give the foundation a mild shake.

"You're not telling me everything."

"No."

"Why not?"

"Because there's a thing I have to do." I flashed him an exaggerated grin. "Chin up. I just caught a serial killer for you. That's a pretty nice gift, right?"

He didn't look convinced. "People love George Diplas."

"They love George Diplas the weather man. George Diplas the serial killer won't be Greece's sweetheart."

He paced for a moment before folding his arms. "We need to talk."

"Later."

"Later," he said. "And right now you're going to do whatever it is you're keeping from me?"

"Yes."

"I could follow you."

"Trust me."

He pulled off his beanie and shoved his hand

through his hair before resettling the woolen hat. "I trust you." He grabbed me by the waist and reeled me in for a kiss. "But I don't trust whatever it is you're keeping from me."

"It's the same thing."

"No," he said. "It's not.

The news about George Diplas wouldn't stay buttoned up for long. I needed to explain things to Angela. I also needed to go find Eleni and her dead, weird boyfriend. When that was done, I was supposed to meet Adonis Diplas near Kyria Yiota's house. Would he renege on his promise to help me once he found out about his cousin's penchant for snuffing cute, young men and my involvement in his arrest?

Wouldn't blame him if he did. Discovering a family member is a serial killer is a bit of a shock to even the most steadfast system.

First, Angela.

With Cerberus balanced on my bicycle again, I rode over to her sterile villa and rang the bell.

A *bing-bong* echoed through the house.

Alfred opened the door. His gaze landed on Cerberus with a horrified and borderline-audible *clank*.

"What is that?"

"Dog. Do you want him? He's looking for a home."

"Does the pope use the lavatory facilities in the woods?"

"If he's in the woods, sure."

"The last thing Mrs. Angela wants in her home is a canine."

Angela wasn't really a pet person. Even something

small, white and fluffy was too much color in her mono-chrome mansion.

"Could you please get her? There's a teensy bit of a problem."

His eyes lit up. "With Mr. Diplas?"

"Afraid so. Let's just say he won't be talking weather on the TV for approximately twenty years to life."

He wrestled with that new knowledge. A smile threatened to break out on his face. Finally, he stuffed the glee down inside and adjusted his butler outfit.

"Wait there with your … dog."

"He's not my dog."

Alfred raised a sardonic eyebrow. "It appears as though he has other plans."

Cerberus was leaning against my thigh, gazing up at me adoringly while I waited for Angela.

"I can't have a dog in my apartment," I told the pup.

His tail thumped the white marble porch. If I did have room for a dog, Cerberus would be the perfect candidate. He was smart, affectionate, and took protecting me seriously, which was nice. But my place was small and he was a lot of dog. He needed a house that could accommodate his size.

The door opened. Angela stepped out in a cream sweater and soft vanilla flannel pants. She recoiled when she spotted Cerberus.

"What. Is. That?"

"Elephant," I said. "I need to tell you something about George Diplas before it takes a ride on the gossip train and ends up mangled beyond recognition."

"He's married," she said flatly.

"Not that I know of. He's a bit of a serial killer."

She hesitated before asking, "How many victims?"

"At least twenty-seven."

The new information took a few seconds to process. "I could live with fewer than ten, but more than twenty is a lot."

My eye twitched. "George is in police custody, so he probably won't be able to make it to dinner or whatever you had planned for this evening."

Behind Angela's back, Alfred was on the verge of smiling.

Angela wasn't deterred. "Can you find me another date for this evening?"

Was she nuts?

"No. I'm done. I'm not scrounging up or vetting any more men for you. You need to take a break from dating and work on yourself. Maybe introduce some colors to your life. Get some friends—real friends."

That confused her. "Where am I supposed to find friends?"

"It's tough when you get older, I know. I only have a couple myself. But any time you want to hang out as friends, let me know. There's always room for another person in my life."

Her mouth fell open. She blinked. That was her best effort at looking surprised.

"By the way, Alfred looks like he could use a good meal. Why not have dinner with him tonight instead?"

Alfred's eyes widened.

Angela's forehead tried wrinkling, but the Botox slapped it back into place. "Alfred? The butler?"

"A butler who is also a man. He's single, straight, and he's house trained. Which makes him practically perfect. Just a serving suggestion." I winked at a spluttering Alfred, then whistled to not-my-dog, and we rode away to see a woman about a ghost.

CHAPTER TWENTY

ELENI WAS WAITING at the old church. Sitting on the ground. Shielded by two stubborn walls that had refused to fall when earthquakes shook up the island for funsies. Vladimir hovered close by, unseen by Eleni but protecting her anyway.

Love makes people crazy, even when they're dead.

She stood when she saw us approaching.

"You came."

"I said I would."

"Any luck with the dress yet?"

"Ask me again this evening."

She smiled. "I hope we won't be here by then."

"Are you leaving?"

Perfect. Eleni could box up Vladimir, transport him across the Aegean, and they could live and not-live happily-ever-after.

"Not exactly," she said, whatever that meant. She took a deep breath. "We need your help. Vladimir told me he already asked, but he's not confident you want to help us."

"*Asked* is an understatement. He bullied, cajoled, misled

me, and subjected the island to bad weather. If he'd asked me for help from the beginning, and told me who he was, this would have gone differently."

Vladimir threw his hands. "I told you, I am Vladimir!"

"He struggles with anxiety," Eleni said. "Will you help us?"

"With the anxiety, sure. A trip to the Afterlife for some Ghostzac should fix that. But getting off the island? I can't. Not if he wants what I think he wants."

"Vladimir says there's a way for us to be together. He can go back in time and warn himself not to leave Merope. Instead, if his plan works, I'm going to back to Russia or wherever with him. We're going to get married back in the 1990s and have our happily-ever-after."

I shook my head. "What Vladimir wants, it's impossible. He's dead. He died. His life is over. Going back in time and warning himself will change the future. He'll be inserting himself into the world after he already stopped existing in live, human form. The result will be catastrophic."

"But there has to be something …?"

"There's not," I said gently.

Vladimir's face was sour. "*Nyet!* I do not believe it."

"The truth doesn't care whether or not you believe in it."

"I need to think," Eleni said. "I can't stay here. I'm wanted for murders I didn't do. Unless the police find out who really killed my parents, I am going to prison."

"Leo is a good cop. He'll find out who murdered your parents."

She didn't look convinced. "How good can he be if he thinks I did it?"

Not fair, and yet totally fair. "He's following the

evidence. Right now all he knows is that you bought rat poison from the More Super Market."

"Because Mama asked me to buy it. She swore we had rats, even though I hadn't seen any evidence of them. I bought the poison because it made her feel better to have it close by. Honestly, she should have just fed them some of her *revithia* and they would have packed up and left on their own. That stuff tastes like a dead man's *kolos*."

As someone who hated chickpea stew, I wanted to high five her.

As someone who made a living finding things and connecting dots, alarm bells went off in my head.

"*Revithia*. When did you last eat them?"

"Me? Not since I was a child. Once I became an adult, I refused to eat them. When I took over the cooking, I made them occasionally for my parents, but I never ate them myself."

"When was the last time you made them for your parents?"

"The day they died."

The Zervases both had bellies full of chickpeas—chickpeas they'd eaten at home. Not the last supper I would choose. I'd hold out for a dish of *yemista* or a New York pizza with cannoli for dessert.

"And was your *mama* present in the kitchen while you were cooking?"

"Always. I couldn't trust her or *baba* around the fire or gas, so I took over the cooking a few years ago. She oversaw most of my cooking to make sure I prepared her meals, her way."

"Did you leave the *revithia* unsupervised at all?"

"A few times. Why?"

"I don't think you killed your parents, and I don't think they were murdered at all."

"What are you saying?"

"I have to go, but I'll be back. Will you be okay here?"

"Vladimir will keep me warm and safe, won't you, *moro mou*?"

Vladimir didn't look like he had ever been anyone's baby, but Eleni loved him. Her words lit him up. "*Da. Always.*"

"See you soon," I said.

I raced home as fast as I could while balancing a dog behind me. What I needed was a dog trailer.

Doh!

No, I didn't. What I needed was to find Cerberus a new home before I got too attached to him.

He chuffed gently in my ear while resting his chin on my shoulder. Could be it was already too late. His being utterly adorable wasn't helping the situation.

At home, I jogged up the stairs.

Jimmy Kontos was sitting cross-legged outside Lydia's apartment, fiddling with his phone. "Stop running," he said. "You'll bring the whole building down."

"Totally worth it if it takes you out in the process."

"Not me. I'm compact. That means I can fit into small pockets off air until the rescue teams show up."

"What are you doing in the hallway?"

"Waiting for *mon amour*. She's getting ready for our date."

Good for them. Now if Angela and her butler could get it together, everyone in my life would be paired up and leave me alone to get busy with Leo.

I stopped. "I don't suppose you know anyone who can

humiliate a man and crush his *archidia* with their high heels?"

"Sounds like something you'd be good at."

"It's the kind of thing I've only ever done by accident. I need a pro."

"Why? You smuggling something we don't know about?"

"Yeah, a heroic amount of restraint."

The door opened. Lydia stuck her head out. "I know someone."

"Who?"

"Me. What does it pay?"

I glanced at Jimmy. The little guy didn't look fazed by Lydia's "consulting" job.

"She's great at humiliating men," he said. "Except me."

Lydia shrugged it off. "I humiliate him all the time and he just eats it up."

That got a grin out of the little guy. "It's not humiliation if you love it."

"I'll have to try harder," she said.

Both eyes were twitching and my feet wanted to flee. But I couldn't move.

"I love these two," Yiayia said, emerging from my apartment via the wall. "I bet they last forever."

"Manolis will pay whatever I tell him to pay," I said.

"That's a good attitude." Lydia made a face. "Manolis? Not the *malaka* from the Hotel Hooray?"

"That's him."

"Tell him for him the price is double."

I texted Manolis, gave him the good news, and he agreed to pay Lydia's fee. Now all that was left was to locate his doll and have the poor plastic thing delivered.

Cerberus pushed into my apartment. He leaped up

onto the couch. Purring like a train, Dead Cat plonked down on his fur and cued up his next nap.

I dropped my things on my desk and unraveled my scarf. "Kyria Zerva? Kyrios Zervas?"

Pop.

The elderly couple appeared. "Did you find out who killed us?" Maria Zerva demanded.

"Yes," I said. "I think you did it."

Maria Zerva crossed herself. "I would never!" She stopped. "Probably. Now that I think about it, maybe I did. But it was an accident. The rat poison was just there and I mistook it for pepper."

I knew it. Now I had to make sure the police knew it, too.

"Eleni is on the hook for your murder. Is that what you want for your daughter?

"After all we did for her," Stathis Zervas said, completely oblivious, "this is how she repays us? By murdering us?"

"Your wife killed you both," I told him. "By accident."

"Why would she do that?"

Maria Zerva clutched her chest. "We cannot be dead." Her eyes narrowed. "If we are dead, then why are we here? Why are we not in the underworld? Why are we not meeting God and waiting for our resurrection?"

Oh, brother. This was going nowhere fast. I had a confession, but what could I do with it? Nothing. I couldn't go to Leo with "A ghost told me so." Well, I could. But he couldn't exactly close a case without something more substantial than hearsay from the dead. His higher ups weren't dating me. They didn't know I wasn't fruitier than a daiquiri.

But crazy or not, this *was* new information. Maybe Leo could do something with it anyway. Eleni didn't commit parricide. It would be every kind of wrong if she got stuck doing the time instead of finally living her life, free of her parents' control. Leo was a good human and a good policemen. He didn't want to lock up the wrong person. Once her name was cleared she'd be able to live her life. Getting a 1990s do-over with Vladimir was impossible without blowing up the world, but maybe Eleni could move forward in some other happy chickpea-free way.

I called Leo. He answered immediately.

"Eleni Zerva didn't kill her parents," I said before he could squeeze the first word in.

"Right now the evidence says she did."

"Sure, the evidence looks like that, but you're reading it wrong."

"I'm listening."

"The coroner found chickpeas in their stomachs along with the poison, right?"

"Correct."

I told him what Eleni told me, that she was following her mother's recipe with her mother supervising—her mother who could no longer be trusted to perform the cooking alone.

"… and when Eleni was out of the room, Kyria Zerva sprinkled in some extra seasoning. A pinch of poison to add some kick. But she thought it was pepper."

He sounded dubious. "She mistook rat poison for pepper?"

"It could happen. I mean, it did happen. Probably. Kyria Zerva admitted to it."

"You mean her ghost."

"Well, yes."

"I can't do anything with the word of a ghost, not when the evidence suggests otherwise."

"I know. That's why I was hoping you could … I don't

know … reorient your investigation or something. Approach it like it was an old woman with dementia making an honest but deadly mistake. Look, were Kyria Zerva's fingerprints on the rat poison box?"

They had to be. I knew it.

"No. The only fingerprints belonged to Eleni Zerva and Stephanie Dolas. Stephanie's were present because she stocked the shelves."

My stomach plummeted. Had Eleni lied to me?

I heard Leo tapping on something. Thinking. Trying to find that new angle, even though the whole thing was thinner than Michelle Pfeiffer's thigh.

"I'll take another look," he said. "But I want to ask you something, and I need you to tell me the truth."

"I don't dye my hair. At least not yet."

He laughed. "Me either."

"You want to know if I know where Eleni Zerva is hiding out, right?"

"Right."

"Yes, I know."

"You're not going to tell me where she is, are you?"

"Not yet. But I will."

"Okay. Good enough. For now."

He ended the call without so much as a promise or a goodbye. I told myself it was because he was busy, not because I was souring our fledgling relationship with my circumspection.

My heart felt like a lump of doggy doo-doo. All I wanted to do was flop down on the couch with a pillow over my face, but it was covered in dog.

I slumped on the floor, facedown. Cerberus leaped off the couch and sprawled out next to me. Dead Cat sat on my head. Purrs vibrated through my skull.

Yiayia poked me with her shoe. The touch registered as a cold spot. "Are you feeling sorry for yourself?"

"Ungh."

"Do you want some advice?"

"Ungh."

"If you want to pick up a man, lift from the knees so you do not hurt your back."

"That's good advice," I admitted. "I should tell Angela."

"If you get up I have more for you."

"I'm not getting up. I live here now. Eleni Zerva will spend the rest of her life in prison unless I can find a way to prove she didn't kill her parents."

In the kitchen, where she was using the "facilities" again, Maria Zerva gasped. "My Eleni cannot go to prison! I never taught her how to cook rats."

"Well, that's where she's going unless you can give me proof that you accidentally seasoned your chickpeas with rat poison." The rug muffled my voice.

"Accident?" Kyria Zerva sounded outraged. "What accident? I did it on purpose!"

I rolled over. Dead Cat didn't budge. "What?"

"Do you think I wanted Eleni to waste the rest of her youth taking care of her two old parents?"

Why not? That was the norm for Greek parents from a certain generation. Children were expected to be caretakers for their parents; otherwise they were ungrateful little *malakes* who obviously never loved their poor *mama* and *baba*.

"Yes?"

"No!"

The trashcan rattled slightly. Most of the time ghosts couldn't affect the living world. Unless they were poltergeists or they were flipping out. Maria Zerva was the second one.

She clomped soundlessly into the living room and glared down at me. "I want more for my daughter! We already did enough damage sending that Russian boy away. I had to kill us before we lost all our eggs and baskets! My daughter was not destined to wipe my *kolos*!"

"I have eggs," Stathis Zervas announced.

She smacked her husband upside the head. "You have no eggs. Only I have one egg left, and I used that egg to save Eleni. And now you tell me she is going to prison?" Maria Zerva spat on the ground. "*Ah-pa-pa*! That cannot happen."

"Your fingerprints weren't on the box."

"Because Eleni made me wear oven mitts! She did not trust me not to ruin my own cooking. My own recipes!"

"Death finds a way," Yiayia said.

"Give me proof I can use to save her," I said. "Please."

Maria Zerva shook her fist at me. "You find something! That is what you do, yes?"

She was right, finding things was my business. But how could I find an exonerating clue where there wasn't one?

CHAPTER TWENTY-ONE

Pappas was at the Zervas house, lurking outside the yard, drinking coffee from a thermos. The front door was barricaded with *Do Not Cross* tape.

The constable scratched his head. "How am I supposed to get in there?"

I flicked his ear. "They don't mean you. You're the police, you *vlakas*."

"Ow! My ears are sensitive when it's cold. What are you doing here?"

"Looking around. You?"

"Investigating," he said. "Leo sent me over."

"We should go in," I said.

"I don't think you are supposed to be here."

"If you give me permission, I can go in there with you."

"I don't know …"

"You know I'm good at finding things."

He swished the ground with his boot. "Okay, but don't touch anything."

Given that he didn't make me promise, I figured I had all kinds of leeway.

We ducked under the tape. The Zervas house was airless. Nothing moved. Even the dust was napping.

"Stay out of Eleni's underwear drawer," I told Pappas.

"What if there is evidence in there?"

He had a point, and he was the police. "Okay, fine. But don't make it weird."

While he was busy rifling through drawers, I searched the kitchen. Leo had already combed the house himself, but he and I weren't necessarily hunting for the same things. Maria Zerva mentioned that Eleni insisted she wear mitts in the kitchen for safety reasons. I wanted those mitts.

Because the kitchen was old and had precisely zero modern updates, there were no cabinets. The kitchen had two options for storage: shelves on the wall, and shelves under the counter. The shelves below waist level were hidden from view by a yellow curtain dotted with white flowers.

I crouched and quickly located the matching pair of mitts sitting on the cutting board. I dropped them into a plastic bag and sealed up the opening. If Maria Zerva wore them while pouring rat poison into the chickpeas, could be they were covered in trace amounts.

What I really needed was damning evidence. Something more solid than circumstantial. A signed "I done it" affidavit was too much to ask for. I'd settle for video of Maria Zerva pouring pellets into the stew. But without that, the mitts would have to do.

I hoped it was enough.

Pappas wandered out, holding up a pair of underwear. Nothing snazzy. Eleni picked her undergarments for comfort.

"No wonder the daughter was single with underwear like these."

"Pappas?"

"What?"

"What did I say about not making it weird?"

"This underwear is making it weird, not me."

"If it's not evidence, put it back. Folded. Neatly."

He hesitated. "Do you think they make these for men?"

"Pappas? Weird."

"Okay, okay."

I left Pappas to his own investigation, half positive he wouldn't find anything Leo's original investigation hadn't uncovered. They were looking for evidence of a crime that wasn't a crime; therefore they'd find nothing.

I took the mitts to the police station, where Leo was poring over files on his computer screen. George Diplas. Dozens of missing and dead men from all around Europe.

He gestured at the screen. "Know any of them?"

"Know? Not personally. But I recognize some of their faces."

"From after they were dead."

"They were crowded around George at Angela's place. Then I saw them … after. They want me to solve their murders, which I'm trying to do. Do the dates and murders match?"

His face turned hard. His cop face. "Yes. He's been active for a long time. He never made it onto anyone's suspect list. Not for any of them. We can put more than two dozen murders to bed now."

"You're welcome." I held up the bag with the mitts. "Don't be mad at Pappas, but he let me into the Zervas house. I found these."

"Mitts?"

I told him what I knew. "Might be worthwhile checking

them for traces of rat poison, seeing as how Kyria Zerva always wore them in the kitchen." I bit down on my lip. Changing the story seemed hokey, but this wasn't my usual case. Things were in flux because of the Zervases' mental states. "The poison, it wasn't an accident. Kyria Zerva wanted to give Eleni her life back before she was forced to become a full-time caretaker. If anything it was a mercy suicide."

"And Kyrios Zervas, what was his role?"

"Hard to say. He's less lucid than his wife. Unwitting victim or participant."

He leaned back in his chair, hands laced behind his head. "You've got nothing, and I've got slightly more than nothing."

"I've got the alleged murder victim's confession to her own compassionate suicide." I blew out a frustrated sigh. "Yeah, I've got nothing. I have to go." I didn't have to go. "My big plan for the evening is to find Cerberus a home. Should be easy enough. He's a sweetheart and I'm good at finding things, right?"

"Okay."

No mention of dinner or meeting up later.

Well, okay then. Eventually I'd push him for a conversation, but not now while things were raw and we were both in a mood.

Maybe it was his time of the month.

Or worse, about to be mine.

The night was thickening. Nice that we were on the other side of the solstice. Bad that we were still months away from spring. Shivering was getting old.

By the time I rode over to Kyria Yiota's neighborhood,

I was warm, but it was a fake, womanmade heat. My snotty nose told the truth about the ambient temperature, which was hovering close to zero.

I kicked my stand, hunkered down in a shadow, keeping Kyria Yiota's house in sight. That dress was in there. The burning question: would Adonis Diplas show up?

Footsteps struck stone. Headed in my direction. Heavy. Confident. Purposeful. Not exactly subtle, if they belonged to Adonis Diplas. He struck me as a guy who wasn't unfamiliar with breaking and entering, so why wasn't he better at stealth?

I shrunk back into my shadow, hoping it would function as a perfectly good blanket fort, hiding me from any passing boogeymen.

A figure appeared. Tall, shadowy, and obviously lost on his way to the nearest misty moor.

What was *he* doing here?

The Man in Black stopped when he drew level with me. He moved until we were both in the shadow fort.

"You cannot help them," he said. "Not the way they wish."

No point pretending I didn't know which "them" he meant. There was nothing I could do for Eleni and Vladimir. All roads led to him remaining dead while she lived on without him in solid form.

"I know. But I keep hoping I'll find a way."

"Some paths simply end, and when you turn around you find the path that was behind you has vanished."

Bleak, but okay. "Then what happens?"

"You remain mired in your present. Or you leap."

"That's a terrible metaphor."

"Who said it was a metaphor?" He nodded to Kyria Yiota's house. "What you seek is in there, am I correct?"

I nodded. Duh. As if he could see that in the dark. "Yes."

"Remain here. I will return."

Was he high?

Definitely high. Or maybe insane. The way he was striding up to Kyria Yiota's door was sheer folly. This would end badly, probably with a broom in a hole that wasn't intended to take a broom. Any second now the shrieking would start, filling up the night with curse words and threats and madness.

I squeezed one eye shut, unable to watch the inevitable carnage with two.

The Man in Black opened the front door to Kyria Yiota's squalid house and stepped through as though he belonged in the home beyond.

The night remained quiet. No yelling. No brooms in tight holes. No furious Kyria Yiota, insulting the Man in Black's forebears and his mother's chastity.

Huh. How did he do that? He really needed to teach me his ways.

I kept lookout. In case of what, I wasn't sure. Seemed to me like the Man in Black had things under control.

When he emerged moments later, he was walking with his usual purposeful gait. No limping. No missing limbs. Clearly he hadn't run into thirty or so mousetraps. Draped over his arm was Kyria Zerva's wedding dress.

He stepped back into the shadow with me. "This, I believe, belongs to your client."

"How?"

I imagined his lips quirking. "Magic. But there are limits, so it would be best if you returned the dress to its owner before—"

Inside the house, Kyria Yiota exploded.

"Before she notices it's gone?"

"Yes."

I bundled the dress into the bicycle's basket. "Thank you."

The air shifted as he nodded. "You are welcome, Allie Callas."

One of us vanished first. I wasn't sure if it was him or me.

One more stop before I turned tail for home. With the dress safely in my basket, I peddled toward the old church to find Eleni.

Vladimir had damaged my island. Scared my neighbors. Performed some sloppy renovations. And yet I wanted those two crazy kids to get their happy ending.

Depressingly impossible.

Eleni had spent her youth scrambling to fulfill her parents wishes, only to become the parent herself. Her mother did what she believed to be the compassionate thing, even though she'd taken a drastic and deadly route. There was help out there for the Elenis of Greece. But her parents wouldn't have agreed to move out of their home or allowed someone else to come to their home and care for them.

Now she was free.

Unfortunately, not to be with Vladimir.

The very least—and only thing—I could do was to return her mother's dress so she could bury Kyria Zerva according to her wishes.

Outside the church's ruins, I kicked the stand on my bicycle. I left the dress in the basket. Eleni was on the run from the police. A dress would slow her down.

"Eleni?" I called out.

She stepped out of the shadows. "Allie?"

"Good news. I got the dress."

"How?"

Good question. One I wasn't sure I could answer. I simplified as best I could. "I had help."

"Can you take it to the funeral home for me? I can't go. Not without being arrested."

I nodded once. "I'll do that first thing in the morning. Sooner if I can."

She smiled. "Thank you. You really can find anything, can't you?"

Almost. I hadn't found a solution that would let Eleni and Vladimir be together again, this time without parental interference. It was killing me that I couldn't fix the problem. I'd finally stumbled on something I couldn't find.

"Most of the time, but not always. I'm so sorry, Eleni."

She hugged me. "It's okay. We found our own solution."

That perked me up. "Really?"

"There's a way to be together. It's so obvious. I can't believe we didn't think of it immediately. Vladimir doesn't love it, but he does love me."

"Obviously it's not time travel. Did you find a necromancer? Is it possession? Is he going to live in another body? Because I'm pretty sure there are rules about that sort of thing." At least it seemed like there should be rules. I'd have to find out.

Eleni laughed. A bright, merry sound with summer in it. "No. It's much simpler."

There was a loud and sudden buzzing in my ears. I shook my head but the buzzing wasn't in any hurry to leave. Something wasn't right about this.

"What's the plan?"

Vladimir appeared. His expression was stormy. I sensed

more bad weather in Merope's future. "I do not like." The wind picked up.

"My sweet Vladimir," Eleni crooned. "He will be fine once we are together. It's worth it. *He* is worth it."

"Eleni, what are you doing?"

She was moving slowly backward, toward the cliff's corrugated edge, where it looked like giant teeth had scraped frosting off the island.

"It's okay, Allie. I promise. I have already arranged for you to receive your fee."

"I'm not worried about money! Stop. Stay right there."

She was close to the edge. Too close. Down on the rocks, the sea was foaming at the mouth. The sound wasn't gentle here. More like a famished roar. *Om-nom-nom, feed me people.*

"Tell me something," she said. "Did my parents come to see you? Did they come to you the way Vladimir came back to me?"

I nodded. I couldn't do much else. Sudden moves were a bad idea. I could lose her if I leaped forward.

"Your mother poisoned the chickpeas. In a moment of lucidity she told me she did it for you. She regretted separating you from Vladimir, so she sacrificed their lives. This way you would have yours back, before it was too late. Don't throw it away. Please. *Please.*"

"See you soon," she said.

Eleni jumped.

CHAPTER TWENTY-TWO

I LUNGED. My fingers brushed against hers, then she was gone and I was holding nothing but thin, empty air. A wild gust of Vladimir-wind sent me flying backward, away from the cliff.

"No!"

Vladimir materialized. "This is vhat my flower vanted."

"You could have stopped her!"

He shook his head sadly. "*Nyet*. My Eleni has mind of own. That I luff about her."

He sat on what had one been a wall. Now it was a low row of stones, the perfect height for sitting. "Here I vill vait for her."

I sat next to him. Fifteen minutes or so passed. Then thirty.

"Why did you team up with Xerxes and Mehmed?"

"They vanted to conquer vorld. I vanted to come back to get my Eleni. No chance of that vhen I vas alive. Greece vould not giff new wisa. So I made plen: come back vhen dead, take leetle power from those two fools. But I make big mistake. We come to island now, not 1995."

"So why all the wind?"

"Xerxes and Mehmet haff bed tempers. It took much strength to take their power." He snatched the air with his fist. "After that, I hed to learn to control power. Not easy. Power is … power."

"I didn't know ghosts could do that."

He touched his chest. "I do what I must for my luff."

"How did you die?"

"Eleni's parents gave money. Told Vladimir to leaf Greece and never come back or they would call authorities. Authorities are beeg deal to Russians. I vas scared. After I left my luff behind on island, I vent home to Russia. I vas crossink road when taxicab hit me. Hit. Run. Then a bus run ower me." He stared at the horizon, where the sky was stitched to the sea. "Vhen vill she be back?"

"Forty days. She'll be back in forty days."

"I haff vaited this long." He smiled. "Forty days is nothink."

Adonis Diplas caught up with me as I was fleeing the More Super Market. I made the mistake of stopping for comfort food. Refined carbs or die. Enough death had happened on my watch today, so sugar was my lifeline. With the Cake Emporium out of commission, I was forced into the More Super Market for my fix.

"Allie!" he called out.

"Don't even think about getting between me and this ice cream," I said, holding up the container of baklava ice cream—a local specialty. "Or me and this chocolate." The other hand was gripping a bar of ION chocolate with almonds.

"We were supposed to meet about that thing we were supposed to meet about."

"Too late. I already got the dress. It's at the funeral home as we speak."

I'd planned to run it by there in the morning, but the light was still on as I rode past the funeral home. Kyria Yiota would be out for blood, and I didn't want her spilling mine on the wedding dress.

Adonis folded his arms. "Glad you got your dress."

I placed my snacks in the bicycle's basket and went to push off before this conversation veered off course and crashed into the subject of his psychopathic condom-hoarding cousin.

He stepped in front of me. "So that's it? You're just going to avoid me?"

"Why not? It was working so well. I'm hoping it will become a habit."

"Couldn't you have given me a heads up about George? Now the whole family is furious at *me*."

"Why? He killed all those men, not you."

He shook his head. "I don't believe it. Not George. He's always been a decent person. Best one in the family."

"He tried to strangle me with his pants, and he knocked out a barista from Merope's Best."

"Okay, that looks bad, but the George I've known my whole life wouldn't hurt anyone."

"Do you honestly believe that?"

He had a face like rock. A frown like a scythe. "Yes."

"People believe in things all the time. Doesn't mean they're true."

I pushed off. This time the More Super Market's new owner didn't try to stop me.

Yiayia was in front of the television, laughing at a bad 80s sitcom where everyone was insufferably loud and unfunny. The hair was big. The colors were violently vivid. Everyone had shoulders like linebackers. Cerberus was snoozing next to her. His tail thumped the couch like a drum as I hung my coat, beanie, and bag on the coatrack.

Exhaustion and sadness took turns slapping me. All I wanted was to cram sugar into my face and then fall into bed. Instead I had to tell the Zervases that their daughter was dead and that the next time they saw her she'd be mist. So much for Maria Zerva's sacrifice.

I found them in the kitchen. Maria Zerva had her head in my refrigerator while her husband picked his ghost nose and inspected the ghost nugget. He flicked it on the floor.

"I have to tell you something," I said.

Maria Zerva pulled her head out. "Where is your food? *Po-po-po*. Nobody cooks for you? Come, I make *moussaka*."

"I cook for me sometimes," I said in my defense.

"No wonder you are too skinny. No man will ever marry you if you are a bag of bones." Her gaze snapped to the ice cream and chocolate in my hands. "*Po-po*. What *malakies* are you eating? You will get fat."

Greek mothers. There was no winning with them.

"The good news is that Eleni isn't going to prison, now or ever."

Stathis Zervas crouched down and retrieved his nose nugget. "Was my mother going to prison?"

His wife shook her hands at the ceiling. "It is a miracle!"

Crap. They weren't making this easy.

"The bad news is that she's no longer with us," I explained.

Eleni's mother peered into my cupboards. "Where did she go?"

"She jumped off a cliff so she could be with Vladimir. So technically I guess you could say she's dead. I'm sorry." Greek social protocol meant I was supposed to say "May you live" but under the circumstances, what with them being dead, I figured that was in poor taste.

Stathis Zervas's eyes rolled up in his head and he passed out. *Plop.* He hit the floor and kept on going directly into the apartment below me. Hopefully Kyria Antigone wasn't in her kitchen, foraging for snacks.

There was a heavy sigh from the dead woman. "I gave her life and this is how she repays me?"

A cool mist rose up through the floor and solidified into Stathis Zervas.

"What happened?" he asked us.

"You went looking for your booger," his wife said.

"Did I find it?"

"Check your pockets, *vre vlakas*!"

"You'll see her again," I said. "Probably. Death is only the beginning."

When in doubt, fall back on a quote from *The Mummy.*

"That is not so bad, I suppose," Maria Zerva said.

Except it was pretty bad. I'd failed Eleni and Vladimir, and now my heart felt like someone had attacked it with a melon baller. I should have tried harder to find a way to reunite the lovers without blowing up the world in the process.

What had I missed?

Anything?

Nothing?

Which was worse?

Maria Zerva's eyes lit up. "Ah! There it is. Stathis, grab your underpants."

The dead man was dazed. "Who are you? Where are we going? Have you seen my gold? I left it right here in my nose for safekeeping."

Eleni's mother looped her arm through her husband's. "Come. You can always get more gold."

The elderly couple stepped forward. Vanished.

I ate my ice cream. I ate my chocolate.

I texted Leo to let him know Eleni Zerva was dead.

I went to bed.

Light slanted through the shutters and puddled on the floor. My apartment smelled like frying bacon with a side of fresh bread. The sugar rush had worn off while I was sleeping, leaving behind a void that demanded to be fed. In its desperation, my poor brain had conjured up a deluxe breakfast. Couldn't be real. Had to be an olfactory mirage.

In my pajamas, I followed my nose to the kitchen. Adonis Diplas was poking bacon with tongs. Cerberus was keeping him company. Figured that a dog could be won over with bacon.

Adonis threw a grin at me like he wasn't trespassing. "How do you like your eggs?"

"Unfertilized. What are you doing here?"

"Making breakfast."

"Why?"

"A man has got to eat. So does a woman."

"I'm seeing someone."

"And I'm engaged. Doesn't mean we can't eat breakfast together. Unfertilized, eh?"

"Fine, I guess I could eat. Crispy around the edges, gooey in the middle."

"Same way I eat them."

I plodded into the living room to find my phone. There was a lone text message from Leo, indicating that he'd read my text about Eleni's suicide. Nothing else except work stuff. People wanted things, and they wanted me to acquire those things for them. Life went on.

"Need help?" I asked Adonis.

"Sit and talk to me. Oh. Before I forget, when I got here there was a woman downstairs, spitting on your bicycle. She was muttering something about going *kaka* in your soul and cursing you for all eternity."

"Kyria Yiota. She's upset about the wedding dress."

"Thought I recognized her. She seems nice."

I snorted. That got a laugh out of him. Nobody had ever accused Kyria Yiota of niceness. The woman was born mean. Probably she'd punched her own mother on the way out of the womb.

Adonis removed the bacon to a paper towel covered-plate and cracked eggs into the sizzling pan. "My mother would say you need to do something about that curse."

"I figure I'll ride it out," I said.

He flipped the eggs. Let them sizzle for a minute before sliding them onto the plate where they sat in a small puddle of fruity olive oil.

I waved a hand at the food. "Where did you get all this stuff?"

"Didn't you hear? I own my own market now. All the groceries I can eat. The bread came from the bakery around the corner."

He ferried the food to the kitchen table. Cerberus followed, licking his dog lips. He jumped up, grabbed Adonis's bacon, and bolted into the living room to eat his treasure.

Adonis shook his head. "*Vre, malaka!*"

In a fit of benevolence, I did the decent thing. I forked

half of my bacon onto his plate. It was the least I could do, given that Cerberus was in my custody for now.

"What are you really doing here?"

"Calling in that favor."

"Wait, what favor?"

"You said if I helped you get your dress, you'd owe me one."

"But you didn't help me. I acquired the dress without you."

"That's on you. I was there. You weren't."

"No deal."

He gave me my bacon back. "It was worth a try. But I still want your help. What do you say?"

"My fees are on my website."

"They say you're worth it."

Was I? Mostly yes. But yesterday I'd failed. My confidence was a piñata and it had popped its first hole. "What's the job?"

"I want you to find out who really killed those men. No way was it George."

I ate my bacon, eggs, and bread. Adonis Diplas was a great short-order cook. But he couldn't buy me with breakfast foods.

"Well?"

Chin up-down. "No."

"Why not?"

"Uh, because he did it? Because the police will flip out if I get involved? Because the guy I'm seeing is the local detective, and I'm already on his naughty list?" I put down my fork. "Wait, how did you get in?"

"Door was unlocked."

Probably that was true. Last night I was more fried than these eggs.

Someone knocked on the door. I jumped up, eager for

the distraction. I could use this as an opportunity to shove Adonis out and lock the door behind him.

"Could be your cop boyfriend," Adonis said. "How does he like his eggs?"

Leo wasn't exactly my boyfriend, and now he might never be. But I wasn't about to tell Adonis that. Something told me he'd see that as an opportunity.

I stomped off toward the door and flung it open.

It was Toula. My sister was dressed in her Greek orthodox finest, right down to the dowdy scarf around her shoulders.

Crap. It was early. There was a strange man in my apartment, cooking breakfast. A stranger who wasn't Leo. There was no way to make this look good unless I knocked him over the head and disposed of the body before Toula noticed.

Toula blanched at the sight of my face. "What happened?"

"I guess I followed the wrong influencer. Turns out mousetraps aren't a great way to get plumper lips and scrape five years off my age."

If looks could kill and judge me at the same time …

"Allie …"

"Toula …"

"You did it," she said.

I tried herding her out into the hallway. "Did what?"

"There's a future now." Her gaze careened off my face and crash landed in the living room. "Oh."

I glanced back. Adonis had escaped the kitchen wearing a big grin. Fortunately he was also fully dressed. But that smile, it looked *bad*. The kind of smile a guy wears after you've spent all night doing that thing he likes.

"It's not what you think," I said.

"I know," she said.

"I made breakfast," Adonis said.

"Not helping," I told him.

"Wasn't trying to, baby."

"Did you just call me baby? Get out! I'm not your baby. I'll never be your baby."

"But we haven't finished breakfast."

"*I* haven't finished breakfast. You're done. Go. Never come back."

He winked at me on the way out. "You say that now …"

"And forever!"

Low-down, dirty rat.

Toula was staring down her nose at him, eyebrows raised. The kind of look that sent her husband scrambling to the couch and her children fleeing to their rooms. She swung it around to me.

"Don't give me that look," I said. "I woke up this morning and he was in my kitchen, cooking breakfast foods. He wasn't here for me. Leo arrested his cousin yesterday for murder. Adonis wants me to find the real killer."

"You're going to do it."

"Am not."

"Yeah, you will. He's going to offer you something you can't resist, and you're going to take it."

"What?"

"I can't see that much."

"Did his cousin do the murders?"

"I can't see that either."

"What *can* you see?"

She gestured over my shoulder. "Your dog is crapping on the floor."

· · ·

Thank you for reading *MEAN GHOULS*. *Allie Callas will be back in a new adventure soon!*

Want to be notified when my next book is released? Sign up for my mailing list: http://eepurl.com/ZSeuL.

Like my Facebook page at: https://www.facebook.com/alexkingbooks

Or follow me on Instagram: https://www.instagram.com/alex_a_king_books/

All my best,
Alex A. King

ALSO BY ALEX A. KING

Light is the Shadow (Women of Greece #4)

No Peace in Crazy (Women of Greece #5)

Summer of the Red Hotel (Women of Greece #6)

Rotten Little Apple (Women of Greece #7)

The Last of June (Women of Greece #8)

Forever and Never (Women of Greece #9)

Pride and All This Prejudice

As Alex King:

Lambs

Tall (The Morganites #1)

Small (The Morganites #2)

GLOSSARY

Ade (ah-thay): An expression of pleasure or anger. A bit like "c'mon" or "go on".

Ade gamisou (*a-they ga-mee-soo*): Go make sweet monkey love to yourself.

Ai sto dialo (*eye-sto-thya-lo*): Go to the devil.

A-pah-pah! (a-pa-pa): A sound Greeks make when they disapprove of something.

Archidia (ar-hee-thee-ah): Testicles.

Booboona (boo-boo-nah): A moron.

Despinida (des-pe-nee-tha): Miss. As in "Miss Jackson, if you're nasty."

Faka: (fah-kah): Mousetrap.

Ftero: (Fff-teh-ro): Feather.

Gamo (*ga-mo*): Fuck.

Gamos (ga-moss): A wedding.

Gamo tin putana (ga-mo teen pu-tah-nah): Make sweet monkey love to a woman of purchasable affections.

Gamo ton kerato (ga-mo ton ke-rah-toh): Make sweet monkey love to a horn. Why? I don't know.

Hezo (he-zo): The act of pooping on something.

Kalamari (kal-a-ma-ree): Calamari. Squid.

Kalo ste (kah-lo-stay): Welcome! Good to see you!

Kaka (ka-ka): Poop

Katsika (Ka-tsee-kah) : A nanny goat.

Klasimo (Kla-see-mo): A fart

Klania (kla-nee-ah): Also a fart

Kolos (ko-loss): Butt

Koulouraki (koo-loo-ra-kee): a Greek cookie. Harder and slightly less sweet than its American and British counterparts.

Kolotripa (ko-lo-tree-pah): The hole in a butt. You know the one. (Hopefully it's just one, otherwise please consult a physician.)

Kota (ko-tah): Hen.

Kotsoboles (kot-so-bo-lez): Gossip

Koumbara/koumbaros (koom-bah-rah/koom-bah-ross):

Kyria (kee-ree-ah): Mrs. A married woman.

Kyrios (kee-ree-oss): A man, married or not.

Lambada (lam-ba-tha): A long, skinny, decorative candle used at midnight service on Easter Saturday.

Loukaniko (loo-kah-nee-koh): Sausage.

Loukoumada (loo-koo-mah-tha): Fried balls of dough, drowning in syrup.

Maimou: (my-moo): Monkey.

Malakas (mah-lah-kas): A person who touches themselves so much that their brain turns to mush. Can be an insult or a term of endearment.

Malakies (mah-lah-kee-ez): Nonsense or bullshit.

Malakismeni (mah-lah-kiz-men-ee): Crazy from an excess of masturbation.

Mana mou (mah-nah moo): My mother. Or rather, mother my.

Mati (Ma-tee): An eye. Could be the evil eye, could be a regular eye.

Mezedes (meh-zeh-thes): Appetizers.

Mouni (moo-knee): Vagina, pussy, twat.

Mounoskeela - (moo-knee-skee-lah): Vagina bitch. It really loses something in translation.

Moutsa (moot-sa): An obscene hand gesture. Open palm, facing someone. Can mean that they're a *malakas*, or that you're rubbing poop in their face.

Nanos (Nah-nos): A derogatory term for little person/dwarf.

Ouro (ou-row): Pee.

Panayia mou (pah-nah-yee-ah moo): My Virgin Mary. Or rather, Virgin Mary my.

Papou (pah-poo): Grandfather

Parakalo (pa-ra-ka-low): Doubles as "please" and "you're welcome".

Paralia (pa-ra-lee-ah): The beach or waterfront.

Periptero (pe-rip-te-ro): A small, boxy newsstand.

Philotimo (fee-lo-tee-mo): A combination of love and generosity towards other. Does not apply if you disagree with their politics or sports.

Po-po (po-po): An exclamation of sorts. A cross between "For crying out loud" and "I can't believe this person is so boneheaded".

Poutsa (put-sa): Penis, wiener, ding-dong, dick.

Propapou (pro-pah-pooh): Great-grandfather.

Proyiayia (pro-ya-ya): Great-grandmother.

Putana (puh-tah-nah): Person who dispenses nookie for a negotiable fee.

Revithia (re-vee-thee-ah): Chickpea soup/stew.

Servietta (ser-vee-eh-tah): Feminine hygiene product.

Skata (ska-tah): Shit.

Skata na fas (ska-tah nah faass): Consume a meal of shit.

Skatoula (ska-too-lah): Little shit.

Skeela (skee-lah): Female dog.

Taverna (ta-ver-nah): A small restaurant that sells Greek food.

Thea (thee-ah): Aunt.

Theo (thee-oh): Uncle.

Tiropita (tee-ro-pee-tah): Cheese pie - typically feta. Can include feta with softer cheese like cottage cheese or ricotta.

Tzatziki (za-zee-kee): A sauce made with yogurt, cucumbers, dill, and all the garlic.

Vaskania (vas-kah-nee-ah): A prayer to remove the evil eye.

Vlakas (vlah-kas): A stupid person

Vre/re: Kind of like "hey, you idiot", but not quite. Informal and can be mildly negative but also indicative of familiarity.

Vromoskeelos (vro-mo-slee-los): Dirty dog.

Vromoskeela (vro-mo-skee-lah): Dirty female dog.

Xematiase (kse-mat-ya-say): Removing the evil eye.

Yiayia (yah-yah): Grandmother.

Yia sas (Ya-sas): Howdy, y'all

Yiftes (yiff-tez): A common derogatory term for the Roma people.

Printed in Great Britain
by Amazon